YOUR PERFECT HARMONY

ALAN HAMILTON

with illustrations by
MARCELLA KELLY

Your Perfect Harmony
First Edition

First Edition, First Printing 2015

Illustrations
by Marcella Kelly

Editing and Book Design
by Maria Kay Simms

International Standard Book Number:
978-1-934976-62-3

Library of Congress Control Number
2015956199

ACS PUBLICATIONS
an imprint of Starcrafts LLC
334-A Calef Highway
Epping, NH 03042

Printed in the United States of America

TABLE OF CONTENTS

And Now I'm Introducing THE ZODIACS—

Pythagoras

INTRODUCTION

"IF MUSIC BE THE FOOD OF LOVE...PLAY ON"
(SHAKESPEARE TWELFTH NIGHT)

So who are YOU dining with tonight? Can you imagine a world without music? I personally do not know anyone who does not like music, whatever the genre!

" 'Money makes the world go round,' but without music there would be no soul and the world would grind to a halt" (My quotation by the way. Feel free to use it!)

The origins of music may well date back to first man or woman and the first instrument could have been their voice, but the ¨modern¨ system of dividing notes into a scale mathematically is thought to have arisen from the ancient Greek philosopher PYTHAGORAS when he first heard the different tones that a blacksmith's hammer made on the anvil!!

Or possibly the simple way of measuring water in a glass and hearing the different tones from adding more or taking away the liquid! You must have done this at school? OK only if you are as old as me! Try it with alcohol it's amazing what tunes you can come up with!

Pythagoras realized this was all mathematical and the first scales were based on his theory with 12 semitones (half tones) and thus 12 the Major chords. Numbers were (and still are) thought to be mystical and magical.

According to most scholars Pythagoras divided the Universe into 12 segments. The first was the Empyrean, the dwelling place of the Immortals.

The next 7 were the then celestial bodies of Saturn, Jupiter, Mars, Sun, Venus, Mercury and the Moon in that order. The Sun and the Moon were considered planets in those times! The last 4 sections were Fire, Earth, Air and Water. (The Elements).

This is **not** a Pythagoras biography.
Please carry on reading, boring stuff over soon!

I have been a professional entertainer/musician for most my life and have studied astrology for the last 30 years. I have always been fascinated by personalities of people—how different but also how similar we all are. Also it's very interesting how we can sometimes instantly get on with someone and likewise, instantly dislike someone!!

As a result I have studied astrology more for the personality traits than for predicting someone's future,and then thought of this theory of twelve signs, twelve major chords and their connection with each other.

We've all heard the phrase, "I felt in total harmony with him or her." Well, that refers to musical harmony and this book will let you know if you were right and perhaps find MR. OR MRS. RIGHT?

Please note that I hold no responsibility if you find a partner from the suggestions in my book and end up separated or divorced, and then have long-term expensive court battles over possessions!!

THIS BOOK IS FOR ENTERTAINMENT
PURPOSES ONLY !!!
....or is it?

THE GENERAL AIM OF THIS BOOK
is to show that the relationship between every musical note—how each note relates to each of the other notes—can correspond with the re-lationship between each of the astrological signs.

CHAPTER 1

BASIC MUSIC THEORY

DON'T PANIC!
PLEASE DON'T THROW AWAY THIS BOOK!
THIS IS NOT ESSENTIAL TO KNOW
BUT IT WILL HELP YOU UNDERSTAND MY THEORY!!

I will try to explain in as simple and as easy to understand way as possible, but if you want to skip this section and just find out who you may fancy or who may fancy you?

THEN JUMP TO CHAPTER 4...!   No problem !

OK if you are reading this then you want to discover more! Great!
If you are a musician or have at least basic music knowledge, you will understand quite quickly (I hope!)—but hopefully this will interest you anyway!!

So let's look at a keyboard.

All keyboards are the same whether electronic or a simple piano.As you can see the white notes are all letters of the alphabet.A,B,C,D,E,F and G and they are always in the same place as shown in the diagram above, e.g., C is always found before the two black notes that are together and F is always found before the three black notes that are together.

The black notes have two names and are called sharps (#) or flats (b), e.g.The black note after C is called C SHARP(C#) and also called D FLAT (Db).

In general the rule is...

If the music goes higher (to the right of the keyboard) then it is sharp (#). If the music is going lower (to the left of the keyboard) then it is flat (b).

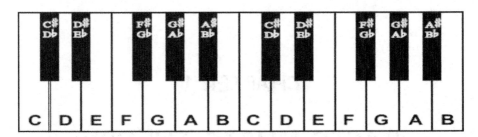

That makes 12 notes altogether which are repeated over and over in the same order to form the complete keyboard

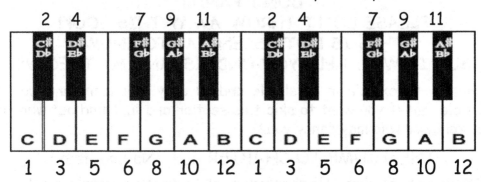

The gap between each note is called a SEMITONE and the gap between 2 notes is called a TONE. So, between C and C#, it's a SEMITONE, and between C and C# it's a SEMITONE, and between C and D, it's a TONE.

C---TO--C# =SEMITONE

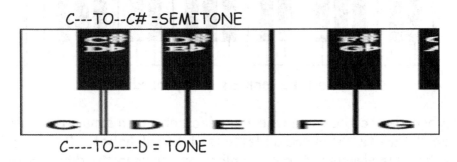

C----TO----D = TONE

Each one of these notes has its own SCALE or KEY, and we are going to be dealing with the MAJOR SCALE, which is formed the same for every note!

Each major scale is made of of 8 of these notes only, the 8th note being the same as the 1st, but an octave (8 notes) higher!

4

We are going to choose the key of C, as it basically uses just the white notes, and as most keyboard players will tell you, are just about the easiest to play!

Now, the "formula" to form a MAJOR SCALE is as follows: TONE/TONE/SEMITONE/ TONE/TONE/TONE/SEMITONE. So, we start with C and the next note is a tone, or in other words, D, which is two notes higher, as was explained before.

C.......TO.....D = (TONE)

The next note is also a TONE which would be 2 notes higher than the D, which would be E.

D.......TO......E= (TONE)

And the next would be a SEMITONE, which is 1 note higher than the E, which would be F.

E....TO...F= (SEMITONE)

The next is another TONE, 2 notes higher than F, which is G.

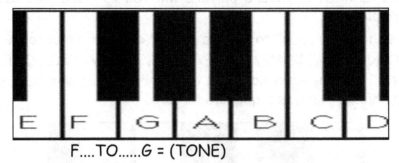

F....TO......G = (TONE)

Another TONE 2 notes higher than G is A

G....TO...A = (TONE)

And another TONE 2 notes higher than A is B

A....TO....B (TONE)

A SEMITONE to finish the SCALE, 1 note higher than B,
brings us back to C (Octave).

B to C + (SEMITONE)

C------------------TO------------------------C = (OCTAVE)

I am assuming everyone has heard of the children's song Do Ray Mi? It is often used, as well, by singing teachers or in a music class at school. Well, these are a substitute for the notes of a scale, ie:

Do=C Ray=D Mi=E Fa=F So=G La=A Ti=B
which brings us back to Do etc.

OK, now let's look at a keyboard and put in the Do/Ray/Mi, etc.

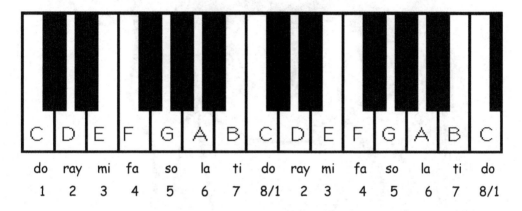

C	D	E	F	G	A	B	C	D	E	F	G	A	B	C
do	ray	mi	fa	so	la	ti	do	ray	mi	fa	so	la	ti	do
1	2	3	4	5	6	7	8/1	2	3	4	5	6	7	8/1

We start then with Do being the note of C and no.1 in the MAJOR SCALE.

A MAJOR CHORD is made up of the 1st/third and fifth note of this scale. i.e., do, mi and so (C/E AND G).

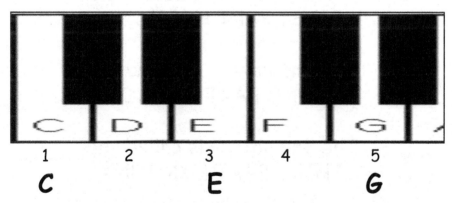

C	D	E	F	G
1	2	3	4	5
C		**E**		**G**

This is the basic and MAJOR chord for C and, in fact, the basic structure for all MAJOR CHORDS!

The three notes of the MAJOR CHORD are all in HARMONY with one another! If you play them on a keyboard, you will hear how harmonious and "in tune" they are together! When we relate these notes to the twelve astrological signs, then the ones that fall in this chord will also be the most harmonious and "in tune"with you!!

The 1st note C is called the
FIRST PART HARMONY

The 2nd note E is called the
SECOND PART HARMONY

The 3rd note G is called the
THIRD PART HARMONY

There are, of course, a multitude of chords, of which the most common will be used in this book. If you are a jazz musician, I am sure you will come up with a totally amazing chord—and good luck with your interpretation!

CHAPTER 2

MUSIC AND ASTROLOGY

NOW!!!.........where does astrology figure in all of this?

If you look at a keyboard as explained in Chapter 1, you see that every note is a half tone or a semitone apart from the others, so starting at C and counting the black keys (or notes) as well as the white keys, we have 12 notes before we arrive back at C.

So, let's now put the TWELVE SUN SIGNS in order
next to the twelve music notes:

The Sun signs in order are as follows...

ARIES is the first sign as it starts in Spring, the beginning of new life. The dates for each sign are from the TROPICAL ZODIAC, the one that is most commonly used by western astrologers. The symbol is the sign glyph.

♈	ARIES	March 21st to April 20th
♉	TAURUS	April 21st to May 21st
♊	GEMINI	May 22nd to June 21st
♋	CANCER	June 22nd to July 22nd
♌	LEO	July 23rd to August 22nd
♍	VIRGO	August 23rd to September 23rd
♎	LIBRA	September 24th to October 23rd
♏	SCORPIO	October 24th to November 22nd
♐	SAGITTARIUS	November 23rd to December 21st
♑	CAPRICORN	December 22nd to January 20th
♒	AQUARIUS	January 21st to February 19th
♓	PISCES	February 20th to March 20th

We will use ARIES as our first keyboard example and then show ALL of the other signs later.

♈

ARIES
THE RAM

C#	D#		F#	G#	A#
Taurus 2	Cancer 4		Libra 7	Sagittarius 9	Aquarius 11

ARIES 1   Gemini 3   Leo 5   Virgo 6   Scorpio 8   Capricorn 10   Pisces 12   ARIES

As explained before we have 12 notes but only 8 notes are used in the MAJOR SCALE, so let's look at ARIES on an 8 note scale.

ARIES 1   Gemini 2   Leo 3   Virgo 4   Scorpio 5   Capricorn 6   Pisces 7   ARIES 1/8

Aries starts the scale as C, so D is GEMINI and the second note of the scale etc. Please refer to this example when I begin to explain harmonies.

Now every note in music can sound good bad or indifferent when played together, and this is easier to understand if you have a keyboard in front of you—e.g; If you play C and C# together, the notes clash and it sounds horrible, so might ARIES and TAURUS also clash and be bad together?

However, if you play C and E together it sounds lovely and is a perfect harmony! So perhaps ARIES AND LEO can make sweet music together!!

OR
JUST ROCK
THE JOINT!!

FIRE SIGNS...
PHEW!!!

So, here are all the other signs in order after ARIES, and where each of them fit into the SCALE!!

TAURUS the BULL

C# Gemini	D# Leo			F# Scorpio	G# Capricorn	A# Pisces	
C	D	E	F	G	A	B	C

TAURUS 1 Cancer 2 Virgo 3 Libra 4 Sagittarius 5 Aquarius 6 Aries 7 Taurus 1/8

GEMINI the TWINS

C# Cancer	D# Virgo			F# Sagittarius	G# Aquarius	A# Aries	
C	D	E	F	G	A	B	C

GEMINI 1 Leo 2 Libra 3 Scorpio 4 Capricorn 5 Pisces 6 Taurus 7 GEMINI 1/8

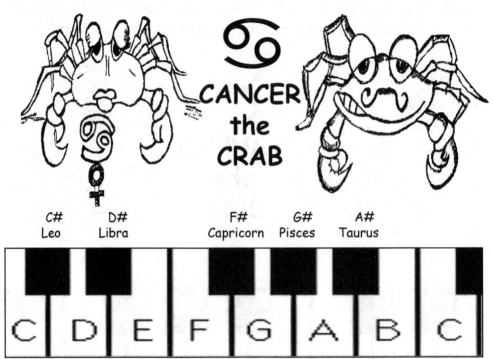

CANCER
the
CRAB

| C#
Leo | D#
Libra | | F#
Capricorn | G#
Pisces | A#
Taurus |

C D E F G A B C

CANCER 1 Virgo 2 Scorpio 3 Sagittarius 4 Aquarius 5 Aries 6 Gemini 7 CANCER 1/8

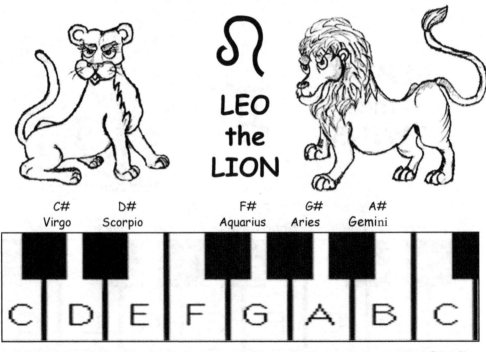

LEO
the
LION

| C#
Virgo | D#
Scorpio | | F#
Aquarius | G#
Aries | A#
Gemini |

C D E F G A B C

LEO 1 Libra 2 Sagittarius 3 Capricorn 4 Pisces 5 Taurus 6 Cancer 7 LEO 1/8

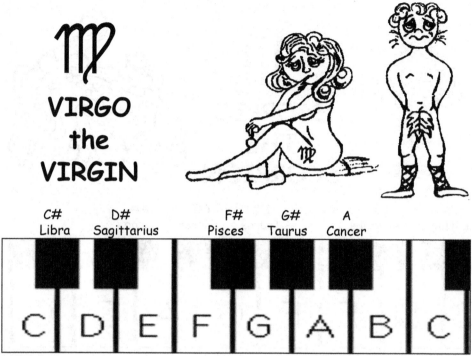

VIRGO
the
VIRGIN

	C# Libra	D# Sagittarius		F# Pisces	G# Taurus	A Cancer		
C		D	E	F	G	A	B	C

VIRGO 1 Scorpio 2 Capricorn 3 Aquarius 4 Aries 5 Gemini 6 Leo 7 VIRGO 1/8

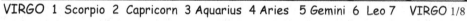

LIBRA
the
SCALES

	C# Scorpio	D# Capricorn		F# Aries	G# Gemini	A# Leo		
C		D	E	F	G	A	B	C

LIBRA 1 Sagittarius 2 Aquarius 3 Pisces 4 Taurus 5 Cancer 6   Virgo 7 LIBRA 1/8

m SCORPIO THE SCORPION

| C#
Sagittarius | D#
Aquarius | | F#
Taurus | G#
Cancer | A#
Virgo |

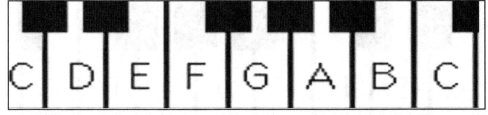

C D E F G A B C

SCORPIO 1
Capricorn 2 Pisces 3 Aries 4 Gemini 5 Leo 6 Libra 7 SCORPIO 1/8

↗ SAGITTARIUS THE HORSE/ARCHER

| C#
Capricorn | D#
Pisces | | F#
Gemini | G#
Leo | A#
Libra |

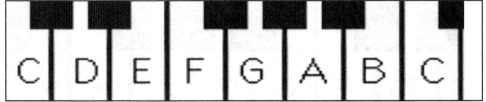

C D E F G A B C

SAGITTARIUS 1
Aquarius 2 Aries 3 Taurus 4 Cancer 5 Virgo 6 Scorpio 7 Sagittarius 1/8

CAPRICORN
THE
GOAT

C# Aquarius	D# Aries		F# Cancer	G# Virgo	A# Scorpio

C D E F G A B C

CAPRICORN 1

Pisces 2   Taurus 3   Gemini 4   Leo 5   Libra 6   Sagittarius 7 CAPRICORN 1/8

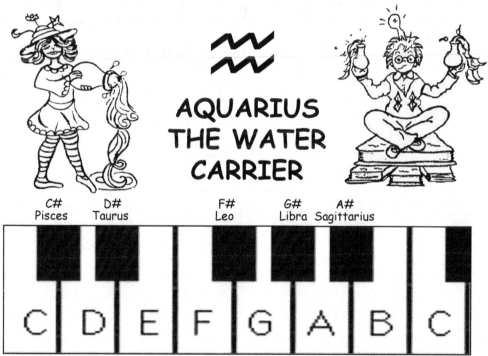

AQUARIUS
THE WATER
CARRIER

C# Pisces	D# Taurus		F# Leo	G# Libra	A# Sagittarius

C D E F G A B C

SAGITTARIUS 1

Aquarius 2   Aries 3   Taurus 4   Cancer 5   Virgo 6   Scorpio 7   Sagittarius 1/8

17

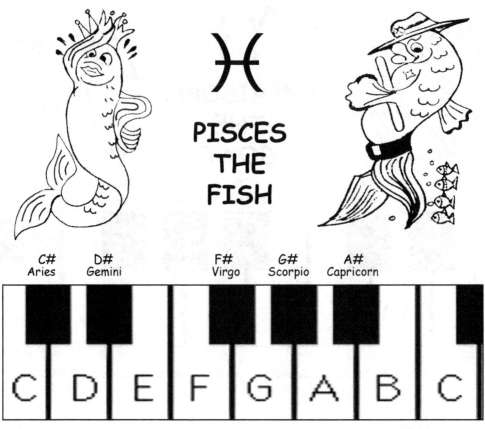

PISCES
THE
FISH

C# Aries   D# Gemini   F# Virgo   G# Scorpio   A# Capricorn

C D E F G A B C

PISCES 1
Taurus 2   Cancer 3   Leo 4   Libra 5   Sagittarius 6   Aquarius 7 PISCES 1/8

Interpretation?

In astrology it is all down to interpretation, following of course, that every sign has positive and negative personality traits of which most astrologers agree in the majority of cases.

I will outline in a little more detail my own interpretation of these personality traits shortly, but first I will give you my basic interpretation of my HARMONY theory!

YOU will be the first or base note C. The base note is also called the ROOT!

C/E AND G are the main harmonies and the
"perfect" harmony for C is E.
i.e., for ARIES the perfect harmony is LEO
and the next perfect harmony will be

SCORPIO (note of G)....

See the first keyboard chart on page 11!

Have we got it so far?

Or you can put someone else in as the first note and work out where you figure in their harmony!

CHORDS

CHORDS are usually made up of 3/4 or 5 notes played simultaneously.

There are more crazy JAZZ combinations, but I am going to use the most common and most frequently used chords in this book!

An explanation of each note and what chord or chords they are in together with my interpretation of whether good or bad for your sign will be given at the beginning of each Sun Sign.

You can use the CHORDS to see if the combination of SUN SIGNS in that order would, for example, make a very good team together or whether they would just NOT get on at all !!

Perhaps you should make your Sagittarian office worker the Sales Manager (they could sell sand to the Arab countries!) and your Virgo the Office Manager (best organizers and know where everything is or should be).

Anyway all possibilities will be covered in the interpretations of each sign. I will go through each note with every Sun sign starting at C, and then work out how all the other signs are in or out of tune with that sign.

CONTROL!!! or (Perspective)

In my opinion, someone always instigates or "controls" the situation, either the boss or team leader at work, or you or your partner may have a certain idea for the house or finances, etc. If so, THAT person would be the base/C note, and the relationship of all the other signs would be shown by following his or her chart at the beginning of every SUN SIGN interpretation.

So consider yourself, and your chart as THAT person first, so that your reading of it is from YOUR perspective. Then check your compatibility with each of the others involved, to see if each of their sign combinations will appear harmonious with yours, or otherwise!

PLEASE NOTE

that YOUR "perfect harmony," with you in charge, may not quite be as perfect with one or the other of them in charge!! In other words they may be good for you—but are you good for them? Check it out!

Then put anyone else you have a "relationship" with, whether it is a personal or work related person, or someone among your family or friends, as the root note C, and find out what they think of you!!

Are you compatible with them?

PERSONALITY TRAITS

Personality traits of Sun signs are first divided into either positive or negative categories: MALE/FEMALE or YING/YANG (Chinese) are also categories. For example, the signs that are called positive or yang are the odd numbered signs of the zodiac 1, 3, 5, 7, 9 and 11, beginning with Aries, the sign of Spring Equinox and the beginning of new life. The second sign, of the zodiac, Taurus, is then the first of the even numbered signs, that are called negative or yang —2,4, 6, 8, 10 and 12

Therefore, we have...

ARIES

GEMINI

SAGITTARIUS

LEO

LIBRA

AQUARIUS

These are thought to be the more
outgoing and extrovert signs, called positive and yang.

Negative (Female/Yang) are the even numbers
2, 4, 6, 8, 10 and 12.   Therefore, we have...

CANCER

TAURUS

VIRGO

SCORPIO

PISCES

CAPRICORN

These are thought to be the
more introvert and cautious signs.

Other personality traits are formed from
your element...

FIRE
ARIES, LEO & SAGITTARIUS
are the fire dragons!

Qualities of FIRE:
ACTIVE
masculine
spontaneous
quick
initializing
vitalizing
energetic

As the name indicates these people can have a fiery temperament and "flare-up" but also have a lot of energy to "burn!" Fire people like action and are purposeful! They are very spontaneous (sometimes too much) and initiate a lot of new ideas and action!! These "hot" people's first emotions are to gain something from life in everything they do.

EARTH
TAURUS, VIRGO & CAPRICORN
are earthy creatures!

Qualities of EARTH:
PASSIVE
feminine   solid
materialization
physical
stable slow-moving
grounded

These down-to-earth people have their feet on the ground and are generally the ¨workers¨ in the Zodiac! They get on with the job in hand and are usually very reliable but often moody. They are the signs who do the action and their first emotional response is to be physical.

AIR
GEMINI, LIBRA & AQUARIUS
are the "clever clogs"!

Qualities of AIR:
ACTIVE
masculine
intellectual
ethereal
abstract
communicative

These carefree air people generally "breeze" through life and are not known worriers but are normally very intelligent! Watch out though, Genius comes with a crazy streak as well! Their first emotional response is to analyze and then intellectually dissect the information.

WATER
CANCER, SCORPIO & PISCES
are the sensitive signs!

Qualities of WATER:
PASSIVE
feminine
receptive
sustaining
subconscious
creative
generative

Still waters run deep for these emotional people. Their hearts can rule their heads and sometimes they "harbor" grudges! But they are also the "caregivers" of the Zodiac, and often are intuitive and psychic! Their first emotional response is to "feel."

The Sun signs are also divided into modes of action, called by these three names: Cardinal, Fixed and Mutable.
Each of the three modes has its own personality traits!

CARDINAL

These signs get things going,
They initiate action, and are very enterprising!

♈ ARIES

♎ LIBRA

♋ CANCER

♑ CAPRICORN

FIXED
These signs hate change!
They don't often initiate, but they get the job done!

TAURUS ♉, LEO ♌
SCORPIO ♏
and AQUARIUS ♒
are the
perfectionists!!

MUTABLE

These signs adapt and adjust to whatever comes up in their lives.

GEMINI
♊

VIRGO
♍

SAGITTARIUS
♐

AND

PISCES
♓

are

the

flexible friends!

CHAPTER 3

SAME SIGNS,
DIFFERENT PERSONALITY ?

Now, many people tell me that they know two people of the same sign that are completely different from each other!! One of the reasons is likely to be that they have totally different Ascendants (also called "Rising signs") from each other.

THE ASCENDANT (also called the Rising sign)

Let me explain as simply as possible for those who do not understand this...Your astrological chart is basically a circle of 12 houses and 12 signs.

Your "Sun sign" is the sign of the zodiac on the day and month of the year you were born. Your "Ascendant" (Rising sign) is the sign that was "rising" on the eastern horizon at the EXACT time and place of your birth. So, while others born at the same time as you were will have the same Sun sign, your Ascendant (Rising sign) is unique to you! It is the cusp of House 1 of your chart, and it's exact position depends on you exact time of birth plus WHERE you were born. In exact calculation of a birth chart, this means the longitude and latitude of your birthplace.

My interpretation of the RISING SIGN is that it shows your outer personality, and sometimes your alter ego. It can also come through as your main personality, especially if you are stressed or intoxicated!

When you find your ASCENDANT (rising sign), try substituting it for your SUN sign, to see if you might often be like your rising sign sometimes, or are you a combination of the two signs?

This is how two people of the same Sun sign could appear to be different—if their Ascendant signs are **not** the same.

There are also many occasions when a person's "true" personality can be so subdued or controlled within a bad relationship that they are not able to be "themselves!"

One other reason for differences in personality between people born with the same Sun sign is that your birth location also figures into chart calcuations. At the exact time you were born in your birthplace. someone else might be born at the same moment, but in a different place, so that person's planets may be in different houses, and one or more of the other planets could be in different enough positions that they would indicate different personality characteristics from others who were born on the same DAY of the same year as you were. Because of the exact TIME of their births, they have different influences in their birth charts.

In any case, we always have to generalize to some extent as we observe that while each Sun sign has its special characteristics and personality traits, how these might show are influenced by other factors within the horoscope that relate to the Sun by aspect.

One other main controlling influence on your personality is the position of the MOON at your birth and which particular sign it was in at that specific time.

Some astrologers even believe Moon is the most important chart influence after Sun! Moon, in astrology, represents your instinctive emotional responses, whether they are good OR bad!!

In other words, there is a bright side to the moon, but also a dark side. So your spontaneous reaction that you can't control, be it joy or anger, is read from your Moon sign!

Also, during the full moon of each month, your personality can change for that day or two, such that you and your friends and associates could be experiencing a different you!

30

On the CUSP/DECANATES!

CUSP

If you were born right at the end or at the beginning of your Sun sign you could have influences from the sign before or after. Also some sun sign dates can vary by a day depending on the astrologer. When you have your accurate birth time though you can determine exactly which Sun sign you are as the sun never enters the next sign at exactly the same time every year! Your strongest personality traits will still be your exact Sun sign but because you are so close to the next sign you could be heavily influenced by it. So check out the personality traits of those signs close to you to see if you think you are more like them!

DECANATES

DECANATES(Decans)are also known as "Rooms" The month of your Sun sign can also be divided into Decanates. Every Sun sign is approx.30 days long and is split into 3 rooms of 10 days and each of those 10 days is split between the 3 signs of that element.

In further explanation, again we'll use Aries as our example. Aries starts on March 21st and finishes on April 20th. Aries is a FIRE sign, so the two other FIRE signs rule the 2nd and 3rd decanates.

ARIES influences the first 10 days of the sign,
LEO influences the middle 10 days and
SAGITTARIUS influences the final 10 days

Anyone born between the 21st-30th March is Aries/Aries.
Anyone born between the 31st March-9th April is Aries/Leo
Anyone born between the 10th-20th April is Aries/Sagittarius

So as an Aries, you are still a FIRE sign, according to your exact birth date, you may also have some personality traits of your fellow fiery friends!

I call this FINE TUNING, as most signs of the same element have similar traits. But, if you are influenced by a stronger or weaker part of your element, this could give you a slightly different personality than other people who have your same Sun sign!

If you want to delve deeper into Decans please contact

www.astrocom.com

On page 32 is a table listing the signs and their decans!!

DECANATES

SUN SIGN	DATES	INFLUENCE
ARIES	21-30 March 31 March-9 April 10-20 April	ARIES LEO SAGITTARIUS
TAURUS	21-30 April 1-10 May 11-21 May	TAURUS VIRGO CAPRICORN
GEMINI	22-31 May 1-10 June 11-21 June	GEMINI LIBRA AQUARIUS
CANCER	22 June-1 July 2-12 July 13-22 July	CANCER SCORPIO PISCES
LEO	23 July-2 August 3-12 August 13-22 August	LEO SAGITTARIUS ARIES
VIRGO	23 August-2 September 3-12 September 13-22 September	VIRGO CAPRICORN TAURUS
LIBRA	23 September-3 October 4-13 October 14-22 October	LIBRA AQUARIUS GEMINI
SCORPIO	23 October-1 November 2-11 November 12-22 November	SCORPIO PISCES CANCER
SAGITTARIUS	23 November-2 December 3-12 December 13-21 December	SAGITTARIUS ARIES LEO
CAPRICORN	22-31 December 1-10 January 11-20 January	CAPRICORN TAURUS VIRGO
AQUARIUS	21-29 January 30 January-8 February 9-19 February	AQUARIUS GEMINI LIBRA
PISCES	20-29 February 1-10 March 11-20 March	PISCES CANCER SCORPIO

BIRTH CHART

Basically it would be a good idea to have your complete BIRTH CHART done, which is quite easy to do. Check out www.astrocom.com for an easy way to get your chart. You'll find that there are a wide of variety of decorative styles to choose from, too! You will need your exact DATE (month, day and year), TIME (hour and minutes, be sure to state AM or PM) and your PLACE of birth (city, state, country) to order an accurately calculated chart.

When you have your chart, and thus know your Ascendant, the signs of your Moon and each of your planets, as well as your Sun sign, and your house cusps, you'll be prepared to make up a far more interesting and complete profile of yourself!

On page 35 is the Birth Chart of the illustrator of this book, whose name is Marcella Kelly. The chart shows the exact position of her Sun, Moon and every planet at the exact time and location of her birth, and so it is very unique to her!

Someone else who was born on the very same day as Marcella, but (for example) twelve hours later, will have the same SUN sign, although a different degree, and each of the planets would be in different position, too—and some may have changed signs! The ASCENDANT of the chart would be in a quite different degree and and possibly also in a different sign! The houses would likely also be different, if the other person was born in a different location.

Below the chart illustration is a listing of the positions in the zodiac of Marcella's Sun, Moon and each of her planets, plus her two primary "personal points," her Ascendant (cusp of House 1) and her Midheaven (cusp of House 10) and her Part of Fortune (which is also called Fortuna). Then the list of Houses shows the beginning degree (cusp) of each House in her chart.

The letter after each placement refers to the element of that planet or the sign that begins each house

F is Fire, E is Earth, A is Air and W is Water). e.g.,Venus is associated with love and Marcella's Venus is in Aries which could make her a "fiery" but demanding lover.

(Hold your horses boys.....no further personal info released... sorry!!)

e.g.,Venus is associated with love and Marcella's Venus is in Aries which could make her a "fiery" but demanding lover. (Hold your horses boys..... no further personal info released...sorry!!)

Of the 12 "houses," knowing which sign is on the cusp (beginning degree) of each house will also add to YOUR personality profile. Note that in Marcella's chart two signs (Cancer and Capricorn) are in the middle of Houses 10 and 3. This is called an interception, and is a factor of the exact location that happens sometimes. Take to mean that both signs, the one on the cusp and the one intercepted are likely to contribute to how we would consider the interpretation of this chart.

A Birth Chart also shows the position of the planets at the exact time and place YOU were born and is unique to you!! Each planet has a sign and the planets make up more pieces of the complicated jigsaw of a person's personality, e.g.,Venus is associated with love and Marcella's Venus in Aries could make her a "fiery" but demanding lover. (Hold your horses boys...no further personal information is offered regarding "houses.)

Just be aware that depending on which sign begins (is on the cusp of) which house adds information to an astrologer's understanding about YOUR personality profile.

Although there are many details that an experienced astrologer might consider, just the basic information of just your Sun, Moon and Ascendant will give a pretty good idea of your general personality—but if you want to get a complete and more detailed profile please make sure you have the correct information of your date of birth, time of birth and place of birth (longitude and latitude).

If you are asking an astrologer to read your chart for you, be sure that he or she is reliable, and above all accurate!! It is not unreasonable to ask for a resume and/or references.

Check out www.astrocom.com for further information.

Also, when you analyze your chart you can see how many FIRE, EARTH, AIR or WATER signs make up your chart, and see how "balanced" you are!!

Marcella's chart, counting planet and house placements, has 5 in Fire signs, 4 in Earth signs, 8 in Air signs and 7 in Water signs. A very quick synopsis shows a balanced chart with the extrovert Fire being doused by the emotions of Water. The Earth signs are in strong positions, as both the Sun sign (Taurus) and the Ascendant (Virgo) are Earth, bringing with the Earth element a person who takes pride in her work, but sometimes is too work orientated and security conscious!

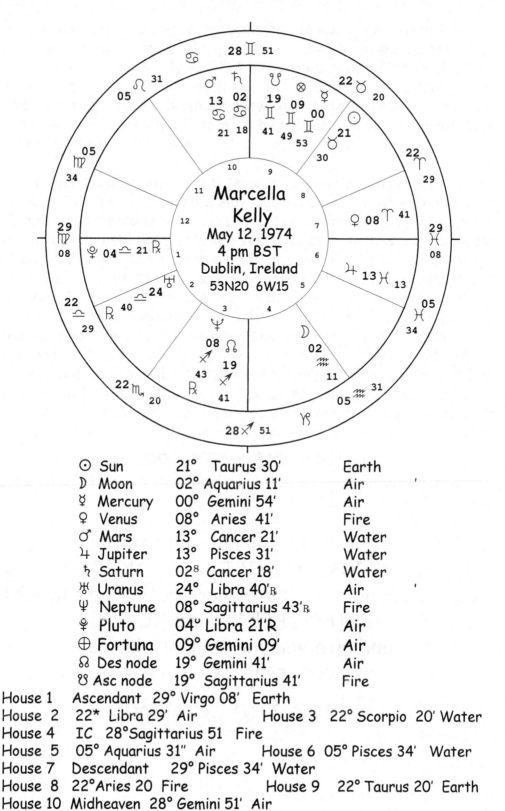

☉	Sun	21° Taurus 30'	Earth
☽	Moon	02° Aquarius 11'	Air
☿	Mercury	00° Gemini 54'	Air
♀	Venus	08° Aries 41'	Fire
♂	Mars	13° Cancer 21'	Water
♃	Jupiter	13° Pisces 31'	Water
♄	Saturn	02ˢ Cancer 18'	Water
♅	Uranus	24° Libra 40'℞	Air
♆	Neptune	08° Sagittarius 43'℞	Fire
♇	Pluto	04ᵛ Libra 21'R	Air
⊕	Fortuna	09° Gemini 09'	Air
☋	Des node	19° Gemini 41'	Air
☊	Asc node	19° Sagittarius 41'	Fire

House 1   Ascendant 29° Virgo 08' Earth
House 2   22* Libra 29' Air   House 3 22° Scorpio 20' Water
House 4   IC 28° Sagittarius 51 Fire
House 5   05° Aquarius 31" Air   House 6 05° Pisces 34' Water
House 7   Descendant   29° Pisces 34' Water
House 8   22° Aries 20 Fire   House 9   22° Taurus 20' Earth
House 10 Midheaven 28° Gemini 51' Air
House 11 05° Leo 31' Fire   House 12 05° Virgo 24' Earth

The Air signs indicate intelligence, especially when Moon sign is in the strong sign of Aquarius—although she's apt to act a little "crazy" at times, and definitely during the full moon!!

Your Birth Chart also shows the position of your planets at the exact time and place when YOU were born and so this chart is unique to you!! Each planet has a sign, and each of the planets make up another piece in the complicated jigsaw puzzle of a person's own unique personality.

There are also twelve "houses" in each Birth Chart, and depending on which sign is in which house, this will also add to YOUR individual personality profile. However the basic information of just your Sun, Moon and Ascendant signs will give a pretty good idea of your general personality. Still, if you want to get a complete and more detailed profile, please make sure that you have the correct information of your birth (month, day and year), plus your exact time of birth (hour and minute), and the location of your birth (the longitude and latitude).

Above all, if you are consulting an astrologer for a complete profile, be sure to provide in advance your correct birth information and that the astrologer you consult with is reliable and accurate.

If you are studying astrology on your own, you need to make sure that you have an accurately calculated chart. You can get one by mail or by email from Astro Computing Services.

www.astrocom.com

Astro also offers interpreted reports and many "how to" books from beginner to professional. level.

And now the moment you have all been waiting for!!
The actual COMPATIBILITY (OR NOT) of every
sign. I am going to show every note, starting with
YOUR PERFECT HARMONY
and give you the compatibilities
of every sign for each note.

Have fun...enjoy!!

CHAPTER 4

IN OR OUT OF TUNE?

Please note that in the majority of cases I do not separate the genders, male or female, with the exception of Leo! I associate this sign with the Lion and the Lioness.

The Lioness, in fact, does most of the work, looks after the kids, gets the dinner which our lazy but lovable King Leo will insist on eating first before trying to mate with all of Lady Lioness's girlfriends!! So, there are more specific differences, in my opinion, between the two genders in this case.

CHORD COMBINATIONS

A CHORD is normally a combination of 3/4 or 5 notes as explained earlier e.g., C MAJOR for ARIES is made up of ARIES/LEO and SCORPIO. They would be Aries perfect harmonies, not only in a relationship but also perhaps in a work scenario or sports team.

Leo and Scorpio are the guys/gals to have by your side, Aries! So when I put in the chord combinations for your sign, you'll see how you can also work out the best or worst signs that are good—or not—for you!

YOUR PERFECT HARMONY!!

OK, I am going to start with YOUR perfect harmony which is E.

C   E

GENERAL
Using you as C and the base of everything around you in your life, then E is your perfect harmony and will be "in tune" with you. This is with you being the "boss" in whatever situation you are in.

ROMANCE
This could be the love of your life and not just a fling or a one night stand!!   You feel at one.

WORK
This will not mean a personal relationship, but a colleague who is on the same wavelength, and is supportive of your actions—and can offer good advice.

HOME or personal situation
This could be your soul mate, who helps in all of life's difficult ups and downs, and is one whom you can rely on.

MONEY
If you control the purse strings then this person will agree with your ideas and offer sensible suggestions to add to your security.

PLEASE NOTE

This is YOUR perfect harmony with you in "control," but you are NOT necessarily THEIR perfect harmony when you reverse the roles—but you can be very compatible all the same. It's just from a different perspective.

In every case, you will be your signficant other person's the C+ (C plus), which adds something to that person's life and takes him or her upwards to better things!   (See Chapter 11 on C+.)

On the next page we'll look at all the "perfect harmony Es,"
including their element!

BASE NOTE C	ELEMENT	HARMONY E	ELEMENT
ARIES	FIRE	LEO	FIRE
TAURUS	EARTH	VIRGO	EARTH
GEMINI	AIR	LIBRA	AIR
CANCER	WATER	SCORPIO	WATER
LEO	FIRE	SAGITTARIUS	FIRE
VIRGO	EARTH	CAPRICORN	EARTH
LIBRA	AIR	AQUARIUS	AIR
SCORPIO	WATER	PISCES	WATER
SAGITTARIUS	FIRE	ARIES	FIRE
CAPRICORN	EARTH	TAURUS	EARTH
AQUARIUS	AIR	GEMINI	AIR
PISCES	WATER	CANCER	WATER

NOTE THAT ALL THESE PERFECT HARMONIES ARE OF THE SAME ELEMENT TYPE i.e.: EARTH AND EARTH, ETC.

This makes perfect sense, as the similarities between the signs show that they would have much in common with each other!

ARIES ♈ and LEO ♌

GENERAL RELATIONSHIP

What a fiery combination we have here! You who have Aries Sun signs will find the more laid back Leo a perfect foil to your 100mph lifestyle.

Aries and Leo will have a lot in common—but a Leo will not be nearly as bothered by the fiery Aries up and down temperament, as most other signs would. Leo will go along with the constant need of Aries to be amused or occupied! Boredom is not an option!

The Leo lion would also be a great protector of the sometimes "childish" Aries types, who could get themselves into troublesome situations—but like a good father figure, Leo would come to the rescue!

LEO FEMALES tend to give strength to this partnership as they are not afraid of work and will possibly keep the income coming in.

The Aries, male or female, will also be happy to earn the crust, but can be overly generous with the cash! So Lady Leo might also come to the rescue, but probably more financially than physically!!

LOVE RELATIONSHIP

Think of this relationship as hot and steamy!! Hopefully, you have plenty of cold showers and buckets of ice!!

Most relationships start out very physical, then gradually and hopefully a meeting of minds happens and a stronger love develops. In this case there is nothing to extinguish the fire!! So enjoy and have a permanent honeymoon!!

One word of caution to both of you....You both like to be leaders! Can a "coalition government" work? Keep doing your OWN thing to avoid confrontation!!

CHORD COMBINATION
C MAJOR C/E AND G
ARIES/LEO AND SCORPIO

Scorpio makes up the C Major chord and is covered in Chapter 5

FOR LEO AND ARIES SEE CHAPTER 11 — THE NOTE G#/C+

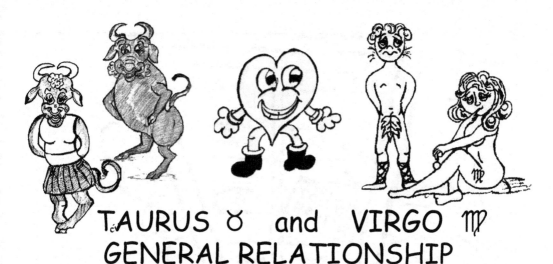

TAURUS ♉ and VIRGO ♍
GENERAL RELATIONSHIP

The Taurean need for security can only be enhanced by a Virgo partner. Their home or business will be obsessively tidy and organized, and although Taureans can make a terrible mess just charging at things, they are also great at cleaning it up!! There is a place for everything and everything is in its place!!

Both of these hard workers' finances should be healthy, with plenty put away for the rainy day! As long as bossy Virgo doesn't try to control things too much, the Taurean will feel contented and secure, in building on this partnership day by day!

LOVE RELATIONSHIP

Taureans are great lovers once they have established complete trust in a relationship. With Virgo's more methodical approach to everything in life (including sex!), sparks may not fly at first.

However, once this relationship is established on a mutual respect for one another, love will grow steadily and strongly and behind closed bedroom doors, a Bull and a Virgin!! I'll leave the rest to your imagination!!

43

CHORD COMBINATION
C MAJOR C/E AND G
TAURUS/VIRGO AND SAGITTARIUS

Sagittarius makes up the C Major chord
and is covered in Chapter 5.

FOR VIRGO AND TAURUS
SEE CHAPTER 11 THE NOTE G#/C+

GEMINI ♊ and LIBRA ♎

GENERAL RELATIONSHIP

The Gemini will be very happy with his or her Libra who will let the Gemini control most situations, or get Libra to run around at Gemini's beck and call! At times, this drives Libra to be pulling out hair because of all the stress!

Our Gemini is not short on compassion when that is what is needed, though, so will soon take the pressure off our lovely Libra and the two can then be friends for life once again. But this happy-go-lucky situation could also involve the demon drink! Both signs are more than happy to be out socializing in the local tavern!

Geminis are clever people who can make, but also lose, a lot of money. The Libra will go along with this, as long as he or she is happy in the relationship. It's easy come easy go. But, if you meet these guys "n" gals in your neighborhood bar, you will be entertained!!

LOVE RELATIONSHIP

Both signs can be a bit flirtatious with the opposite sex...so the main danger is TRUST!

As long as they both are committed to each other and understand that BOTH will need a bit of freedom—but not too much—then the saying,"Don't mind where you get your appetite—just have your meals at HOME!!" is appropriate in this scenario.

There could be lots of laughs here, and a some enjoyable nights going out "on the town" together.

CHORD COMBINATION
C MAJOR C/E AND G

GEMINI/LIBRA AND CAPRICORN

Capricorn makes up the C Major chord and is covered in Chapter 5

FOR LIBRA AND GEMINI SEE CHAPTER 11,
THE NOTES G#/C+

CANCER ♋ and SCORPIO ♏

GENERAL RELATIONSHIP

The normally home loving, caring Cancerian will gain strength from a solid Scorpio, who is not as emotional on the outside as their Cancerian water sign counterparts tend to be.

The Cancerians will let their hearts rule and the Scorpios will keep their heads, and possibly also their finances, on the straight and narrow. The Scorpio friend or lover is faithful and true, and would never divulge a secret—but also he or she will expect the same of you!

If you don't deliver, then beware the sting in the tail !!

The combination of the strength of Scorpio with the caring attitude of Cancer could benefit not only those with planets in these signs, but probably a lot of very worthy causes as well !!

LOVE RELATIONSHIP

Cancerians are likely to fall head over heels in love with Scorpios.

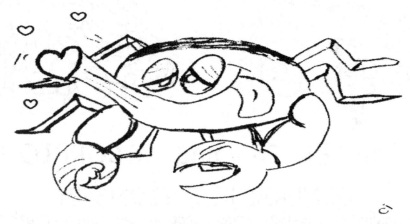

At last they have found someone that they can completely trust to not divulge all their inner secrets and insecurities! Scorpions may take on the role of "caregiver" in this relationship—and watch out for any enemies of a sometimes vulnerable Cancer.

This Sun sign has a balanced combination of emotion and strength, although Cancer may overdo the tears....and getting inside the Scorpion's heart may be harder than you think!!

CHORD COMBINATION
C MAJOR   C/E AND G
CANCER/SCORPIO AND AQUARIUS

Aquarius makes up the C Major chord and is covered in Chapter 5

FOR SCORPIO AND CANCER SEE CHAPTER 11,
THE NOTES G#/C+

LEO ♌ and SAGITTARIUS ♐
GENERAL RELATIONSHIP

Leo is the only sign I generally split between male and female, as I associate the Lion and Lioness roles.

e.g.,The lazy LEO MALE will normally wait for the food to be brought to him, eat first, then make love and go back to sleep!!

The King needs courtiers to praise and love him!! And you do—you can't help it!

However, our hard-working LEO FEMALE will catch the food, bring it to the table, wait till Dad and unruly kids have eaten and might grab a bit before fighting off Dad's lovers and trying to catch 40 winks and then starting all over again the next day!...

WHO SAID LIFE WAS FAIR ?

So how would a LEO MALE be with a Sagittarian? With his expectation of being the "boss," he should find a Sagittarian to be a perfect foil. Both have outgoing personalities, both crave attention and generally like to get on with life, but the lazy lovable Leo will be quite happy for his Sagittarian to do the work! The Sagittarian will back up the Leo in every way but be careful they do not use aggression to achieve this!!

A LEO FEMALE would find her Sagittarian helpful, and be supportive of the Sag need for "freedom." The Sagittarian would respond by being closer and even protective of Leo.

Both of these signs are social "experts" in the art of charming people. Likely, the Sagittarian would be unusually faithful in this partnership. Sag might flirt a lot and check out the hot guys or chicks, but will then get back home to mama or papa!

LOVE RELATIONSHIP

As with all fire signs, sparks fly in the bedroom....King Leo's favorite room! In fact he could live there all day and night as long as regular meals were brought to him. The Sagittarian, however, would have the guile to tempt Leo to new pastures (and rooms), and also be a bit experimental, with a "Life is too short, so get off your butt and live a little,"Leo! "Sag can show you so much!!"

LADY LEO should have no trouble in going along with the Sagittarian's zest for life, and will enjoy being taken away from household chores for a change. Just YOU keep an eye on the expenses, Lady Leo, and don't let sexy Sagittarius charm you into giving him the credit card!!

CHORD COMBINATION   C MAJOR   C/E AND G
LEO/SAGITTARIUS AND PISCES
Pisces makes up the C Major chord and is covered in Chapter 5
FOR SAGITTARIUS AND PISCES
SEE CHAPTER 11 THE NOTE G#/C+

VIRGO ♍ and CAPRICORN ♑
GENERAL RELATIONSHIP

What a strong combination!! The partnership in this case may well result in more mutual respect and admiration for each other in other ways beyond just a than a strong sensual desire!!

The normally bossy Virgo, especially when in control of the situation, would find the amiable but hard working Capricorn to be a willing accomplice in business. Capricorn may even help the Virgo achieve desired ambitions even at the cost of Capricorn's own!

These two workaholics could rule the world, if their ruthless streak would let them! Even in desperate times they would both survive and give strength and support to each other. Beware that the Virgo does not over step the control he or she so likes!!

LOVE RELATIONSHIP

This is a very down-to-earth relationship based mainly on security. Behind closed (bedroom) doors, these two may take a while to get the action going than you might think, as both signs would not like to reveal their intimate secrets, and both signs may be a bit unadventurous to to start with. They need to build up a long term relationship before completely baring their souls to one another. Capricorn, in particular, may be guilty of this, but will also be the most loyal of partners.

This is a good long term relationship that could last for years and years. The only setback may still be the "bossy" Virgo trait that eventually could even try the saintly patience of the goat!!

CHORD COMBINATION
C MAJOR   C/E AND G
VIRGO/CAPRICORN AND ARIES

Aries makes up the C Major chord and is covered in Chapter 5

FOR CAPRICORN AND VIRGO
SEE CHAPTER 11
THE NOTE G#/C+

LIBRA ♎ and AQUARIUS ♒

GENERAL RELATIONSHIP

.Now here are 2 happy go lucky souls!

Librans will love the quiet but serious and intelligent Aquarian personality that will give the Libran a free reign to live their life as

they please. Librans are generally caring people that try to please everyone but sometimes end up not pleasing anyone especially themselves. "Indecisive? Not me at least I don't think so, well maybe sometimes do you think?"

The Aquarian will be more than able to make helpful and correct decisions in this relationship without hurting the feelings of the Libra who in turn has a great eye for quality and their home could be full of antiques or beautiful things providing that the Aquarian can keep up the payments!!

LOVE RELATIONSHIP

These 2 air signs will say to each other that they will not tie them down and are free to be their own person and as a result of this it will draw them closer together. Aquarius being a free thinker will not feel threatened or bored with

their lovely Libran and Libra will not have to try and please their adoring Aquarius it will just happen.

This is not necessarily a full on lustful relationship, but both of these two Sun signs can relax in each other's company and also in each other's bed!!

CHORD COMBINATION....
C MAJOR   C/E AND G

LIBRA/AQUARIUS AND TAURUS

SCORPIO ♏ and PISCES ♓

GENERAL RELATIONSHIP

The determined Scorpio will temper the Piscean trait of sometimes being too bossy and Scorpio will also console Pisces when his or her tears arrive, but then the Scorpio will also say:

"OK, that's over...now get on with life and don't look back!!"

On any rare occasion that the Scorpio might need support, the Piscean will be in there at the double with all guns blazing!

Don't make enemies of these two2!!

You can"t beat these two in a verbal competition—and physically? Well, I hope you've been working out regularly at the gym!

LOVE RELATIONSHIP

Still waters run deep for this couple but it is a very strong combination and could be a sizzler in the bedroom!! Pisces has a lot of imagination and this would excite and stimulate our Scorpion. More than a match

55

for each other will bring mutual respect but no bedroom secrets will be revealed especially by our secretive Scorpion.

As for the Pisces, if you reveal anything too personal about your Piscean lover, then you better quickly go swimming back to the ocean for protection!!

CHORD COMBINATION
C MAJOR..C/E AND G

SCORPIO/PISCES AND GEMINI

Gemini makes up the C Major chord and is covered in Chapter 5

FOR PISCES AND SCORPIO
SEE CHAPTER 11 THE NOTE G#/C+

SAGITTARIUS ♐ and ARIES ♈

GENERAL RELATIONSHIP.

Aries are probably the only sign that a Sagittarian respects fully and completely!!

Sagittarians can be honest to a fault but often in a very sarcastic way. For example, the old saying, "The truth hurts," was made for the sarcastic Sagittarius!!!

A Sagittarian might tell you, in no uncertain terms, things such as They will tell you in no uncertain terms things such as, "You are not wearing **that**, are you?" Then, if you object or seem sad, he or she would then say, "I was only being honest!"

Now most people will take offense at such things, but and Aries will generally either just accept this unusual form of wha the Sagittarian might consider to be constructive criticism, or will just not give a damn anyway!

Both of these Sun signs like to party but you had better make sure you have two or three alarm clocks set, if you know they have to get up early the next day!!

Sagittarians will love the caring Arian's attention and Aries will not steal the Sagittarian's thunder or craving to be center of attention and be quite happy to share the glory with his or her fiery friend and lover!

LOVE RELATIONSHIP
Come on baby light my fire!!...

And it will be a burning furnace when these two get together. For how long? As long as they both want!

Aries and Sagitarrius-signs, both fire signs, will understand each other — and both are sexy signs, too.

When the Sagittarius is is in "control" of this situation, though, the primary danger could be his or her roving eye!

But be prepared for a Ram raid, our Sagittarius—if you are caught at some place where you shouldn't be!!

CHORD COMBINATION
C MAJOR C/E AND G

SAGITTARIUS/ARIES AND CANCER
Cancer makes up the C Major chord and is covered in Chapter 5

FOR ARIES AND SAGITTARIUS
SEE CHAPTER 11 THE NOTE G#/C+

CAPRICORN ♑ and TAURUS ♉

GENERAL RELATIONSHIP
Work,work and more work....

What are you doing on your day off? Oh, just working on something!.

There is more to life than just work—or is there, for this down to earth, security conscious couple?

Capricorns will find their Taurean partner more than their equal in strength and stubbornness and determination to always pay the bills!!

More than often, though, the Taurean will rescue the situation, since the normally decisive, but control freak Capricorn, will sometimes play "Peter Pan" and want to be a child forever!!

The Taurean will want to be as secure as possible— but that can be times too much sometimes. .

It's a case of "putting something by for a rainy day.... but not a whole rainy year!!

Capricorn's control of self is very important to this Sun sign. It is just as important to Capricorn as one's home would be important to a Taurean.

So, just as os long as the goat and bull don't lock horns too much this relationship will be a successfu lone.. if possibly slightly emotionally starved someties.

Lighten up a little...both of you!!

LOVE RELATIONSHIP

Capricorns can be surprisingly shy at times but are nearly always in control of themselves and their emotions. This strength is an attractive attribute for our security conscious Taurean, but once behind closed doors The Taurus will expect his or her Capricorn lover to be a bit more adventurous and open up a little more.

A Capricorn and a Taurus can be prolific lovers, once they have finished eating!!

The Capricorns will find the Taurean to be one of the only signs to which he or she can reveal all, without fear of deceit.

This love relationship actually grows over time— and even an often solitary person, such as a Capricorn can be, needs a little loving sometime!

CHORD COMBINATION
C MAJOR   C/E AND G
CAPRICORN/TAURUS AND LEO

Leo makes up the C Major chord and is covered in Chapter 5

FOR TAURUS AND CAPRICORN
SEE CHAPTER 11
THE NOTE G#/C+

AQUARIUS ♒ AND GEMINI ♊

GENERAL RELATIONSHIP

"Great minds think alike" is a saying made for this couple. They each have simple respect for each other's intellect and general attitude, ad share the belief that life is there for the taking!

Gemini will only enhance and carry out the amazing and possibly even crazy ideas of his or her Aquarian partner. After all, geniuses are often regarded as being crazy!

If this is a boardroom combination then heaven help the opposition—they won't stand a chance!

At home, if these two are sharing a home, they will need some household help to keep the place tidy for them. This is because they will too busy planning their next adventure togehter!!

So, be careful—both of you—not to be looking for the meaning of life through a bottle!! This could be your only potential downfall to have an amazing life together.

LOVE RELATIONSHIP

A relationship between an Aquarian and a Gemini can be a successful combination, because these two will love each others intellect, just as as much as each others bodies!! They will be open and honest to each other about what they need and want in the relationship.

Aquarius will be one of the few signs to accept a Gemini's sometimes "what's in it for me" attitude. Also, Aquarians are generally not jealous types, which is just as well considering that Gemini can be quite flirtacious.

Still both of these two Sun signs are "free spirits" so, in a partnership, they will also give each other that freedom—NOT to be with other partners—but for each of them to feel free to be just as he or she is—to be himself or herself withou pressure to change.

As stated before, though, beware the demon drink or other substances! Neither of you need them to have a happy partnership!

CHORD COMBINATION
C MAJOR C/E AND G

AQUARIUS/GEMINI AND VIRGO

Virgo makes up the C Major chord and is covered in Chapter 5

FOR GEMINI AND AQUARIUS
SEE CHAPTER 11
THE NOTE G#/C+

PISCES ♓ AND CANCER ♋

GENERAL RELATIONSHIP

Cry me a river...in fact cry me an ocean!!!.

These two Sun signs are such emotional creatures that they could put the stock price of Kleenex through the roof!!

However they can control their emotions enough to be very good together. This partnership could also be very good news for animals in distress or other caring causes that they share.

I could imagine a Pisces controlling a charitable institution with the Cancerian secretary carrying out the commands of his or bossy Piscean!!

But regardless of the type of relationship between these two Sun signs, it will be one partnership that could live and work together for a better world.

Possibly these two are ar-tistic even "hippy" like idealistic people, such that even the normally home loving

Cancerian would travel to the ends of the earth for his or her Piscean partner!

One warning however! Take care that you both avoid any possi-ble drinking or drug abuse, because then your emotional involvement with each other could cause depres-sion.

LOVE RELATIONSHIP

Sexy and sensual, these two roman-
tics! Passions run high, but beware
that these water signs don't overflow
or drown each other! Too much of a
good thing? At least initially, this will
be emotional overload, and all sorts
of experimentation in the bedroom,
as they both will understand each
others needs to be open about their
feelings. Someone at last that under-
stands!

If the sometimes bossy
Pisces can control this trait inside
the house and let Cancer be an equal
then this has every chance of long
term success with probably a few
little break ups but the making up is
always fun!!!

CHORD
COMBINATION
C MAJOR   C/E AND G

PISCES/CANCER AND LIBRA

Libra makes up the C Major chord and is covered in Chapter 5

FOR CANCER AND PISCES
SEE CHAPTER 11
THE NOTE G#/C+

CHAPTER 5

The THIRD PART HARMONY G

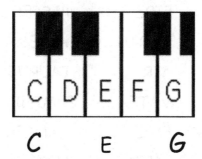

C E G

This note is often played an octave lower.

e.g. The chord of C is C/E and G. If you start with the G below the C and then the E you are playing the same chord but with an inverted G.

SO THE G IS THE BASE NOTE!!

G......... C.......E G...........C......E

WORK.............this will be your most dependable co-worker a reliable and steady base to build your team around.

HOME.............if this is your partner then he or she will be your rock and will always support you especially in times of crisis, etc.

ROMANCE ....this could be a lover who will never cheat on you, will be honest and dependable and will always be there for you if needed!

MONEY..........this would be the treasurer in a club or society...the wages clerk, security, bank guard etc.

So here are your G perfect harmony combinations:

BASE NOTE C	ELEMENT	HARMONY G	ELEMENT
ARIES ♈	FIRE	SCORPIO	WATER
TAURUS ♉	EARTH	SAGITTARIUS	FIRE
GEMINI ♊	AIR	CAPRICORN	EARTH
CANCER ♋	WATER	AQUARIUS	AIR
LEO ♌	FIRE	PISCES	WATER
VIRGO ♍	EARTH	ARIES	FIRE
LIBRA ♎	AIR	TAURUS	EARTH
SCORPIO ♏	WATER	GEMINI	AIR
SAGITTARIUS ♐	FIRE	CANCER	WATER
CAPRICORN ♑	EARTH	LEO	FIRE
AQUARIUS ♒	AIR	VIRGO	EARTH
PISCES ♓	WATER	LIBRA	AIR

The G harmony in most cases will be more of a support in times of trouble or someone you can always rely on to tell you the truth!

This may not be the most romantic partnership in the world and some combinations may clash more than others but, but if your friend and partner was not there for you, he or she would be much missed.

ARIES ♈ and SCORPIO ♏
"THE ROCK"
GENERAL RELATIONSHIP

The Scorpio will definitely be the ROCK in this partnership. He or she will back up the fiery Aries in every way and be a friend or lover for life!

The Aries habit of rushing into things sometimes too quickly will be controlled by the cynical Scorpio who won't be taken in by "too good to be true opportunities!"

As long as the water element does not dampen the Aries fire too much, this will be a solid combination. If this was a detective team, it would be a scenario of Aries (the good cop) vs. Scorpio (the bad cop) !!

LOVE RELATIONSHIP

Both Aries and Scorpio are passionate signs and Aries fire could have the Scorpio's water boiling over at times in the bedroom.

In my experience, I think that this combination works well as a team, and in love could work out OK, as long as the Scorpio's jealous streak can be controlled in relationship with the flirty Aries.

(The Aries types are just like that, Scorpio—so don't get your stinger out yet—just accept it and your Aries will always come home to you.)

CHORD COMBINATION
C MAJOR C/E AND G
ARIES/LEO AND SCORPIO

This trio can be a strong team, if perhaps a little bit overly enthusiastic at times, with the fiery combination of Aries and Leo.

Scorpio may have a hard time keeping control of the "children"" here, but if anyone can do it, a Scorpio can.

TAURUS ♉ and SAGITTARIUS ♐

"THE ROCK"
GENERAL RELATIONSHIP

At first glance, the down to earth Taurean would not normally be seen dead with a fire sign!!

But both of these signs have some great things in common. Both are incredibly honest. Even if Sagittarians are a bit blunt with the truth, the Taurean loves nothing more than directness and honesty. So, call a spade a spade, etc.

A Sagittarian also has lots of energy, which is a common trait and appeals to the alter ego of the Taurean, who actually would like a sporty fast car, and to go out dancing now and again! The Sagittarian doesn't need to be asked twice to accommodate this.

Taurus would be better off looking after the wages in this combination, as the Sagittarius might have spent them in the bar on the way home, buying drinks all around for their posse of friends and hanger ons!!

Sagittarians can also be fiercely loyal and want to protect their partner with a passion—so don't criticize these two without a good reason!

LOVE RELATIONSHIP

Opposites attract, so they say—and this could be a wonderful sexy affair to start with....

and if Taurus can keep the green-eyed monster "Jealousy" under control, then this could be a lot of fun all around!

Sagittarians are extremely "versatile" in the bedroom, and as all earth signs really want to break free from their general personality of being non-adventurous, this will be exciting for them.....at least to start with.

Sagittarians are better, in my opinion, as a great support for their earth partner in this situation, as the initial sexual attraction will be hard to maintain over a long period of time. Sagittarians can get bored and have a roving eye!!

Can you keep the love interest going long enough Taurus? You have the most stamina and are the most loyal of all the signs, so if anyone can do it, it is you!

CHORD COMBINATION
C MAJOR C/E AND G
TAURUS/VIRGO AND SAGITTARIUS

Sagittarius may be the perfect foil for the two sometimes "dull" Earth signs, and just keep your input like this, our Archer, and all will be well.

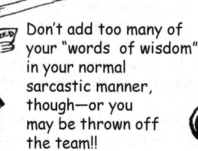

Don't add too many of your "words of wisdom" in your normal sarcastic manner, though—or you may be thrown off the team!!

70

GEMINI ♊ and CAPRICORN ♑
GENERAL RELATIONSHIP

For the Gemini, Capricorn could be the perfect partner to carry out Gemini's wonderful inventive ideas and lifestyle, as the Capricorn will just do what is asked! Brains and Brawn? Well, in a small way, since Capricorn is quite high on the IQ stakes, as well, but is also happy to work hard to support the clever Gemini.

These two enigmatic characters are not shy in public and may well form a double act on stage!! As long as Gemini does not keep piling too much on Capricorn's side of the table, and pulls his or her weight, this is a hard act to follow!!

LOVE RELATIONSHIP

Capricorn is a steadying and very supportive influence in this combination—but also Gemini could find Capricorn's reserve just a little boring in the bedroom. Geminis crave freedom to express themselves and as long as the goat does not hold Gemini back this could work.

Capricorns long to break free from themselves as too tied down to earth, worriers, and etc. If so, the Gemini could attract them to be more adventurous in all of life's departments!

CHORD COMBINATION
C MAJOR C/E AND G
GEMINI/LIBRA AND CAPRICORN

Capricorn is there in this combination to keep our two "up in the air" signs from floating away altogether!!

Gemini's are leaders, not followers, but at times they need someone to control their sometimes extravagant lifestyle, which they may want, but are not quite able to afford!

Call Goat and Co. Accountants, though, and be assured you will be kept within your budget!

You may not be happy about it, Gemini—but you won't have to hide if the Landlord comes to collect his rent!!

FOR CAPRICORN AND GEMINI, SEE CHAPTER 9.

CANCER ♋ and AQUARIUS ♒
GENERAL RELATIONSHIP

The emotional Cancerian will find the Aquarian to be an interesting and stimulating partner who will use intelligence to conquer any difficulty that arises and avoid any possible panicky Cancerian outburst!! In fact, the Aquarian "air" element will create quite a few nice "bubbles" in a water sign partner to make him or her think and be excited for the future! Aquarius can be a steadying influence on the Cancerian, without too much emotion, and this will bring some calm to most any situation.

　　　　The Cancerian will be able to feel his or her emotional burden a little bit lighter whenever the water carrying friend has been available.

LOVE
RELATIONSHIP

Most of the G harmony combinations are more supportive than sensual, however I think Cancer would be attracted to the cool Aquarian exterior and wish sometimes to be like that.

If our Aquarian really cares for the Cancerian, he or she will nurture and demonstrate how to have less stress in life, and this could relax Cancer such that sparks then could fly under the sheets. If however the Aquarian is too remote and aloof then Cancer could feel totally alone. Cancers are normally very nice caring people, Aquarius so you be nice and caring too, and this relationship could work very well.

CHORD COMBINATION
C MAJOR   C/E
CANCER/SCORPIO AND AQUARIUS

And
the
wise owl
says:

In the picture that you see above of that very happy couple walking hand in hand, think about them as a Cancer and a Scorpio, happily walking side by side.

You may recognize that these two might not need anyone else, since the Scorpion is able to look after and handle most any situation. Still, Scorpios can, at times, be their OWN worst enemy—so, Cancer, **you** may then need the services of a wise Aquarian!!

LEO ♌ and PISCES ♓
GENERAL RELATIONSHIP

A MALE LEO will find the female Piscean a good partner to back him up especially in battle!! The Piscean is known for love of the "underdog" and will be at her man's side when trouble brews, as it may often do in this partnership, since the proud Leo may not back down or be very diplomatic in a disagreement. A Pisces (male or female) will be more inclined to back up his or her partner without thinking of the consequences! This can be a formidable duo in sports, though, so make sure you back up yourself, if you are confronting these two!

A FEMALE LEO will probably have a softer approach to this pairing, but don't underestimate the cat woman! She will do battle for her Piscean partner just as much, and could have very sharp claws!

Still, it is a strong partnership, these two, and many charities could benefit from some volunteering from both of these caring souls.

75

MALE LEOS will find the relationship ben-
eficial in a practical way more than in a
physical way. Pisces in love with the Leo
will be supportive to the bitter end and
also be very sensual in the boudoir to keep
the lion interested. As long as King Leo
does not treat his emotional fish like a
servant to cater for his every pleasure, then this will be a strong relationship. Don't even think about straying, your highness, or you'll face
an uprising!

FEMALE LEOS will treat their Pisces partners more on equal
terms and benefit from their support. They'll even have interesting
conversations of a spiritual or psychic nature.

Don't go too far off the wall, though, Pisces, or the fairly down-
to-earth Lioness may just ignore you and get on with her chores!! In
this chord combination you may think that Pisces could be left out of
the party that the two Fire signs have arranged.

Well, Leo, you had better keep our Fish's cell phone handy if you
need rescuing from a tricky situation that you and the Archer have
found yourselves in. Perhaps our Sagittarian upset a few guests with
some blunt speaking and now you are surrounded in the car park. Don't
worry—a school of Pisces Piranha is on the way!!

CHORD COMBINATION
C MAJOR C/E AND G

LEO/SAGITTARIUS
AND PISCES

VIRGO ♍ and ARIES ♈
GENERAL RELATIONSHIP

Earth and fire do not often mix well, since the earth can smother and extinguish the flame—but still, opposites often attract, and the Aries can be a surprising and lighter influence on the normal controlling and serious side of Virgo.

The Aries childlike energy can soften the Virgo heart, but their unending energy would be a great temptation for Virgo to tell Aries to complete the 1000 tasks a day that the Virgo has planned!!

Virgo would act like a caring, but also a disciplinarian parent.

But Virgo—
don't overdo the
discipline,
or the
"child"
may throw
a big tantrum!

LOVE RELATIONSHIP

On paper you would not give these two opposites much of a chance to-gether, with Virgo's disciplined life in comparison to the Aries energy and non-stop action. But, although the passion may be more evident in their arguing than in the bedroom, they each have something that the other wants or craves.

      In this situation, The G harmony acts like the "rock" for you both.   Aries would certainly be there for you, Virgo, if you needed help, even if you had just had a blazing row and thrown all of his or her clothes in the street!

**CHORD
COMBINATION**

**C MAJOR
C/E AND G**

**VIRGO/CAPRICORN
AND
ARIES**

Virgo and Capricorn will only need their Aries team mate on this occa-sion to add a little bit of "light" into their sometimes quite dull, effi-cient and stable existence!

      Don't worry about our down-to Earth-workers, though. You can imagine Aries to be like grandchildren.They may wear you out, but they'll liven your day and even make you laugh.

The best bit in that?
You can send them home
afterwards.

After all,they are your grandchilden! You can love them and enjoy them, but you don't have to live with them all the time...

Phew...!!

LIBRA ♎ and TAURUS ♉
GENERAL RELATIONSHIP

Our Libra person will love the secure and trusting back up of a Taurean partner because the Taurus will keep things together and back down-to-earth from all of the Libran's flights of fancy!!

Although the Libra may prefer to be boss in this relationship, he or she will be happy to relinquish control and let the Taurus take

over the management of their home, so long Libra is free to go out as desired, with a little pocket money!!

The Libra's eye for quality, especially for the things in their home, will be pleasing to the very home-loving Taurean... although the Taurus may well have to earn the money to fund the lavish Libra lifestyle!!

LOVE RELATIONSHIP

Librans are, in general, pretty easy going and lovable because they try to please everyone and Taureans are easy to please, so long as you just tell them the truth! You couldn't wish for a stronger or more trustworthy partner.

Libra if you keep to the truth, even if you've just maxed the credit card, you'd better own up. Taurus may be angry initially, but will come up with a plan to get your finances back on the straight and narrow.

Taureans can be very sensual with the right partner, and a Libran could make Taurus float on air in the bedroom—but the Taurean could come down to earth with a bump if the Libran strays. Don't expect your freedom to flirt with whomever, Libra. Your Taurus is waiting at home, horns sharpened!

CHORD COMBINATION C MAJOR C/E AND G

LIBRA/ AQUARIUS AND TAURUS

Taurus in this team will be the backbone for Libra and Aquarius! The Taurus is strong, reliable, and honest as the day is long!

Libra and Aquarius may find Taurus a little boring—but sometimes one or the other of of you may need a lift home from that distant planet that you both sometimes visit!!

Aquarians may even ask you to stay up all night, Libra and just look at the moon!!   Aaaah!!

SCORPIO ♏ and GEMINI ♊
GENERAL RELATIONSHIP

This is a terrific combination of secrecy and subversion! These two could be spies for BOTH sides and still not let the other know what is happening!!

Gemini's tend to play the game of life quite well—although in their "two in one" person mode, they can be quite changeable.

Scorpio, a fixed sign, does not so easily change, once his or her mind is made up about a partner. Scorpio can be your very best friend or your worst enemy!

If the Gemini is true to Scorpio, this pairing will have all they need to be successful—but beware, as BOTH signs can turn as easily and as quickly as making a cup of tea!! This relationship could be the subject for a best selling thriller!!

LOVE RELATIONSHIP

As a support to you, Scorpio, your Gemini will be very strong and clever and could get you through any difficult periods of your life. Not that you need much help in this department, as you generally just get on with life regardless.

You will be fascinated by Gemini's quick mind and often very sexy and good looking persona. You are also very sensual, and the honeymoon period could last quite a long time—as long as Gemini can remain faithful!!

Scorpio will be a one woman or one man person and will not accept second best. Can you be the Scorpio's best friend and lover, Gemini—or will your flirtatious ways get the better of you?

CHORD COMBINATION
C MAJOR   C/E AND G
SCORPIO/PISCES AND GEMINI

Strong emotions are in play with the Scorpio and Pisces combination, such that it may lead to conflict with others. Scorpions and Pisceans are unlikely to hold back, when difficult situations arise.

At such times, diplomacy and a strategic withdrawal may be needed, and who better to organize that for you but your General Gemini.

You may have lost a small battle, but the war is not over yet! Leave it to the charming Gemini persuasion techniques!!

82

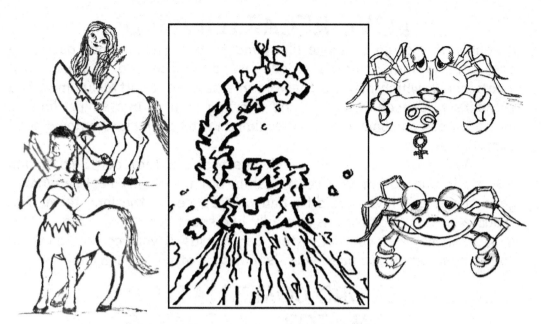

SAGITTARIUS ♐ and CANCER ♋
GENERAL RELATIONSHIP

The Cancerian in this partnership is more likely to be left at home to do the washing, ironing, cooking, cleaning and look after the kids until the Sagittarian gets home and inspects your work!

So don't cry, Cancer, if the Sagittarian gets a bit blunt! Sag is only are trying to help and "correct" your mistakes!!

This is OK for a while, as long as the Sagittarius also adds a lot of praise and takes you out to dinner now and then!.....Oh, or perhaps buys you a puppy or 6, just to keep you happy!

Cancer, however, can be a strong emotional support for the confident Sag, if Sagittarius is having an "off day," because Cancer is always prepared to listen.

So don't be so harsh, our fiery horse,
and you could find a true friend!

LOVE RELATIONSHIP

Probably this could be more like good friends rather than good lovers? Still, in a lot of cases a close friendship can lead to a good love relationship, which may be possible in this case. Sagittarius may find the sensual Cancer intriguing and exciting at first in a sexual liaison, and also good company when out socializing, as both signs enjoy a good party!!

Will this relationship last? It's possible that our Sagittarian may be in and out of the relationship, but eventually realize what a good friend and lover could be had with Cancer in the long term. The trouble is that Sagittarians normally like short term romances.

You may kick yourself later, Sagittarius, if your caring Cancer is not at home when you need your "significant other"....mmmmm?

CHORD COMBINATION
C MAJOR   C/E AND G
SAGITTARIUS/ARIES AND CANCER

At first glance you most likely wouldn't think that our caring Cancer could offer anything to these two overconfident Fire signs.

When Sagittarians and Arians get together, though, really anything could happen, and sometimes situations need "dampening down" a little. Actually, then, having a Cancerian Fire Brigade Team on standby may be more appropriate!!

CAPRICORN ♑ and LEO ♌
GENERAL RELATIONSHIP

Both are capable leaders. The Leo would take a slight back seat to the sometimes controlling Capricorn—but what a back up! The goat may scramble the way onward and upward slowly, but surely—especially with a Lion in their tank who could put a stop to it!

A lot of Capricorns are also very laid back, at least on the outside, which is a trait that most Leo males have in common.

Capricorn may show a "lazy" streak, particularly if the subject is of no real interest. Again, the male/female Leo each have different traits that may come in to play.

For example, the Leo female would be the most likely to finish the task in hand, but the Leo male may just yawn, agree with the Goat and say, "We'll do it tomorrow?!"

Both signs are very proud leaders and charmers—so beware of some real smooth talking!!

LOVE RELATIONSHIP

Wouldn't you like an angry Lion to fight for you in times of trouble? Well if your Leo male loves you, then it's an unbeatable partnership. Fire signs always attract down-to-earth signs at least initially, and they can bring all the pleasure you crave. Unfortunately, you will come to your senses, Capricorn, and you may become too boring for our Leo, who has to be kept amused, especially in the bedroom! Even when the Capricorn is the support player, and even if the physical attraction wanes, a strong mutual admiration could be formed here.

LEO FEMALES would be better at making this a long term relationship, as they would have more patience, will try to make a success of this combination and be happy that Capricorn is more than willing to share life's daily chores.

Capricorns also never give up until the end, and even in a bad relationship, they'll at least give love a chance! They are more likely great partners than great lovers!

CHORD COMBINATION
C MAJOR C/E AND G

CAPRICORN/TAURUS AND LEO

Try getting past an old Goat, a stubborn Bull and an angry Lion!! That's a tough team to beat here. Don't try and match them for strength.....instead, play on their weakness. They are all softies inside. Give them the hard luck story of the century.

They may not shed a million tears, but might help pay your mortgage and clean your house!! The trouble is that when they find out that you have not exactly been totally honest with them—watch out! And hopefully, you can run fast!!

AQUARIUS ≈ and VIRGO ♍
GENERAL RELATIONSHIP

The Aquarian will love his or her Virgo "right hand man/woman," who will get the Aquarian's zany, but probable genius ideas, find a way to help turn them into reality. Virgos may be bossy and try to control everything, but in this case, the Aquarian will be happy to let the Virgo do the hard work! After all it was Aquarius who had the idea!

On the other hand, if the Aquarian should get into a very sticky situation and not be able to think his or her way out of the trouble, don't worry.

The Virgo will come to the rescue, and take over the entire situation.

After all, our Virgo types can be the best of signs to assist when there is a "crisis."

LOVE RELATIONSHIP

These two will have mind sex! Both are intellectual and interesting people, so they will be attracted to each other mentally—and if they are attracted physically, as well, then wonderful!

Your Virgo will be a fantastic "rock" in a close relationship with you, Aquarius as long as you aren't too overly generous with your cash and freak out the Virgo bank manager!

This combination of a "thinker" and a "doer" should be a great pair, so long as Aquarius doesn't crave too much time on his or her own, and Virgo does not try to control or subdue the Aquarian's longing for freedom and space, then all will be ok. Yes or No?

CHORD COMBINATION
C MAJOR C/E AND G
AQUARIUS/GEMINI AND VIRGO

Virgos may have a tough time on their hands trying to find out what the two enigmatic Air signs are thinking!

So, don't think Virgo—just be there when the Aquarius or Gemini schemes to either find the fountain of youth or build the biggest nuclear weapon that could destroy us all, or cause the world to come to an abrupt and dangerous end.

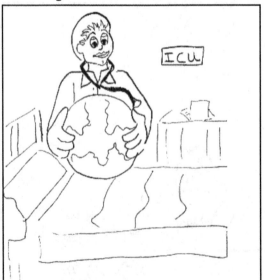

Then they will need you, Virgo, to dig them out of the largest hole anyone could make.

Or... one or the other of them—or maye the pair of them together— may have won the Nobel Peace Prize!!

PISCES ♓ and LIBRA ♎
GENERAL RELATIONSHIP

The partnership in this case may NOT be about being a ¨rock¨ physically or involving hard work. Pisceans are not normally shy about getting their hands dirty! Librans may wash them every 5 minutes to get rid of dirt, but emotionally I can see the Libra being a positive and great friend to the sometimes overemotional Pisces who would just need someone to talk to on most occasions!

Librans have a sympathetic ear as they try to please, then weigh things up then agree with both sides! But they can also lighten your life and cheer you up, when you need it, they can also be a shoulder to cry on!

This is just right for the caring Pisceans, who sometimes give off a hard exterior, when they really are more like big softies inside!

LOVE RELATIONSHIP

This will be a fun and exciting relationship, at least to start with! The Pisces has a hard outer shell but a very soft interior that could melt with an easy going and extrovert Libra who wants to go dancing every night and still has energy to make love in the mornings!!

If Pisces can keep up with this pace of life, then fantastic —but all too often the Piscean moody, deep emotional side takes over and your Libra would not cope very well with a partner in depression! He or she would listen, however, and try to help, which is what Librans do, but he or she may be feeling weighed down, if the Pisces is in a dark place. So, keep things as light as possible, then Pisces and Libra will make each other laugh!! That's better than crying eh?

CHORD COMBINATION
C MAJOR C/E AND G
PISCES/CANCER and LIBRA

Librans will feel quite comfortable with these two caring souls and not feel pressure to make too many decisions. Pisces and Cancer will also feel they have found someone who will listen to their "concerns!"

Although the Libra may not actually DO anything about it, just being there is all that the Pisces and the Cancer may need.

After all, that's what friends are for!!

CHAPTER 6

Your NOT SO PERFECT harmony C SHARP (C#)

Ok so the next note we are going to look at is
No2...C SHARP(C#)

The note in between C and D, and as explained earlier, can also be
called D FLAT (Db).

C#/Db

This is the very first note after C going up, and is hardly ever played in
a C chord because it clashes when played together.

If you have a keyboard handy, play the two notes together and
hear what it sounds like!

The illustration at the top of the next page was given the title
"Clash"—because the image matches the sound! It's hardly harmonious!

This illustration, for me, relates that most zodiac signs that are next to each other are seldom harmonious, as well! One of the few times the note could be used is to get to the next "note," but in general the adjacent signs are not a very happy mix!

There are always times, though, that two signs very different in temperament can actually get on well—at least for a little while!

Opposites attract and often you can see something in another sign

 type that you are lacking in your own sign, and wish that you could be more like that other sign!

This will work for a while, before you realize that it is just "not you"—and you cannot be someone else!

In the short term, your relationship with an adjacent sign type could be exciting and fun, but I do not see long term relationships without problems when adjacent signs are prominent.

Also for this note there are no chord combinations! That is, unless you are a funky jazz man or a crazy classical conductor!

Here are all the C# combinations:

SUN SIGN	ELEMENT	C#	ELEMENT
ARIES	FIRE	TAURUS	EARTH
TAURUS	EARTH	GEMINI	AIR
GEMINI	AIR	CANCER	WATER
CANCER	WATER	LEO	FIRE
LEO	FIRE	VIRGO	EARTH
VIRGO	EARTH	LIBRA	AIR
LIBRA	AIR	SCORPIO	WATER
SCORPIO	WATER	SAGITTARIUS	FIRE
SAGITTARIUS	FIRE	CAPRICORN	EARTH
CAPRICORN	EARTH	AQUARIUS	AIR
AQUARIUS	AIR	PISCES	WATER
PISCES	WATER	ARIES	FIRE

When you look at the elements together you have....

FIRE with EARTH
FIRE scorches the EARTH/EARTH puts out FIRE.

EARTH with AIR
Too much EARTH in the air causes sandstorms of trouble.
AIR blows EARTH all over the place...chaos.

AIR with WATER
Too much AIR in WATER causes storms.
Too much WATER in AIR causes storms.

WATER with FIRE
WATER puts out the FIRE
FIRE boils the WATER.

ARIES ♈ and TAURUS ♉
CLASH

GENERAL RELATIONSHIP

The Ram and the Bull may have a complete clash of horns here in the situation where Aries calls the shots.

Taurus will be thrown completely off balance with Aries running around giving orders and Taurus trying to keep up with them.

Eventually Taurus could just put a hoof down, and probably right on top of Aries, if he or she doesn't slow down and give Taurus time to think, and to complete the 100 jobs that Aries has allocated!

If you want to keep bulls happy, Aries, just slow down a bit, give them one job at a time and give a little praise at the end of each one —and you may keep Taurus contented and working hard for you for a long time.

Oh, yes—
be sure you
don't forget
to feed them...
lots!!

LOVE RELATIONSHIP
Arians like freedom and want to check out all that
love's menu has to offer!

Taureans can be jealous creatures,
so more conflict is likely here.

If the Aries can survive for a period of time,
he or she may come to appreciate the security and reliability
that a Taurean has to offer.

Could this be their only chance together?

As with all these combinations,
there could be a thrill.... and a challenge and wow!
....For a one night stand only!!

Living together? How long will it last?

NO CHORD COMBINATION
FOR TAURUS AND ARIES
SEE CHAPTER 14, The maj7th

TAURUS ♉ and GEMINI ♊
CLASH

GENERAL RELATIONSHIP

Nearly every time a Taurus gets with a Gemini, Taurus will be used and abused afterwards. At the time, all is smiles and laughter from charming Gemini, who agrees to work hard and be loyal to the Taurean cause.

Loyalty and honesty are No. 1 on Taurus's list in a relationship! However at some time, whether they intended it or not, Gemini will let Taurus down, in one way or another. It may be a simple thing like not turning up on time—or not turning up at all! Then Gemini types will probably try and smooth talk their way out of trouble—maybe with a few little white lies?

Taureans, however, are expert readers of people, so may very likely see it as a betrayal and high treason!

I don't think Geminis realize that they can be like this, and some signs will react in a less dramatic way than Taurus. Still, the effect will stay with the Bull for a long time before the rift is healed...if ever!

LOVE RELATIONSHIP

I think Taurean demands for loyalty and the "you should be home every night—**not** in a bar" scenario would stress out restless Gemini, who has a natural longing for stimulation from the new people he/she just may meet in a bar!

Taureans can be very passionate however and this could keep our Gemini at home.

Gemini can be a charmer, so could soften the Bull's heart—and no one will try harder than Taurus to keep the relationship going...but still, I feel that in the end, there are too many differences. This could cause conflict, and the Gemini may well be tempted to escape!!

...for a few hours anyway!!

No Chord Combination
For Gemini and Taurus, see Chapter 14,
the Maj7th.

GEMINI ♊ and CANCER ♋
CLASH

GENERAL RELATIONSHIP

Cancer, I think, will probably irritate Gemini more than Gemini irritates Cancer. Gemini, in control, will expect things to be done according to his or her ultimate plan of Global domination!

Does that sound a bit extreme?...OK....just controlling most all of the other things at home or work will do!

Actually Geminis can be really great to get along with, especially socially. They are talented, clever and either good looking or at least able to charm the pants off you....But! They do have a selfish streak and in general, will do most anything, if it is advantageous to themselves!

Cancer may be too emotionally involved for Gemini's slightly more carefree attitude, and will probably try and get too close to Gemini's inner secrets, of which there are many!

Or Gemini could play the "twins" game...
good twin/bad twin ...
and then Cancer would be confused!

Loves me/Loves me not.

This can be very confusing for Cancerians,
who wear their hearts on their sleeves.
Gemini likes interesting mind games ...
but would a sensitive Cancer?

No Chord Combinaton
For Cancer and Gemini,
see Chapter 14, the Maj7th

CANCER ♋ and LEO ♌
CLASH

GENERAL RELATIONSHIP

Well here we have KING LEO again—who asked to be subservient to an emotional fool!

Well that's what he may think in private, if not in public! Cancers, though, wear their heart on their sleeves and express their feelings.

King Leo just wants his dinner and then to bed, especially if he doesn't have control of the TV remote!

If the King was injured however who better to come to his aid than caring animal lover Cancer! Once patched up though he would probably revert back to his old self but with a new story of his bravery at fighting off a whole pride of lions on his own with no mention of his nurse!

LADY LEO as always will react slightly different to this combination and at least listen to Cancers concerns and worries even if she is thinking to herself why don't you just get on with life like the rest of us!

LOVE RELATIONSHIP

For this to work Cancer will have to play up to (Male) Leo's ego but may be grateful of the fire sign, fun sign attitude which a sometimes melancholy Cancerian would need.

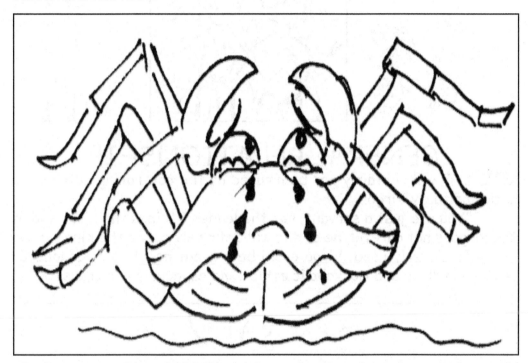

The lioness would probably be a better partner, however, as she would at least try to make the Cancerian happy—which may be a hard task, but one that Cancerian females would see as a challenge!

NO CHORD COMBINATION

FOR LEO AND CANCER
SEE CHAPTER 14 The maj7th

LEO ♌ and VIRGO ♍
CLASH

GENERAL RELATIONSHIP

KING LEO will certainly not be amused at the controlling actions and antics of fussy Virgo!

"You are just a servant, not the leader," thinks the Lion. And if the Virgo is not careful, he or she will definitely ruffle the King's mane!

If cleverly used, Virgo could be a great asset, with undoubted organizing skills and workaholic ethic—and especially in a crisis!!

However it is not likely that Virgo will accept second best to a proud and sometimes haughty leader, and the Leo will think Virgo is out to get his crown!

LADY LEO will probably think more carefully about this union, and if she and Virgo can work together, a lot could be achieved. But again, Virgo is not very good at playing second fiddle!

LOVE RELATIONSHIP

Neither of these two signs may easily understand the other!

The male Leo will secretly admire Virgo's control and strength, and would see it as a challenge to seduce and then break down that hard Virgo exterior, probably with little success—and then frustrations would creep in, and their differences would be exposed even more!

LADY LEO would have a softer approach to this relationship, and as a hard worker herself, would be admired, even for a short time, by the unforgiving Virgo.

    However, cracks would appear in time. Who would dominate in the bedroom first?

NO CHORD COMBINATION
FOR VIRGO AND LEO
SEE CHAPTER 14 The maj7th

VIRGO ♍ and LIBRA ♎
CLASH

GENERAL RELATIONSHIP

Virgo will find the Libran's general attitude to a more relaxed carefree life very irritable. Normally a Virgo's first concern is security through work and more work, and Virgos hate to not be in control.

Virgo won't have any trouble controlling Libra, but Libra will most likely find this liaison very uncomfortable and feel a bit oppressed!

LOVE RELATIONSHIP

Can the Libran find in the hidden sexy Virgo what they secretly want to be? Most earth signs tend to see openness and sexual freedom as a weakness, or at least keep it private! Librans have a more relaxed attitude to life, while love is not always on the Virgo agenda. I think that the only way this relationship is likely to work well, is behind closed doors.

Don't tell anyone, Libra. or you'll be in trouble. Is it worth the effort?

NO CHORD COMBINATION

FOR LIBRA AND VIRGO SEE CHAPTER 14 The maj7th

LIBRA ♎ and SCORPIO ♏
CLASH

GENERAL RELATIONSHIP

Again, Libra may well sit back and do nothing in this relationship. The Scorpio may well not control things, as such but will be irritated by Libra's often indecisiveness, and then the Scorpio may possibly be a little verbally harsh on the Libra.

If Librans can be a little stronger they may well get more respect from Scorpios who are able to bend a little and show a softer side than their Water element normally indicates!

Scorpio, then, may well come to be a Libran's friend for life, but eventually the open Libran lifestyle may well give away too much of Scorpio's secrets, and then there could be trouble ahead!

LOVE RELATIONSHIP

Scorpions are known for being sensual, but very jealous lovers! Librans will not want to be tied down by Scorpio's rules and may well go off and flirt with strangers, just for fun! This would totally drive the Scorpio to go out looking, with sting poised for the strike.

You will always try and please your Scorpion lover, Libra, so take care that you don't get in to a difficult relationship where you feel you that you can't escape!

It's better to speak your mind honestly, even if it causes a row that could at least "clear the air!" It's possible, then, that your Scorpio will admire your courage and improve the relationship.

If you keep it all inside, though, it could lead to illness and a feeling of being trapped. So, be very careful, Libra. Is this really what you want?

NO CHORD COMBINATION
FOR SCORPIO AND LIBRA

SEE CHAPTER 14
The maj7th

SCORPIO ♏ and SAGITTARIUS ♐ CLASH

GENERAL RELATIONSHIP

"And in the blue corner we have the stinging Scorpio!!"
"And in the red corner we have sarcastic Sagittarius!!"
Shake hands (no chance) and come out fighting (definitely)!!

Need I say more?

OK, it was a little bit dramatic perhaps—but not that far from the truth, in certain cicumstances.

Who can say the most hurtful and sarcastic sting- ing comments?

Could it be a draw!

Scorpions will not back down to even a hail of pos- sible abuse from anyone, and Sagittarians will give as good as they get.

Sticks and stones? Words would definitely hurt most other signs, but with this two, it could be a battle to the death! Yes, I am going to the extremes. The amazing thing though, is that if these two got their heads banged together, and then actually **look** at each other, they may see that they have a lot more in common than you would think.

LOVE RELATIONSHIP

Scorpio will be attracted to outspoken, funny and probably good looking Sagittarius AT FIRST!

As the affair develops, however, it could become clear that Scorpio would not like a saucy Sagittarian's flirtatious ways and would demand more loyalty and respect. Will Sagittarius reform? Not much chance of that, methinks!!

Scorpio may think he or she has a "hold" on the Sagittarian's often carefree attitude to money and security, etc., and try to keep the Sag tied down, but this is a recipe for disaster—and likely with love lost eventually!

For any chance of a long relationship, Scorpio will have to give a lot, because the Sagittarian will probably take a lot! (That is, emotionally speaking!!)

So Sagittarius, if you really want your Scorpio, who could just turn out to be the best friend you EVER had, then you will have to give a little as well!!

NO CHORD COMBINATION
FOR SAGITTARIUS AND SCORPIO

SEE CHAPTER 14
The maj7th

SAGITTARIUS ♐ and CAPRICORN ♑
CLASH

GENERAL RELATIONSHIP

From a distance each of these signs will find the other interesting mainly because they are poles apart in personalities!

Capricorns could actually charm the Sagittarius and probably talk themselves up to be something a little more than what they are... just a little exaggeration?

Sagittarians will be fascinated at first, but then see through any deceit or excuses from Capricorn. Especially if finances run out, then off they go into the night together— Probably to the nearest party!

There is probably a complete clash here, in most cases, and especially when Sagittarius is in control. This is because Capricorn will try to please, but then the personal criticism may be too much for the Goat to carry on.

LOVE RELATIONSHIP

There may be some attraction to start with here. Most Earth signs, like Capricorn, would secretly love to let go of their stuffy image and be free in life and love and sex. This is exactly what the Sagittarian could offer them, party on, with freedom, sex, and rock 'n roll!!

Ok, this could last a while before Capricorns regain their senses and also see how much money they have just 'wasted'!!

Sagittarians, though, want to keep the party going and soon will tire of boring Capricorn ways!!   NEXT!!

NO CHORD COMBINATION
FOR CAPRICORN AND SAGITTARIUS

SEE CHAPTER 14,
The maj7th

CAPRICORN ♑ and AQUARIUS ♒
CLASH

GENERAL RELATIONSHIP

Air typically can blow Earth around especially on a windy day! Here we have a combination that could well respect and admire each other's traits e.g. the Capricorn's strength, reliability and work ethic, etc., and the Aquarian's intelligence and thought process, etc. But these two signs will most likely have totally opposite views on life and how to live!

Aquarians are the thinkers, but not really the doers, so would likely irritate a Capricorn who wants to be in control in this relationship, so the goat may doing whatever he or she wants, and just ignore the Aquarius!

Aquarians will not like feeling suppressed, though, so just might simply walk away—or if their "crazy" side comes out, they may well surprise Capricorn with an untypical outburst of contempt!! If these two just don't mix, and leave each other to do their own thing then...

Peace and Harmony!

LOVE RELATIONSHIP

The best way for these 2 to be lovers would be through a meeting of the minds. Capricorns respect intelligence and love provocative conversations, which Aquarians could provide in abundance. Aquarians eventually would find that a meeting of the bodies would be nice as well!

Capricorns are sensual in a private situation and this could work to start with but Aquarians also like to be able to have their independence which a sometimes controlling goat does not give away easily! This would cause problems and the wild, crazy Aquarian head would just find another chess opponent!

NO CHORD COMBINATION

FOR AQUARIUS AND CAPRICORN
SEE CHAPTER 14, The maj7th

AQUARIUS ♒ and PISCES ♓ CLASH

GENERAL RELATIONSHIP

If Aquarians think that the Capricorn was a control freak, then watch out for bossy Pisces!!

Aquarians are meant to be in control in this situation but will find an unwilling partner in Pisces who may well throw tantrums at any suggestions made by any Aquarius, if they don't like him or her!

"You don't want to be doing it like that...do it **this** way!" says Pisces, even if the Aquarian's careful thought process has worked out the correct way to do whatever he or she is doing!

Aquarians will therefore find it to be hard work every time that it becomes necessary to try to explain anything and/or everything to the Piscean on every occasion, and as a result, the Aquarian could feel a severe energy drain!

Pisces emotions run deep, while Aquarians reveal little, but these "Waterbearers" can sometimes appear to be quite shy, shy people.

If so, Pisces may find it hard to draw out his or her Aquarian partner's feelings, and as a result, the Pisces could feel neglected!

LOVE RELATIONSHIP

As in most cases of all the signs that are right next to each other in the zodiac, they are quite different from each other, so a relationship between them can be another case of "opposites attract."

Ｔhe Piscean's sensual sexy attractiveness will get the Aquarian's blood pressure rising, and this could be the beginning of a passionate affair.

Piscean insecurities, though, makes them look for a strong dependable partner in the long term—which they probably cannot easily find in an Aquarian's free thinking, free living, and "don't worry about tomorrow" attitude" toward life!

So, the Aquarian's air may cause some early bubbling within the emotional Piscean water.... but as with most bubbles, they can all too easily burst!!

**NO CHORD COMBINATION
FOR PISCES AND AQUARIUS**
SEE CHAPTER 14 The maj7th

PISCES ♓ and ARIES ♈
CLASH

GENERAL RELATIONSHIP

The emotional bossy tidal wave of water sign Pisces will have the fiery Aries running for the hills! And they can run 100mph...

What's the alternative? Confrontation!! Aries fire may well have the Pisces water boiling or the water may put out the fire? Not likely, I think, so a difficult collaboration is needed here, in my opinion!

The Pisces will want to do it his or her way, and Aries may appear to listen, but will then go off and do something completely different! It's like the Pisces' words went in one Aries ear and out the other!

However, there is a chance that some degree of agreement can be found between these two, however unlikely it may appear on the surface, because both Pisces and Aries have extremely caring natures, especially when it involves animals or downtrodden people!

If having these caring natures can help sustain the relationship, then fine...but I feel that each of these two Sun signs will think that he or she is the one who knows best, and for this reason, confrontation between them, again, is quite likely!

LOVE RELATIONSHIP

A Piscean's water element could be brought to boiling point by the fiery passion of Aries.

When these two signs meet for the first time, there could be an instant sexual attraction and "never mind the small talk—let's go back to my place...NOW!!"

But, can the two of them maintain this steaming ardor?

Well, then, we might ask, "How long does a kettle boil before the steam starts evaporating?

In the short term, it would probably be hard for these two to get out of bed, or whichever room they happened to be in at the time!!

Over the long term, they both like to argue and they'll both think they are right. Aries may flare up regularly, but will then calm down. Pisces will dwell on feelings a bit longer and quite probably might plan revenge.

So, can these two be good partnership material? It's up to you to decide!!

NO CHORD COMBINATION

FOR ARIES AND PISCES
SEE CHAPTER 14 The maj7th

CHAPTER 7
THE SECOND and/or THE NINTH
(+2/9 and or sus 2/9 or maj9)
The NOTE OF D.

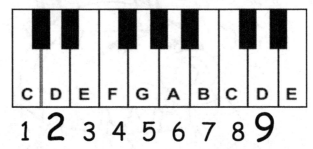

This can also be played as a sus2nd, when playing it lower on and off between the C and the E.

Basically what this means is when they are played together, they clash badly and will keep you in suspense (see Csus4 for example). Sometimes they are there, and sometimes not.

However when played as part of the maj7th chord, and you ADD their note, it can be beautiful!

AS LONG AS YOU ARE KEPT FAR APART!!

CHORD COMBINATIONS are:
Csus2 ...the notes of C, D, E, G
Cmaj9......the notes of C, E, G, B and D (octave)

There are other combinations you can play with like C+9/Cm9 but the 9 effect is the same regarding the compatibility!
So let's look at these combinations with 2 possible outcomes.
Which one is yours??

BASE	ELEMENT	sus2 (9th)	ELEMENT
ARIES	FIRE	GEMINI	AIR
TAURUS	EARTH	CANCER	WATER
GEMINI	AIR	LEO	FIRE
CANCER	WATER	VIRGO	EARTH
LEO	FIRE	LIBRA	AIR
VIRGO	EARTH	SCORPIO	WATER
LIBRA	AIR	SAGITTARIUS	FIRE
SCORPIO	WATER	CAPRICORN	EARTH
SAGITTARIUS	FIRE	AQUARIUS	AIR
CAPRICORN	EARTH	PISCES	WATER
AQUARIUS	AIR	ARIES	FIRE
PISCES	WATER	TAURUS	EARTH

Note that
FIRE signs are matched with AIR
EARTH signs are matched with WATER.

This means that when AIR is put onto a FIRE it can have two effects....
Blow the FIRE out OR cause an explosion!!

When WATER is poured onto Earth it can be beneficial, but too much can drown plants and end up as a muddy mess!!

ARIES & GEMINI   CLASH OR CHERRY?

GENERAL RELATIONSHIP

This can be an amazing combination OR confrontation!! When Gemini is used in the maj9 this is harmony indeed!

The real cherry on the cake is for the frantic Aries who wants to achieve a goal! Gemini is the perfect back up to give that Aries fire a boost!! ("relight my fire")!! When kept apart and from a distance, so as to not get too close, Gemini will create all kinds of wonderful new opportunities for you, Arians...

BUT (there's always a but!), Geminis rarely do things totally for others without first checking out what's in it for them! So, when they get too close for comfort and perhaps want to take over then the +2 Gemini appears and the clash of the Titans is In the cards!!

They will create the confusion then blame it on someone else or just shrug their shoulders or just disappear and all without the slightest bit of conscience!! So Arians keep them away from YOUR plans and just use them to complete the team or just be not close friends but friendly all the same and you will survive!

120

LOVE RELATIONSHIP

This could be a no holds barred/no inhibitions partnership for both sides. Aries sexual energy is matched with the clever Gemini who will always come up with new ideas in the bedroom, and it's not re-painting! Will the overly enthusiastic Aries be too much for Gemini, and the fire burn itself out, or will it be blown out by Gemini?

If you reveal too much in this relationship, Aries you may regret letting Gemini get too close and then be hurt later. Being Aries you would probably bounce back quickly—but be careful. In my opinion, a passionate occasional love affair with no ties would be the perfect answer for these two explosive combinations.

CHORD COMBINATION 1
C2 or sus2.. (C/D/E and G)

ARIES/GEMINI/LEO
AND SCORPIO

Ok you have your "perfect harmonies" of LEO and SCORPIO by your side and up pops Gemini now and then just to disrupt the Dream Team!

Gemini might also be attracted to your other Fire harmony Leo and try secretly to take him/her away from you? Gemini would only be "playing" doing this as part of his/her hobby or sport! So, Aries—watch out for this sneaky Gemini.

CHORD COMBINATION 2
Cmaj9   (C/E/G/B +D octave)

ARIES/LEO/SCORPIO/PISCES
AND GEMINI

In this combination, however, we see a
different side to Gemini!

(They are a twin after all!) You have your loyal Leo and Scorpio and by adding Pisces to make the maj7 sweet music indeed but for the "piece de resistance," in comes Gemini and you are complete!

This is because Gemini is just used as your secret substitute in sport or a specialist to complete your project, etc. A real ace up your sleeve!

Note it is YOUR project Aries, so you are not to let Gemini take credit. That is why Gemini is far apart from you in this scenario!

FOR GEMINI AND ARIES
SEE CHAPTER 13, THE 7th

TAURUS & CANCER   CLASH OR CHERRY?

GENERAL RELATIONSHIP

Ok, the maj 7 + 9 combination will work here, and in fact Cancer could feed the earthy Taurus with some emotion which at times is lacking.

Not that Taureans are uncaring people; they just show it openly and honestly and sometimes abruptly which at times can lead to trouble! They charge in when they think an injustice was done and wait for the consequences later! It's best that Taurus leave this side to the Cancerian, who will deal with issues on a gentler basis, then they can still be friends, not enemies! It's Taurean bluntness that could fail to make this +2 close combination a success. Taurus might find that the Cancerian is trying to calm down a situation, when Taurus would rather

Cancer just get out of the way. The Taurus' thought is, "Just let me at them!!"

In most cases Taureans are correct in their assumptions and are very good at "reading" people. They spot dishonest characters a mile away!!

So, do not interfere very much, Cancer, or you'll be trodden upon. Just lend a helping hand when you are ASKED for help, and peace will reign.

LOVE RELATIONSHIP

These two could actually work as they have a lot of similar goals. Taurus likes to be secure financially with a nice home and Cancer likes to be secure emotionally with a nice home! Taurus would have to be in charge of the finances, etc., and Cancer the painting and decorating! If Cancer gets too close to Taurus, he or she may be hit with an emotional brick wall until such time as there is confidence that the crab can be totally trusted. If this trust is established, a Taurean will love you forever and fight any battle against all odds for you, Cancer.

x

123

Just be sure that you don't betray your
Taurus —or get too crabby and critical—or you may be chased by a raging
bull for the rest of your life!

CHORD COMBINATION 1
C2 or sus2...(C/D/E and G)
Taurus Cancer, Virgo, Sagittarius

In the Csus2 scenario, Cancer will just come in and out of Taurus' life—
not good. If Cancer can't commit 100%, then bye-bye. This would drain
Taurus emotional energy, which could cause depression. A Taurean will
give 110% and total commitment, once the trust is established!
        Cancer can be attracted to many other signs who will lis-
ten to emotional concerns, and Taurus can be insanely jealous! Are you
ready, Cancer, or do you want to keep your distance a little longer?

CHORD COMBINATION 2
Cmaj9.... (C/E/G/B and D octave)
Taurus/Virgo/Sagittarius/Aries
and Cancer

So if the Cancerian has fully committed and has earned the trust and
respect of the stubborn bull then heaven awaits! If all the above signs
are involved, Taurus, then life is bliss. Virgo and Sag are your perfect
harmonies. The only danger is if the trust comes under scrutiny.

FOR
CANCER AND TAURUS
SEE CHAPTER 13
THE 7th

GEMINI & LEO   CLASH OR CHERRY?

GENERAL RELATIONSHIP

We three kings ... well, two kings and a queen. Gemini will love to be able to use KING LEO as back up and "cavalry to the rescue" when need-ed. Not that Geminis really need rescuing much, as they generally get through life at the pace they want—but USE is the operative word in Leo's case.

A lion or lioness LEO may not feel that he or she is being used. In fact, the Leo ego will probably be boosted by Gemini, when Gemini wants Leo to come in and complete the battle!

KING LEO will probably only work out that he is being used some time later—and then turn into the +9 combination. And then, Gemini, your ally has become a dangerous enemy! Let Leo too close, Gemini, and the King (or Queen) could make a meal out of "both of you!"

You will have to use all of your persua-sive powers (which are many) to only use King Leo when YOU need to!

QUEEN LEO, as always, can be a different case altogether, as she will happily help, but without the "sickly charm offensive." It's best that you just explain clearly what is needed and when, then she will oblige. But, if you overdo the wooing, beware the fiery Lioness!

LOVE RELATIONSHIP

Gemini with MALE LEO. These two could have a lot of fun together and sparks could fly in the bedroom as well. Both flirtatious creatures but they will probably be amused at the others attempts to seduce a stranger and see it as a game before going home together, probably having overdone the partying!!

Gemini will use Leo to full advantage. Gemini will stand behind Leo in a possible bar fight encouraging from the rear! Leo will love the attention until realizing he's really on his own!

A LIONESS, however, may not be as gullible as her male counterpart and would be able to see through the Gemini charm. Also, Gemini would have to be extra careful when whispering "sweet nothings" in this lady's ear. She's heard it all before!!

CHORD COMBINATION 1
C2 or Csus2.... (C/D/E and G)
GEMINI/LEO/LIBRA and CAPRICORN

The worst scenario for Gemini in this chord is relying on Leo to be there when needed.

KING LEO may be too busy with his courtiers to be bothered to come and be there for you, Gemini. Possibly because Gemini had let Leo down too many times in the past and Leos pride will not let it happen again. LADY LEO may very well turn up all the time, but will be sure to give Gemini a piece of her mind if Gemini had treated her badly in the past! Hell hath no fury, etc.

CHORD COMBINATION 2
Cmaj9... (C/E/G/B and D octave)
GEMINI/LIBRA/CAPRICORN/TAURUS and LEO

Gemini now has everything and everyone in his or her place for his or her dastardly plans! Libra, as the perfect harmony will bow and scrape at every demand, and Capricorn as the second perfect harmony will be the ROCK and stability for Gemini and Leo. Then in comes Taurus as the maj7 to further strengthen the whole organization . KING LEO will then add the masterpiece or final chess move for supreme ruler Gemini...unstoppable.

Even LADY LEO will add her own magical touch in this situation...what could go wrong? Well, nothing, unless Gemini is deceiving the whole lot of his followers by not sharing out rewards at the end as promised? Have you all been taken in or will Gemini realize that all need to be happy or the organization will collapse!!

For Leo and Gemini, see Chapter 13, the 7th.

126

CANCER and VIRGO   CLASH OR CHERRY?

GENERAL RELATIONSHIP

Cancer will definitely have to keep Virgo at a distance here to have any-thing from this relationship, but will benefit greatly from some down to earth straight talking and doing! Especially as problems seem to occur frequently in a Cancerians life, leave it to Virgo to sort it all out! Virgo is a very useful partner on occasions like this.

That was the maj9 combination. The normal sus2 will get Virgo too close for comfort, and Cancer, you won't feel very comfortable with Virgo looking over your shoulder at everything you do or say!

Virgos will pop up just when you don't need them; put their two penny's worth in (more like $200 worth), then go off doing their own thing. You will feel a bit battered and bruised—more mentally than physically and emotionally—if you let yourself be drained by a con-trolling and bossy Virgo!

LOVE RELATIONSHIP

Each of these two signs have what the other wants, so this relation-ship could quite possibly be a success. Cancer craves security, both emotionally and materialistically. Virgos, inside, want to have their ice

127

melted by a passionate lover, but they also want to control the whole scenario. Cancer will happily let fussy Virgo go about his or her bossy ways, if the result is security and a bit of love. Will a financialy secure life bring happiness to you, Cancer, if the emotions are not forthcoming from the hard exterior Virgo portrays? It's all about "give and take." If you don't give too much, and you don't receive too little, this relationship may be just what you are looking for. Is it what YOU are looking for, Virgo?

CHORD COMBINATION 1
C2 or Csus2 (C/D/E and G)
CANCER/VIRGO/SCORPIO
AND AQUARIUS

This normally indicates a sign that will be in or out of your life and mess you around a lot by not being there when you need help. In this combination it will probably be a case of Cancer NOT wanting Virgo around as much, as all Virgo does is criticize everything the Cancerian does! Scorpio, as your perfect harmony, is also a strong secure sign and your best friend. Aquarius will provide all the knowledge you need to help you in this emotionally stressed life. So if Virgo knocks on the door just to give their opinion....you're not in!!

CHORD COMBINATION 2
Cmaj9 (C/E/G/B and D octave)
CANCER/SCORPIO/AQUARIUS/GEMINI and VIRGO

Now Cancer, you readily open the door for Virgo in this situation. You have your two perfect harmonies, Scorpio and Aquarius, giving you everything you really need, and then there is General Gemini with all the skills to get you just where you want to be. So, finally you open the door to Virgo, who just tops it all off by arranging your mortgage on great terms or even showing you how to pay it off!!

You feel on top of the
world!!

FOR VIRGO AND CANCER SEE
CHAPTER 13 THE 7th

LEO and LIBRA   CLASH OR CHERRY?

GENERAL RELATIONSHIP

LORD LEO will dominate the sometimes shy Libran but could benefit from the lightness and carefree approach of Libra who will be happy to please. This is the maj9 combination, and Librans could be used here, or could become the court jester, if they are not careful, and as such, could be made fun of!!

Trying to get close to Leo will be a mistake, as Leos just do not suffer fools easily, and will banish you from their kingdom. King Leo will, however, be impressed by your eye for quality, and if you play up to his ego, then gifts may be showered on you.

Is this really the way you would like it, Libra? Just be a trusted adviser or friend from a careful distance and all will run smooth.

Again, LADY LEO will be a much better proposition for Libran ways, and will be quite happy to hear and listen to a Libran's point of view, but will almost certainly do it HER way in the end. She will also like the Libran's eye for good looking things and will be happy to let Libra take her to the hairdresserer every week, or to Harrod's for weekend shopping.

129

But who pays?? The Csus2 option is probably what will happen here, with Leo not being totally happy with the indecisive, carefree attitude of Libra.

You can't please everyone, Libra so why try in the first place?

LOVE RELATIONSHIP

Fire and Air together can always be a dangerous mix—but danger can be very sexy for the Lions, who are not afraid of anything!

Librans will also be excited at first, but will the passion continue into a long term relationship? I have my doubts, unless the Libran, in a relationship is happy to play a subservient role.

CHORD COMBINATION 1
C2 or Csus2   (C/D/E and G)

LEO/LIBRA/SAGITTARIUS
AND PISCES

Leo will find the intrusion of Libra in this combination more of a nuisance than a confrontation. With Sagittarius as their 1st perfect harmony they can have all the fun they want and Pisces as their other perfect harmony to provide emotional stimulation and protection, what more could King Leo ask for? Not an indecisive Libra popping up now and again like an itch on his back that he can´t reach!

"If you are not here to amuse me then go away "says the King but Libra wants to please his majesty—and also everybody else when the King only wants Libra to be HIS court jester!

LADY LEO will be more tolerant of the Libran jester and not be bothered if Libra is in her life or not. She has too much to be doing to be stressed about the occasional appearance of Libra. "See you when I see you"....no problem for the lioness.

Libra you had better make an appointment—
if you want or need to be close to your Queen!

FOR LIBRA AND LEO SEE CHAPTER 13 THE 7th

CHORD COMBINATION 2
C2 or Cmaj9   (C/D/E and G)
LEO/SAGITTARIUS/PISCES
CANCER AND LIBRA

In this combination Libra will just provide that extra stimulus and even intelligent conversation.

Even KING LEO needs a rest from partying at times, especially with Sagittarius!

Pisces and Cancer will provide all the emotional needs to last several lifetimes and Librans will talk about anything to keep anybody happy. Still, they are also part of the clever Air signs, so will come up with perfect solutions to most any problems the King may have.

But don´t be expected to be invited to the court's inner circle, Libra. King Leo will prefer you to act as adviser, but keep your distance!!

LADY LEO will also be happy to have some decent gossip after a long day working, looking after the cubs, etc. A bit of diversity from the stress of life is welcome—but, again, don't get too comfortable, Libra and end up becoming the dish of the day!!

VIRGO and SCORPIO   CLASH OR CHERRY?

GENERAL RELATIONSHIP

Well, this is a very strong combination if these two can work together. If Scorpio is adding the cherry on the cake as the final piece of the maj9 jigsaw, then unstoppable! Scorpio as colleague or friend or even lover will not let you down, Virgo, and will keep your innermost secrets just that, a secret!

Do not let your control freak nature get out of control with Scorpio, our Virgo, or you will be unpleasantly surprised! Scorpio may then turn into the +2(sus2), a too close for comfort person who could cause you major problems and also upset your plans and your orderly way of doing things. You will not like this at all, Virgo, and may say or do something that you will regret. Keep the harmony with Scorpio albeit at a distance and you will be pleased you did not act in haste!

LOVE RELATIONSHIP

Sexy, sensual and secretive is this partnership. What goes on behind closed doors stays behind closed doors. Scorpio will probably be more adventurous in the bedroom and Virgo, for once, may be happy to comply and not be the leader. Both signs feel safe and secure in this partnership, but would feel safe and secure on their own as well. So if love fades away, they will both just move on. If they can keep a respect for each other as individuals and each do their own thing, then this could be a strong union. The main problem could be if either wants to be in "control" of everything—then watch out!

All's fair in love and war. Or is it?

CHORD COMBINATION 1
C2 or Csus2
(C/D/E and G)

VIRGO/SCORPIO/
CAPRICORN AND ARIES

This will probably feel uncomfortable for control freak Virgo. Although the old saying of "keep your friends close and your enemies closer" may be Virgo´s best option.

A Scorpion, when scorned, is not a nice friend or enemy! They will plot revenge—or at least tell everybody on Facebook how you let them down, and probably with a few choice "French verbs"!!

So what do you do Virgo? Probably it might be best to pretend to be a friend for the sake of peace? Or you could consult your canny Capricorn friends when the going gets tough—and call up the Aries army if it gets nasty!! Would you like to be in the middle of an angry goat or a ram?

CHORD COMBINATION 2
Cmaj9 (C/G/E/B and D octave)

VIRGO/ CAPRICORN/ARIES
LEO AND SCORPIO

If you can get this team together Virgo you could be unbeatable! Capricorn is your perfect everything, partner, lover, your security. Aries as your rock, with ram like strength that will support you to the end. On top of that you have the Lion or Lioness as back up, and then a Scorpio to add the "sting in the tail." What could you not achieve?

A Scorpio in this situation would add the final touch and be your best friend, but from a distance! As mentioned above, if you let the Scorpio in too close, and then you don't want to be close anymore, then be very careful!!

FOR SCORPIO AND VIRGO SEE CHAPTER 13 THE 7th

LIBRA and SAGITTARIUS   CLASH OR CHERRY?

GENERAL RELATIONSHIP

At first glance I can't see a fruitful relationship here, as Sagittarians would normally find Librans too indecisive for their "up and at 'em" way of life. Librans might also feel dominated by a more powerful personality.

HOWEVER there is light at the end of this tunnel, if a softer Sagittarius accepts the Libran fairness to all, and the basic "what will be will be" attitude, then they could enhance a Libran party by being the entertainer or just give the night a boost!!

This would be the maj9 combination, and could be party on! The trouble is, though, that parties don't last forever. In time, you may end up in the morning with Sagittarius a little too close for comfort, and wondering how you might be able to sneak out...with all your clothes!

LOVE RELATIONSHIP

This could be an exciting, full of fun relationship, as a romantic and clever Libran could appeal to a Sagittarian who normally regards other signs as having an inferior intellect to them! Librans would be more likely to make roots first, as Sagittarians like to be footloose and fancy free for as long as possible! You coud find this exhilarating at first—As for Libra with Air and Fire in the bedroom...kerbang!

But it could all fizzle out if the Sagittarian isn't quite ready to stick to one partner, or if our indecisive, but fair and kind Libran eventually gets fed up with waiting, or receiving verbal abusive from a sarcastic Sagittarian. That would be just too much!

CHORD COMBINATION 1
C2 or Csus2   (C/D/E and G)
LIBRA/SAGITTARIUS/AQUARIUS
and TAURUS)

This combination would be too much for our lovely Libran. A Sagittarian with the negative traits of sarcasm and flirtatious ways would really upset a sometimes nervous Libra personality. You would have to rely on your perfect harmony of Aquarius to be at your side in any "pub quiz" against the confident Sagittarian and your other dependable Taurean rock to counter a Sagittarian who at the end of the night in a bar sometimes turns from Jekyll into Hyde!

Good idea everyone... HIDE!!

If you get this team together, Libra, your head could be spinning with delight. All the other signs have the personality traits you would like. Aquarius, your perfect harmony, is another Air sign like you, but without the indecisiveness. Aquarians are thinkers like you, but will not try to please everybody (an impossible task, after all). They will be fair and kind whenever they can. Taurus is your other perfect harmony and will be steadfast and strong to protect you in your time of need.

Add on the maj7 sign of Virgo to organize everything, (from a distance...Virgo, there is no taking over now!!). and then to finish it off with the "strengths" of Sagittarius, which are straightforwardness, energy, full of life etc. With all of that aiding you, Libra, you basically won´t have to do anything Libra...leave it up to the team!!

For SAGITTARIUS and LIBRA,
see Chapter 13, the 7th.

♏ SCORPIO and CAPRICORN   CLASH OR CHERRY? ♑

GENERAL RELATIONSHIP

This combination is normally recognized as one of the strongest in the Zodiac! However, strength can come in many forms. It can be a real force for good and be there when you most need it, or it can overwhelm you such that you feel deflated and defeated. In other words, when these two are together, they will make a formidable pairing IF they can work together cooperatively.

Remember Scorpios can be your best friend, or your worst enemy. Scorpio, in charge in this situation, will benefit from Capricorn's work ethic and reliability, if they can keep Capricorn doing his or her own job and not trying to control the whole situation.

This would be the maj9 combination and great things could be achieved together...BUT, if Capricorn gets too close to Scorpio without being asked, Capricorn will then feel the sting and soon need to move on!

138

LOVE RELATIONSHIP

I feel that emotions may be kept hidden too much between this pair for a lot of passion to be here! Scorpio will have to try and break down Capricorn's emotional defense system to succeed romantically...a difficult task!

What these two do have in common, though, is being secretive, and if the sexy, sensual Scorpio did get inside the Capricorn's outer layer, a willing partner in the bedroom would be found.

As long as you don't tell anyone!!

CHORD COMBINATION 1
C2 or Csus2   (C/D/E and G)

SCORPIO/CAPRICORN/PISCES AND GEMINI

Scorpios and Capricorns will normally work well together, but there are times when they both think they are right and then the disagreement could end up nasty. Scorpios are very scathing if they think a job is not done well, and the Capricorns think they always do a good job. The Scorpio may well be surprised at the normally reserved Capricorn puffing his chest and sharpening his goat horns ready for battle! In the end, no one can remember what the fight was about in the first place! Pride comes before a fall, but who will fall?

It's better to just keep away, Capricorn—or Scorpio allies of a Pisces, or a bossy General Gemini may be too much for even a stubborn old goat to handle!

CHORD COMBINATION 2
Cmaj9 (C/E/G/B and D octave)

SCORPIO/PISCES/GEMINI/LIBRA AND CAPRICORN

This would be the maj9 combination and great things could be achieved together...BUT, if Capricorn gets too close to Scorpio without being asked, Capricorn will then feel the sting and need to move on!

Assemble this team, Scorpio, and who will dare criticize you?

Pisces your "perfect harmony," will defend you to the death. Gemini, another perfect partner, will plot and scheme on your behalf (theirs as well of course!).

Librans will lighten your day and Capricorn will organize the celebrations. In this scenario you will work well with the goat because you let each other be the boss of whatever task is at hand.

Just leave the goat to take care of his department and you will reap the rewards of this partnership. Interfere and you will go back to the Csus9 situation on the previous page!

War or Peace?

FOR CAPRICORN AND SCORPIO
SEE CHAPTER 13
THE 7th

SAGITTARIUS and AQUARIUS CLASH OR CHERRY?

GENERAL RELATIONSHIP

If Sagittarians are clever here, they will use their Aquarian friend's brain power to achieve their own Sagittarian needs—and will also find the general AIR sign quality of going with the flow quite endearing, Why? Because it would not put any pressure on them to be what they are not—and **that** is "security and hard work come first!?"

No, that's not for party animal Sagittarians, if they can help it! So use the Aquarian wisely and you will achieve your goal, Sagittarius —and then you can party together to celebrate using Aquarian's credit card!

On the other hand, a Sagittarian could find Aquarians a bit too deep thinking and quiet for their taste and get bored with them. So, the Aquarian would have to be fairly outgoing, and would need to amuse the Sagittarian partner and certainly boost his or her ego from time to time—although most Sagittarians are able to do that for themselves!!

141

LOVE RELATIONSHIP

I think these two could actually get on well as both are idealistic thinkers and look to the future. As with all Fire and Air signs, there can be an explosion of ideas in the bedroom!

Aquarians are happy to be taken out night after night and can party with the best of them until the money runs out! There's always tomorrow for both these signs!

However if the Aquarian gets too close, as in the sus2 combination, then Sagittarius will feel his or her space has been invaded and move on rapidly—with probably a few chosen sarcastic comments before leaving!!

CHORD COMBINATION 1
C2 or Csus2   (C/D/E and G)
SAGITTARIUS/AQUARIUS/ ARIES AND CANCER

Sagittarius has Aquarius in between his or her perfect harmony Aries. Would YOU like to be in the middle of these two fiery beasts?

So, Aquarius, you will be taking a chance every time you pop in and out of a Sagittarian's life and can expect a hell like furnace if you continue.

The Sagittarian's other perfect pal, Cancer, will probably stay out of the battle and even perhaps have some sympathy with you. and Cancer will, in this situation, also be there to heal any wounds inflicted.

Have you got good insurance Aquarius?

CHORD COMBINATION 2 Cmaj 9 (C/D/G/B and D octave)
SAGITTARIUS/ARIES/CANCER SCORPIO AND AQUARIUS

Now in this situation, Aquarius—this is where Sagittarians can really love you!! Your intellect and your interesting conversation will stimulate the Archer, who's already drawing back the Cupid's bow that he just "borrowed" for the occasion! If Sagittarius gets this gang together, there could be no stopping the resulting party!

In this maj9 role, Scorpio may control the celebration, so as not to commit the crime of having too much fun, but even the emotional Cancer will be crying tears of joy in this company!

The Aquarian's air will keep the fire burning long into the night. If you go too far, though, Sagittarius—perhaps with the demon drink—then Aquarian air might blow out the flames, and then there may be trouble ahead!!

FOR AQUARIUS AND SAGITTARIUS
SEE CHAPTER 13 THE 7th

CAPRICORN and PISCES CLASH OR CHERRY?

GENERAL RELATIONSHIP

Capricorns have trouble with showing their true feelings and emotions, so they will not be happy if Pisces gets too close, as they will probe Capricorn's inner soul and make him or her feel insecure, which they hate!!

From a distance, though, Pisces could add an emotional and caring side to Capricorn's life, without being too intrusive or asking a lot of personal questions. This would be OK with careful Capricorn, he or she would take that care on board, and digest all the info gained by it to be used at a later date!

When Pisces does try and break the Capricorn's barrier down , then he or she they might be a little aggressive and try to boss the Capricorn around!

Capricorns are very resilient creatures, however, so will not take kindly to the Piscean's control methods. Whereas Capricorns are normally very gentle goats, if they feel threatened or "verbally," abused they can stick their horns down and retaliate, by often catching their opponents off guard, since the opponents would not be expecting such a reaction from this normally reserved creature.

LOVE RELATIONSHIP

There is too much emotional conflict here to avoid plenty of ups and downs in this relationship. Capricorns may well be tempted by the sensual and erotic Piscean and even be controlled in the boudoir!

Pisces will love the stability a Capricorn can give and feel safe. After all, some ancient astrologers have depicted Capricorn as a goat with a fish tail!

Perhaps these two have more in common than at first appears. If the Piscean can control his or her own natural urge to delve deep into someone's soul, then this relationship could have a chance. You will have to be patient, though, Pisces. before Capricorn will bare all !!

CHORD COMBINATION 1   C2 or Csus2   (C/D/E and G)
CAPRICORN/PISCES/TAURUS and LEO

This first combination will definitely not be comfortable for our goat. The Piscean will likely be an annoyance for the steady structured life of Capricorn. Just when the goat has finished something, up pops Pisces to disagree with nearly everything that Capricorn has done.

Pisces may not stay around to make changes, but will disappear, waiting for the next opportunity to arise! Capricorn will, of course, just ignore the advice once the fish has swum away!! If the goat was with their perfect harmony Taurus, then Pisces is probably lucky to have gotten got away without being turned into fried fish!

CHORD COMBINATION 2
Cmaj 9 (C/E/G/B and D octave)
CAPRICORN/TAURUS/LEO/ SAGITTARIUS and PISCES

Presenting Capricorn's dream team! Hold on, Capricorn in a team? It is rare for the goat to work with other people, because they are happier on their own little mountain or rock, just getting on with what needs to be done to survive.

We all know, of course, that everybody needs somebody sometime, so when Capricorn is in trouble, who better than their perfect harmony sign, Taurus. Once you have established the Taurean's trust, you have a friend and gallant defender for life!

If you needed further help, then Capricorn's other "rock" harmony is King Leo or Lady Leo. Would you want to tackle an angry bull or lion?

Sagittarius is there to add the fire lacking in the goat's sometimes boring life, and this time Pisces appears as the +9 to sort out all your emotional problems, Capricorn!! What more could you want?

Capricorn will probably say, "Can I go back to my mountain now, please?" Don't lose the mobile telephone numbers of your Taurus or Leo friends, though, Capricorn. You never know when you will need them!!

FOR PISCES AND CAPRICORN
SEE CHAPTER 13 THE 7th

AQUARIUS and ARIES   CLASH OR CHERRY?

GENERAL RELATIONSHIP

There are some Aquarians who are more outgoing than others and will probably enjoy this relationship and in fact keep Aries fire alight for a very long time. There are others who will just want to blow this fire out a.s.a.p., as they will find Aries too overwhelming and energy draining especially during Aquarians time of contemplation! "Thinking time" is very important to them! So Aries will probably be too close for comfort to the Aquarian in most cases and in fact find the childlike quality of Aries a bit irritating after a while.

This would create some tension even for the normally fairly laid back Aquarian and a lot of clashes and Arian tantrums!! The good thing about Aries anger is that it flares up and then calms down just as quick as it started and then they wonder what all the fuss was about!

If they can keep them away from the "sweetie jar" and do a bit of homework they might end up of benefit to head teacher Aquarius! So keep control of your "child" Aquarius and all will be well....let them have a free reign then....

Watch out!!!

LOVE RELATIONSHIP

Both of these signs respect the other's need to be free and will not tie each other down unless it's in the bedroom!

This could be hot stuff, though alright, as they both are quiite inventive and imaginative.

But away from the physical, the Aries would be

attracted to the Aquarian's intellect, and Aquarius is attracted to the Aries forcefulness and leadership skills. The only problem, Aquarius—as always with Aries—is will you be able to keep up with their constant energy, since they are traveling at a different speed than most of the other signs!!

Boredom is definitely not a factor here—but you could be simply worn out, Aquarius! Could that be because perhaps your "baby" Aries is keeping you up all night?

CHORD COMBINATION 1
C2 or Csus2   (C/D/E and G)
AQUARIUS/ARIES/GEMINI AND VIRGO

Aquarius will not be able to rely on their perfect harmony partner Gemini if Aries gets out of control. Geminis are more likely to incite further mayhem. There are two Air signs here both incapable of blowing out Aries fire so might as well join in and watch the firework display. How long do fireworks last? Eventually some control over the energy demon Aries is necessary and Aquarians have their other perfect harmony sign of Virgo to throw some earth over the Aries fire and calm things down a bit.

An Aquarian's main issue with Aries is always going to be if they can cope. All the fun in the world is offered but the Aquarian's "Duracell batteries" need to be recharging all the time!

CHORD COMBINATION 2
Cmaj9   (C/E/G and D octave)

AQUARIUS/GEMINI/VIRGO
CAPRICORN AND ARIES

Aquarians have an interesting "best of both worlds" combination in this situation. Their perfect harmony Gemini will come up with all sorts of amazing plans for work or playtime. Virgo will organize it all and then Capricorn will provide the manpower.

On top of that, Aries is kept at a reasonable distance—but will add the spark to set the whole thing rolling.

If Aries does get a little too enthusiastic for you, Aquarians, then you have the back up of Virgo and Capricorn earth to keep it to a controlled explosion or just a damp squib.

You choose!!

FOR ARIES AND AQUARIUS
SEE CHAPTER 13, THE 7th

PISCES and TAURUS   CLASH OR CHERRY?

GENERAL RELATIONSHIP

Here we have two very strong personalities that could work well to-gether —or end up going ten rounds of heavyweight boxing!!

Taureans are the best and most reliable workers, and they like to have something to do—or they can get lazy and eat too much grass!

So for Pisces to get the best out of this combination, he or she needs to keep the Taurean busy with chores, but always treat them with respect. A little pat on the back will do wonders for these some-times very insecure creatures!!

The problem with you, Pisces, can be your own controlling bossy nature when you get something in your mind like a good cause—and especially when you are fighting for the underdog. In that, you can go overboard and start upsetting a lot of people.

Even if you know you are right, a lesson in diplomacy would not go amiss—and then, you could achieve more!!

So if you treat Taureans in this way—diplomatically—whenever they perhaps get too close and ask a lot of questions, always looking for the truth, then you may find that you have a raging bull on your hands that would take some major effort to stop!!

LOVE RELATIONSHIP

Pisceans are very creative and Taureans are very artistic. Both can be passionate lovers. Taurus will provide the stability in the life of Pisces, since Pisceans often let their emotions get out of control! Pisceans are great seducers and can entice lovers into their fish net. Taureans may then have trouble finding a way out. But, perhaps they don´t want to escape?

CHORD COMBINATION 1
C2 or Csus2   (C/D/E and G)
PISCES/TAURUS/CANCER and LIBRA

What are your motives, Pisces?

You really like Taurus to be close but how close? Taureans will demand all or nothing and this could be uncomfortable for you, so you might prefer them at a distance.

In this scenario, the sus2 comes in and out of your life and you don't know where you stand, Pisces. This would be very irritating to you and you could lose your cool!

To be fair Taurus is not normally like this, and either will be in your life or not in your life—there is no in between!

If you cannot cope with the emotional strain, then Cancer, your perfect harmony, is there to let you cry on his or her shoulder. Your other perfect partner, Libra, should be your rock, but possibly will be crying with you instead and also hoping his or her Taurus is OK! (Just trying to be fair).

CHORD COMBINATION 2
Cmaj9   (C/G/E/B and D octave)
PISCES/CANCER/LIBRA
AQUARIUS ANDTAURUS

This combination is full of artistic, creative and intelligent, but also very emotional ideas.

Pisces, you should be dancing, singing, acting, writing and creating masterpieces, if all these super signs turned up at your house!. Cancer and Libra are very good listeners and will hang on to every word that comes out of your mouth. Aquarius would provide psychic experiences and Taurus your stability and security. What more could a sign want? Just let Taurus be the cream on your cake and fulfillment is yours!

It's PSYCHEDELIC !!
(turn the page to view...)

FLOWER POWER !!

For TAURUS and PISCES,
see Chapter 13

CHAPTER 8

THE MINOR CHORD

The next chord we will look at is a MINOR CHORD

This is made up of the 1st/the "flattened" 3rd (flattened means to go down 1 semi tone) and the 5th...so we have C/Eb and G = C MINOR.

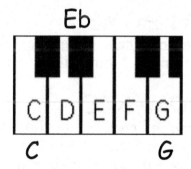

When you hear a minor chord being played it could
mean several things.

A dour mournful sound...this person could be draining your energy with sadness and be a "moan!"

An expressive soulful sound...this person could give you strength and be a strong force at work or in the home!!

Or a strong, heavy dramatic sound...this person could give you strength and be a strong force at work or in the home!!

So, be careful with a "minor" person—
he or she can affect you in different ways.

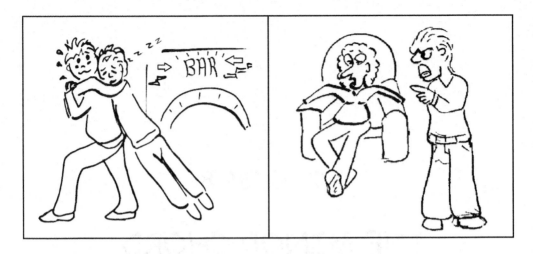

AT WORK
This could be the "complainer" always bringing you or your ideas down—or alternatively, a strong, if somewhat dour, team member. You may not get on, but you will respect each others strengths!

AT HOME
This could be the "nagging" partner (male or female), who is constantly on your case—or could be the "moan, " but still gets something done!

ROMANCE
There may not be a great deal of romance in this partnership, but instead, a possible "odd couple" existence! You are totally different from each other. You can't live with each other but each of you may feel lost without the other.

MONEY
Your "significant other" may tell you that you never earn enough to pay the bills, or alternatively, could be a strong financial adviser, no matter how much the advice you are offering may hurt!

So here are all the minor chord combinations
and their elements.

BASE NOTE C	ELEMENT	MINOR HARMONY Eb	ELEMENT
ARIES	FIRE	CANCER	WATER
TAURUS	EARTH	LEO	FIRE
GEMINI	AIR	VIRGO	EARTH
CANCER	WATER	LIBRA	AIR
LEO	FIRE	SCORPIO	WATER
VIRGO	EARTH	SAGITTARIUS	FIRE
LIBRA	AIR	CAPRICORN	EARTH
SCORPIO	WATER	AQUARIUS	AIR
SAGITTARIUS	FIRE	PISCES	WATER
CAPRICORN	EARTH	ARIES	FIRE
AQUARIUS	AIR	TAURUS	EARTH
PISCES	W ATER	GEMINI	AIR

Let's look at possible element combinations here.

FIRE can make cold WATER comfortably warm BUT also can boil over!!
EARTH can be heated gently or SCORCHED by too much FIRE!!
AIR can "aerate" the EARTH for good crop production or
    blow into a tornado!!
WATER needs oxygen from AIR but too much could cause a whirlpool !!

Which element is YOUR minor partner?

In ALL of the Minor chord combinations your Eb and G are very compatible to each other and so in this team they could work against you if
not handled properly, and even your normally loyal G harmony could be
influenced by the MINOR Eb team member!

Be careful with this combination.

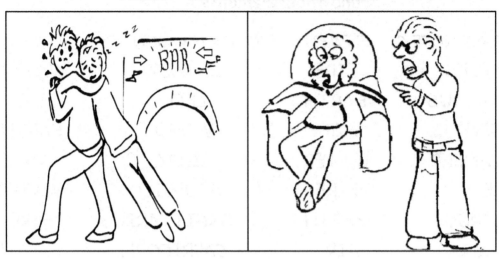

GENERAL RELATIONSHIP

The problem here, for the happy fun loving Aries, is that Cancerians can bring them down with their strong emotional side and make the Aries sad as well!

This is not a particularly strong combination except that Arians normally love animals, especially in distress, and a Cancerian would be very much in agreement with that. As for the watery Cancerian, he or she could dampen the fiery Aries too much, and that could lead to arguments, quite likely short and sharp!

LOVE RELATIONSHIP

Fiery childlike Aries may be too much of an emotional stress for caring Cancer. Aries will like Cancerians keeping a nice home which was probably messed up by Aries in the first place! Emotions can run high both with sexual excitement and lots of niggly fights so a very up and down relationship. If Cancer does not complain too much and Aries not lose control too much? We can only be what we are at the end of the day so long term? Hard work for both of these animal lovers!

CHORD COMBINATION

C MINOR C/Eb AND G
ARIES/CANCER AND SCORPIO

If you upset our emotional Cancer too much Aries watch out for Scorpio coming in to protect their harmony WATER sign to the death!!! Your friend has become your foe!!!

For Cancer and Aries, see
Chapter 12   C6

TAURUS AND LEO
HELP OR HINDRANCE?

GENERAL RELATIONSHIP

Well, the down-to-earth Taurean could actually find strength in this un-likely partnership, if the normally lazy Leo gets off his or her backside and works as hard as the Taurean partner.

If not, then beware of a very stubborn Bull and a proud Lion face-off!!

LEO FEMALES, as expressed before, are more likely to get along in this combination, but Taurean earth could dampen Leo's fire too much in most of these cases!

The Leo would have to conform for this to work! If you are wise, Taurus, you'll use your Leo wisely Taurus and just let Leo do what he or she wants to do, then you will have a chance!

LOVE RELATIONSHIP

Sexually these two Sun signs would be arduous lovers and the animal magnetism of Taurus and Leo could make the bedroom walls shake!!

Sex isn't everything in a love relationship, though, and the obvious differences between these two socially could be the undoing of this combination. Leos are more gregarious and like a bit of praise for their endeavors, whereas Taurus would look on. Then when the two of you got home, Taurus would tell Leo what he or she really thought about Leo's behavior in no uncertain terms. Well, some disagreements can be settled in the bedroom, but for how long?

CHORD COMBINATION
C MINOR   C/Eb AND G

TAURUS/LEO AND SAGITTARIUS

Upset the Lion too much and he could contact his old friend Sagittarius to form a coalition against you, with an arrow aimed at your heart!!

Ⅱ GEMINI AND VIRGO ♍
HELP OR HINDRANCE?

GENERAL RELATIONSHIP

Oh boy, what a combination!

If Virgo adds his or her undeniable strength and workaholic attitude and does not try to control the Gemini (fat chance!!), then this could be of benefit to the Gemini, who would be quite happy to give the orders!

A Virgo, however, would normally do the same, so some things have just gotta give!!!

Too much Gemini air could blow the Virgo earth all over the place!

But, however, if these two signs decide to work together, this could be a very strong combination—as long as the Gemini is able to go out now and again, and show off!

If YOU want this to work, Gemini, then you will have to be straight down the line, and then Virgo will respond willingly...BUT if there is any hint of deception, then pack your bags!

LOVE RELATIONSHIP

Geminis are charmers and they would need all their ability to charm a sometimes dour and critical Virgo! Inside, most earth signs long to be a bit more carefree and let their hair down and Gemini would entice them to be daring and more interesting—especially in the boudoir!

Virgos will enjoy this for a while, then be embarrassed by the web cam set up by devious Gemini for possible blackmail use later!!

If YOU want this to work, Gemini, then you will have to be straight down the line, and then Virgo will respond willingly...BUT if there is any hint of deception, then pack your bags!

CHORD COMBINATION
C MINOR C/Eb AND G

GEMINI/VIRGO AND CAPRICORN

If you do deceive Virgo once too much, Gemini, then prepare for Virgo's Capricorn friend to prepare a court case against you!!

FOR VIRGO AND GEMINI
SEE CHAPTER 12   C6

CANCER AND LIBRA
HELP OR HINDRANCE?

GENERAL RELATIONSHIP

The caring, emotional Cancer would probably find the Libra too lacking in emotional depth for this relationship to work well. While another minor chord could add strength, I can't see it happening within this combination. The Libra partner, though, would likely be happy to join the Cancerian partner in drowning their sorrows—perhaps a bit too much on occasions!!

LOVE RELATIONSHIP

Cancer will probably be looking for a deeper relationship than Libra could provide.

Libra will try and please the Cancerian, but not really feel comfortable with a "too close" relationship, at least to start with. In a first date "out on the town," these two may get along fine, what about the morning after?

Cancer may have already decided this is the "one" after the first date.

Libra, however, will be polite, but may disappear by lunchtime, after promising to call.

CHORD COMBINATION
C MINOR   C/Eb AND G

CANCER/LIBRA AND AQUARIUS

If Libra does a runaway after wrong doing, then it will be probably up to buddy Aquarius to explain their narrow escape!.

Aquarius should give an impartial view based on the evidence.

Is it that Cancer is too clingy? Or is Libra not caring?

The jury is out on this one!

FOR LIBRA AND CANCER
SEE CHAPTER 12   C6

LEO AND SCORPIO
HELP OR HINDRANCE?

GENERAL RELATIONSHIP

This combination could actually work if the Scorpio partner becomes a true friend or an ally of the Leo.

LEO MALES might get some of the shine rubbed off by the Scorpio's "just get on with it" attitude, since Leo is then not receiving the hero worship that he thinks he deserves!

LEO FEMALES may find more of the respect they desire—and also loyal friendship from a strong Scorpion who would back up and defend his or her partner to the death!!

LOVE RELATIONSHIP
Scorpions can be quite intense and sexual, but are very private about it. Leo males are normally "no holes barred, in your face come back to my place....now!"

Initially, this could be quite exciting for both of them, but Scorpio's jealous streak and general secretive nature may drive the Lion to despair.

Leo females as always would react a little calmer than their male counterparts, and even be attracted by the sexy, "What are you hiding?"
image of Scorpio.

If you delve too deep and/or too quickly Scorpios may close up
even more, and you may never get past their defensive walls!

CHORD COMBINATION
C MINOR   C/Eb and G

LEO/SCORPIO AND PISCES

If your Scorpion is not happy, Leo, you'll soon know about it! I do not
expect any long drawn out troublesome relationships between these
two. Either you are together or you are not!

FOR

SCORPIO

AND

LEO,

SEE

CHAPTER 6

C6

♍ VIRGO AND SAGITTARIUS
HELP OR HINDRANCE? ♐

GENERAL RELATIONSHIP

Stand back and watch the sparks fly here!

This will only work if Sagittarius is prepared to take orders (ha! ha!). Virgo in control will really be irritated by the sarcastic blunt Sagittarian comments—possibly telling the Virgo to lose weight and also, "Don't you think that perhaps a bit of exercise would do you good?"

If there is anyway these two can work together, then don't take them on in an argument. You have no chance, and will come out battered and emotionally scarred!

LOVE RELATIONSHIP

Cautious, careful Virgo may be sweet talked by Sexy Sagittarius at first, but these two may well get fed up with each other quite quickly! Free spirit Sagittarius will soon look for new pastures, if Virgo remains a bit boring in the bedroom.

If you are happy to give the Sagittarian freedom and hope that he or she will come home to you every night after spending the rent money at the nearest or furthest bar, then OK......but, somehow I don't think so.

171

CHORD COMBINATION   C MINOR   C/Eb AND G
VIRGO/SAGITTARIUS AND ARIES

The trouble with
this combination
is that
Sagittarius could
take your "rock"
Aries along for
the ride, and
then you would
have to try and
get the two of
them home!!

FOR SAGITTARIUS AND VIRGO
SEE CHAPTER 12   C6

LIBRA AND CAPRICORN
HELP OR HINDRANCE?

GENERAL RELATIONSHIP

Librans may like this combination more than Capricorns would! Capricorns will think the way that Libra runs things is too out of control for their liking! Especially with money!!

Libra will love that the Capricorn is doing things he or she has asked to be done, but may get tired of feeling "controlled."

Capricorn will like that the Libra always tries to be fair, so the goat can likely get away with quite a lot within this partnership. Still, I do not think that this sign pairing is a relationship that is easily built to last, that is if **only** the two Sun signs are considered. Other factors within the two horoscopes, though, may be quite compatible, and it is important to keep this in mind.

LOVE RELATIONSHIP

Behind closed doors Capricorns can be quite sensual and adventurous and Librans who "love to love" will enjoy being controlled under the sheets.

However Librans would like the romance to continue in daily life, too, and will find Capricorns sometimes workaholic and dour way of life too heavy for their lighter airy personality!

Librans will try for a short while, and Capricorns will also feel bound by duty to make an effort. The two of them could end up good friends, but most likely not as long term lovers!

CHORD COMBINATION C MINOR C/Eb AND G

LIBRA/ CAPRICORN AND TAURUS

I can't see too much concern about confrontation here, as both of these signs really like to argue, although Libra, especially, would just avoid it, if possible.

"Life is too short" could be their motto, so the Capricorn would probably have a little grumble with his or her Taurus mate, and then leave it at that!!

FOR CAPRICORN AND LIBRA SEE CHAPTER 12 C6

SCORPIO AND AQUARIUS HELP OR HINDRANCE?

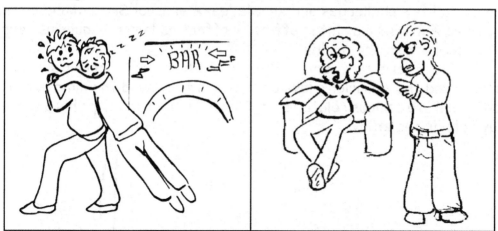

GENERAL RELATIONSHIP

This actually could be a winner as Scorpio would respect the Aquarian intellect, but also may find the Aquarian a bit too much "off the wall."

Still, Scorpions hide their emotions more than most water signs do, and Aquarians could be quiet with their thoughts, as well.

So, it could take time for each of them, on either side, to learn to know just who the "real person" is within this "signficant other," and what he or she wants in this relationship. Who will bare all first?

LOVE RELATIONSHIP

A Scorpio will demand complete and utter trust in any relationship and total commitment. Aquarians think of relationships as a further advance to life's challenges and knowledge. A sensual Scorpio and a free spirited Aquarius may hit it off as an affair, as long as Aquarius keeps it a secret from the world!!

For a long term union, though,, I think that Scorpio's jealous streak and the Aquarian's love of freedom to expand the mind may not bode well in a serious relationship. It may be best to keep this a secret love affair and enjoy!

CHORD COMBINATION
C MINOR   C/Eb AND G

SCORPIO/AQUARIUS AND GEMINI

If Scorpio is too strict about his or her personal life, then Aquarius would rather bare all with a Gemini pal or anyone with an open mind!!

FOR AQUARIUS AND SCORPIO SEE CHAPTER 12   C6

SAGITTARIUS AND PISCES
HELP OR HINDRANCE?

GENERAL RELATIONSHIP

This could be a battle of wits, nerves and emotions! Not that Sagittarians are too emotional unless you criticize them, which a Pisces is more than likely to do!

As one of the Zodiac bossy boots, sarcastic Sagittarian's biting tongue tempers could flare up, and tearful Piscean tantrums and strong emotions will not move the strong totally "I am right" attitude of the Sagittarius.

Pisceans will find that the sometimes very hurtful words they hear from a Sagittarian might be just a bit too much to take without a fight—especially if the words are directed to someone else, because they will fight for the underdog or die in the attempt!!

Pisceans will need to have a flood of their water sign to have any chance of dampening the fire of Sagittarius!

LOVE RELATIONSHIP

Try putting a fish on the back of a horse—flapping all over the place and falling off!! Try it again, but with the same result and you know that it can't be any different unless tied on tight! Sagittarians hate to be tied to anything or anyone so...

Initially. a Sagittarian could talk an emotionally scarred Piscean into bed quite easily and listen intently to his or her troubles for at least 10 minutes—then with a look at the watch, and say "Sorry—must dash!" and off Sag goes into the night, leaving Pisces to add another scar to his or her emotional battle wounds!

Sagittarius would NOT get a second chance, however, with the vengeful Pisces and beware if you try. Once bitten, Pisces can turn from a goldfish into a killer whale!!

CHORD COMBINATION
C MINOR   C/Eb AND G

SAGITTARIUS/PISCES AND CANCER

Pisces will not be a perfect partner for our Sagittarian unless they can soften up their hard exterior. It's a difficult task, and Sagittarians will not accept they could be wrong!! Go get support from your emotional Cancer partner and together you may stand a chance??

Well...you can only try!!

FOR PISCES AND SAGITTARIUS SEE CHAPTER 12   C6

CAPRICORN AND ARIES
HELP OR HINDRANCE?

GENERAL RELATIONSHIP

Again this Earth and Fire combination normally is not very successful and the Capricorn control would irritate the Aries free spirit!

"Stop running around, sit down, think it through" would be the Capricorn way, but before they have even finished talking, the Aries would be off!!

If Aries can stop long enough and control that Arian energy towards his or her own ends, then OK—but **doing** it is another thing!!

Communication, as well, could be a problem, as Capricorns rarely bare all and Aries types have probably been in "hot water" and talked about it (or have been gossiped about by others) more times than anyone else!!

LOVE RELATIONSHIP

Aries will certainly liven up a cautious goat who likes to take things, including sex, at his or her own pace! No such luck with an Aries lover who will wear you out in the first ten minutes!!

Capricorns may enjoy this totally different approach to life than they are used to, but will eventually call time out and revert to their old ways. They hate not being in control of themselves firstly, and they also like to call the shots on all occasions!

So both of these two Sun signs like to take the lead in their own way, which leads to arguments, disagreements about money, sex and pretty much everything. Capricorns, I feel, would have to give more for this relationship to have a chance, but if they get nothing back over a period of time, then the union may be fated to end in tears!

CHORD
COMBINATION
C MINOR
C/Eb AND G

CAPRICORN/ARIES
AND LEO

Aries could have many a tantrum in this combination and go running to loyal Leo for support. Who will you believe Leo? A problem child or a harsh parent?

FOR ARIES AND CAPRICORN
SEE CHAPTER 12   C6

AQUARIUS AND TAURUS
HELP OR HINDRANCE?

GENERAL RELATIONSHIP

Aquarian bosses would normally be the "thinkers,"not the "doers"—so this combination may actually work, as the natural Taurean work ethic would be of benefit to the Aquarian's logical way of thinking!

Well, it's their logic—not necessarily everybody elses!! The Taureans will take orders and get on with the task in hand, as long as they are not overworked. Then the boss had better watch out for the raging bull!

At home Taureans would keep the house in order and go out and do two jobs, as well—but don't push your luck with them or they could fall into a deep depression.

LOVE RELATIONSHIP

Taureans can be very passionate in love, and Aquarians can be very sensual and interesting because you never really know who you are gonna get in bed! Aquarius could be the quiet thinker taking his or her time or the crazy genius who comes at you with all guns blazing. This can be fantastic to start with for the Taurus—but then the Aquarian ups and leaves without a word to go and do his or her own thing—leaving jealous Taurus angry and having to clear up the mess!

Aquarians won't necessarily be unfaithful—they just want to float through life thinking about the meaning of everything and finding intellectual challenges. This is all very well, but someone has to earn a living and clean the house....Taurus!

The Taurean will soon put his or her hoof down without a 50/50 partnership, so be prepared, Aquarius! Although you are an air sign, you are also a fixed sign. Can you handle that responsibility?

CHORD COMBINATION
C MINOR   C/Eb AND G

AQUARIUS/TAURUS AND VIRGO

This could be a very strong combination for you Aquarius but perhaps more in a work situation than romance. Keep both these Earth signs on your side and you will go from strength to strength. Upset them and face the consequences!!

FOR TAURUS AND AQUARIUS SEE CHAPTER 12   C6

PISCES AND GEMINI
HELP OR HINDRANCE?

GENERAL RELATIONSHIP

You may think you are the boss or are controlling the situation with your Gemini, but think again!

Somehow Geminis will always work things round to their benefit so in this case the "bossy" Pisces may believe he or she has control over the clever Gemini, but this may end in tears for the Piscean!!

Pisces types will have their heart on their sleeve, but Gemini will not reveal a thing and will remember everything—to be used in a court of law, if necessary.

This is a strong combination in business and possibly the Gemini's alter ego may be soft enough to listen to the caring Cancerian when they need a shoulder to cry on!

BUT not often!

183

LOVE RELATIONSHIP

Pisces can be possessive lovers, which is far from the Gemini and Air signs in general ways of thinking. Gemini will be intrigued by a mysterious Piscean who can be very psychic! Gemini's charm and intelligence will stimulate our fish for a short time, but if this gets serious, then Gemini's freedom would feel threatened, because Pisces would demand an all or nothing relationship.

Beware the Pisces scorned, Gemini! Pisceans have been known to harbor grudges and will eventually get revenge. Play it straight from the start, and all may be OK, but Gemini...can you keep your word?

CHORD COMBINATION
C MINOR   C/Eb AND G
PISCES/GEMINI AND LIBRA

Libra is Gemini's perfect partner, as well as being Pisces "rock." So... whom do you support when things go wrong in this relationship, Libra?

What a dilemma for our indecisive Libran! "Can't I support BOTH of them ?"

Leave Libra out of your problems guys—you won't get a decisive answer anyway!!

FOR GEMINI AND PISCES SEE CHAPTER 12   C6

CHAPTER 9 the sus4th

Csus4

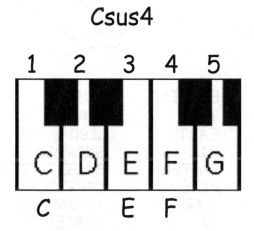

Now the Csus4 (suspended)....means just that—it's the 4th note of the scale. In the case of Cmaj it's the note F, BUT it is not normally played at the same time as the E note. You play the F then the E and sometimes repeat this pattern. You will probably have to listen to a sus4th chord to fully understand, if you are not a musician or don't have any musical knowledge.

My interpretation is that this person is sometimes there, and sometimes not. He or she could give you a little boost, but just when you needed a little more, this person is gone! He or she will not really get along with your "perfect harmony E," as the two of you clash together. So, why? Well, its just that sometimes two people are harmonious with each other, and sometimes they are not.

Ok, it is like here's Mr/Mrs or Ms. F again, putting in two pennies worth of their opinion, but doing nothing really to help—perhaps saying, "You don't want to be doing it like that...do it like this."

On the positive side, the two of you could sound quite nice together if your perfect harmony E is not around—then, why not? Just don't bank on a future together without a little suspense

So here are the sus4 combinations:

These combinations actually appear together earlier as the harmony G, but the boot is on the other foot and the "boss" is now opposite to before! Can these two still be harmonious or will the other not like a change in roles?

BASE NOTE	ELEMENT	SUS4	ELEMENT
ARIES	FIRE	VIRGO	EARTH
TAURUS	EARTH	LIBRA	AIR
GEMINI	AIR	SCORPIO	WATER
CANCER	WATER	SAGITTARIUS	FIRE
LEO	FIRE	CAPRICORN	EARTH
VIRGO	EARTH	AQUARIUS	AIR
LIBRA	AI	PISCES	WATER
SCORPIO	WATER	RIES	FIRE
SAGITTARIUS	FIR	TAURUS	EARTH
CAPRICORN	EARTH	GEMINI	AIR
AQUARIUS	AIR	CANCER	WATER
PISCES	WATER	LEO	FIRE

The controlling element in this case is the C note so we have the following......

FIRE can burn the EARTH but EARTH can put out the FIRE

EARTH can make a sandstorm with AIR,
but AIR can also disperse the EARTH

AIR can whip WATER into a tidal wave,
but WATER can just drizzle through the AIR

WATER can put out the FIRE
but FIRE can also boil WATER into steam

You see you never really know what situation will arise!

ARIES AND VIRGO
SUSPENSE?

GENERAL RELATIONSHIP

This combination appears as Virgo's harmony G, as was covered earlier, but now with Virgo in control! In this case with Aries as boss, the Virgo will appear as the "I told you so" type! Aries will be OK if it's constructive criticism, but Virgo will probably add a little more than is necessary, then get on with his or her own thing.

If Virgo can temper this natural habit of taking over, and actually listen to what Aries has to offer, he or she will have a chance...but the relationship may work OK for a while, and then all be back to normal later!

As stated earlier, when Virgo is in control, then he or she can benefit greatly from Aries energy, etc. But when it's the other way around, with Aries in control, the Virgo probably won't give Aries the same respect, and may often just ignore the Aries.

LOVE RELATIONSHIP

Normally Aries is the one who is running around and disappearing when needed but if he or she is the chaser in this situation, Virgo may seem too distant to get close to. One or two nights of excitement are great, but then Virgo wants to get back to work and will criticize Aries for an untidy bedroom, probably in a note written before Aries wakes up. Aries will of course get over this "rejection,"and smile when Virgo calls back and wants a bit more!! Just have your fun, Aries and accept Virgo's limitations in love, or else you guys will just be arguing over everything!

CHORD COMBINATION
Csus 4   C/E AND F
ARIES/LEO AND VIRGO

I feel Aries would be of more support to Virgo than the other way round as stated in the "G" note. Don't worry, our Aries (you rarely do anyway)—just find a sexy Leo and happiness will prevail!

FOR VIRGO AND ARIES
SEE CHAPTER 5....THE G NOTE

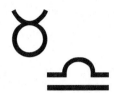

TAURUS AND LIBRA
SUSPENSE?

GENERAL RELATIONSHIP

This reverse combination could actually be OK, if the Taurean can cope with Libra's normally carefree approach to life in general, as this may chill out the sometimes stressed out Taurus! This is OK for a while, until the Taurean's natural work eth-ic takes over and will expect nothing less from the Libran lover, friend or colleague. So, if Libra just comes into your life for a short while, then disap-pears a short while, then comes back again, then the Taurus may actually look forward to that... but, living or working together long term? Not so sure...

LOVE RELATIONSHIP

These two signs are both controlled by Venus the planet of love so you would think they could "get it on" without any problem at all.

Both also have an eye for quality and like a nice home and are sensual creatures...all good so far!!

So what's the problem? Sexually, the gentle side of Libra could sooth the savage bull, and I don't think there would be any problem in this de-partment.

It's just that the general relaxed and carefree attitude of Libra about everything—but especially money—would upset our down-to-earth, gotta pay the bills on time, Taurus!

So for the long term, this would be frustrating for the Taurus, so he or she would likely part from Libra as friends and move on......

"Hey ho, such is life!!"

189

CHORD COMBINATION
Csus4   C/E/F

TAURUS/VIRGO AND LIBRA

Libra flitting in and out of a Taurus life would confuse the Taurus, who prefers routine and likes people to be there when they said they would be. Libra does not really profile as the best partner in this case, but probably is a nice person to know.

FOR LIBRA AND TAURUS
SEE CHAPTER 5
THE G NOTE

♊ ♏ GEMINI AND SCORPIO
SUSPENSE?

GENERAL RELATIONSHIP

In this combination, with Gemini in control, the Gemini will use the occasional appearance of Scorpio to great affect, and to further the Gemini's aims.

Gemini will not be too perturbed about Scorpio flitting in and out, and just use the useful info that Scorpio will offer! If they are working together and have the same "enemy," then Scorpio could infiltrate the opposition and relay the secrets back to General Gemini and then go undercover again! If, however, the Gemini goes after a Scorpio friend, then beware the reaction and you may have a double agent on your hands!

LOVE RELATIONSHIP

These two strong signs will battle it out for dominance in the bedroom. They could even keep the neighbors awake, if they are living in an apartment!! Gemini would not care about upsetting the neighbors, but the private Scorpio would insist on soundproofing!!

Stormy lovers—this pair will likely be—and in this case, not always together, because the sus 4th note is in and out of your life. This wouldn't really bother the Gemini, who likes the freedom it would offer. But if the relationship got more serious and both wanted a little more, the sparks could fly—and then too much of each other would definitely be a battle of control!

These two might be better off with separate homes and secret love affairs, or it will be hard going forming a long term relationship by living together!!

Don't push your luck Gemini!!

191

CHORD COMBINATION
Csus 4th   C/E AND F

GEMINI/LIBRA AND SCORPIO

FOR SCORPIO AND GEMINI
SEE CHAPTER 5
THE G NOTE

CANCER AND SAGITTARIUS
SUSPENSE?

GENERAL RELATIONSHIP

This reverse harmony will not work as well for Cancer this time. Sagittarians will flit in and out of this relationship leaving a bemused Cancerian wondering where they stand!

Cancerians need someone to be there most of the time and will be happy to reciprocate if they get the attention they think they deserve and emotionally need. Sagittarians, in this case may just occasionally be there put in a sarcastic but you possibly truthful statement, then off you go down to the pub with another buddy!!

Just take it with a pinch of salt, Cancer, or you may dwell on it too much, and that could hurt you more!

LOVE RELATIONSHIP

A Sagittarian would open up the mind of our crab and introduce some new and exciting ideas, especially under the sheets! Our sensitive Cancer will then fall head over heels in love and look forward to the next "session" and then get let down at the last minute!

Sagittarius would only shrug his or her shoulders, make some excuse and then seduce the crab again, and again, and...????

How long will it take you to understand, our caring Cancer, that trying to tie down a fiery horse is very difficult, and he or she would most likely bolt at any chance of freedom.

Can you enjoy this relationship for what it is? On/off/on/off? Or might you just find a more caring soul like yourself as a partner, to save further heartache!

CHORD COMBINATION
Csus 4th   C/E AND F

CANCER/SCORPIO AND SAGITTARIUS

Oh, boy! Cancer, you will be on the edge of your seat all the time, once that Sagittarius pops into your life—and then out again! You will either welcome the Sagittarian's brutally honest opinion on what's happening in your life... or you might just wish you had ear plugs!!

FOR SAGITTARIUS AND CANCER
SEE CHAPTER 5
THE G NOTE

LEO AND CAPRICORN
SUSPENSE?

GENERAL RELATIONSHIP

This may actually work a little because Capricorn possibly would add sound advice to his or her majesty...the Leo "king" or "queen" may then ignore this and do his or her own thing anyway, but certainly should at least think about it!

Lady Leo, however, would definitely think it through and accept any offer of help that Capricorn could give her and help her through her long day!

It is rare for Capricorn not to try and take over most any situation, however, and may tread on King Leo's tail. Lady Leo would also put her paw down, as well, if a sometimes controlling Capricorn gets too involved!

Just take the advice, Leo...do with it what you will, and tell the Capricorn to see you next week!

Capricorn may well get grumpy about this, but it's YOUR show, Leo—not Capricorn's!!

LOVE RELATIONSHIP

Well...these two amorous animals, on the male side, normally have lots of female concubines for purely reproductive purposes. So sex may just be a physical thing for the males and not too much romance would happen here.

Female goats(the Nannie goat) and the lionesses normally have to endure partners who just want it when THEY want it!!

So a combination of these two signs may not look hopeful for a romantic liaison! If lovemaking is the only compatible thing they have in common, then the ardor will soon wear off for everyone concerned, as the Lion or Lioness would find the Capricorn male or female a bit too boring and set in his or her ways in the long term!

    Female goats(the Nannie goat) and the lionesses normally have to endure partners who just want it when THEY want it!!
    So a combination of these two signs may does not look hopeful for a romantic liaison! If lovemaking is the only compatible thing they have in common, then the ardor will soon wear off for everyone concerned, as the Lion or Lioness would find the Capricorn male or female a bit too boring and set in his or her ways in the long term!

CHORD COMBINATION
Csus 4th   C/E AND F
LEO/ARIES AND CAPRICORN

This would definitely work better for Capricorn in the G note situation than for Leo in this scenario. Fire and Earth signs, in my experience, have to work together....separately....in order to have any chance of success!! When each can do his or her own thing, the end result is....

HARMONY!!

SEE CHAPTER 5   THE G NOTE

VIRGO AND AQUARIUS
SUSPENSE?

GENERAL RELATIONSHIP

The occasional appearance of Aquarius would not bother Virgo too much as Virgos are quite happy being in control on their own, if necessary. Aquarians could add words of wisdom, however, that Virgo should take seriously, as it takes brains as well as brawn to solve problems and live life, in general!.

Just being there now and then could also annoy a Virgo, who wanted to find out more, but the Aquarian had nipped off down to the library and then probably out on the town!!

LOVE RELATIONSHIP

Both of these two signs can be a little distant in a relationship, as Virgo is always cautious and practical and Aquarians are deep thinkers who like their own space and freedom.

A meeting of intellectual minds would be a better prospect than a meeting of the bodies!!

Probably it would take a while for the relationship between these two signs to grow, as they may have met at a debating society or suchlike, and then over time would get to know each other slowly. Still, with each of them probably not quite trusting the other enough to take the first step towards a sexual relationship. If and when that happens, I don't think the earth will move for either of them. Probably Virgo will try to control the whole scenario completely, which will send Aquarius off to as quiet spot as possible.

A monastery???

CHORD COMBINATION
Csus 4th   C/E AND F
VIRGO/CAPRICORN AND AQUARIUS

If you are clever Virgo, you should try and get all the info you can when Aquarius can be bothered to keep an appointment with you, or you'll be kept waiting for hours!!.....grrrrrrr!!

FOR AQUARIUS AND VIRGO
SEE CHAPTER 5   THE G NOTE

LIBRA AND PISCES
SUSPENSE?

GENERAL RELATIONSHIP

Librans could get frustrated at a brief appearance of Pisceans and probably think they have done something to upset them!

A partnership of these two signs with Libra in "charge" would probably make both of them even more insecure than they might otherwise feel.

Pisces types might pop in for a cup of tea and boss the Libra around a bit, telling him or her all about all their troubles and then leaving the Libran to do the washing up!

It's unlikely that either of these two signs can rely on this being a two sided relationship!

LOVE RELATIONSHIP

Both signs are sensitive souls, but react differently to a crisis in love. Librans will try and please but shrug their shoulders if they can do no more and move on. Pisces will take it all to heart and plot revenge!

So this combination may start out as if you have found your soul mates but as every relationship has it's ups and downs a scolding Pisces would be hard for a carefree Libran to take. I don't think either side will know what they want and could end in a lot of tears.

CHORD COMBINATION
Csus 4th   C/E AND F
LIBRA/AQUARIUS AND PISCES

Ok Libra when your Pisces floats in and out of your ocean what you gonna do? Just remain a gentle breeze or blow up a storm??

FOR PISCES AND LIBRA SEE CHAPTER 5
THE G NOTE

SCORPIO AND ARIES
SUSPENSE?

GENERAL RELATIONSHIP

This time around, with Scorpions in control, they would probably be a little angry—or a little amused—at the childlike Arian's brief appearance in their lives. Aries would probably call Scorpio with the latest gossip and then say "Sorry... gotta dash, plane to catch"...or train... or just whatever the next thing on their long list for the day happens to be!

If you understand your Aries, then this would be normal—if not mostly irritating—and you certainly could not rely on the Aries to be in a certain place at a certain time!

But...if the Scorpion is a good friend to the Aries, then he or she will accept all this without moaning...although if (for example), it's a first time encounter between these two signs, then the Scorpio may cut the Aries friend out of Scorpio's life very quickly!

LOVE RELATIONSHIP

Scorpios are intense in most areas of their life especially in sex!. They are sensual, but very private. Aries, like all the fire signs, are flirtatious and fiery lovers, which would excite our Scorpion, but later Scorpio might hear that Aries has been gossiping about the size of his/her....tail !!

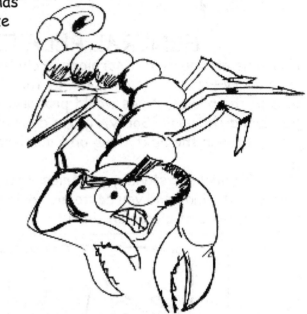

Oh boy (or girl) ! Watch out, Aries! If you can"t keep your bedroom secrets as a private affair,then you'd better start packing!

Your Scorpion lover might soon show you the size of that Scorpio sting!

CHORD COMBINATION

Csus 4th   C/E AND F

SCORPIO/PISCES AND ARIES

On the other hand Scorpio having a "child" around, even now and then, could possibly lighten up your life!!

Be like a grandparent and you can always give the grandkids back!!

Think about it!

FOR ARIES AND SCORPIO
SEE CHAPTER 5   THE G NOTE

♉ ♐ SAGITTARIUS AND TAURUS
SUSPENSE?

GENERAL RELATIONSHIP

Earth and Fire, in general, are not a good mix, so occasional times to-gether would be OK, becuase they both know it's not for the rest of their lives!!

A Taurean could add some strength to any projects that the Sagittarian is up to, but don't ask Sag too much about what is going on, or you'll be told very quickly and bluntly to "mind yours!!"

Sagittarians may also think that Taureans should be around more to help with the chores and not just turning up when they want. Well, you can't have it both ways, Sagittarius, and you would probably complain that the Taurus broke the cutlery with his or her sometimes heavy handed approach......

It's best not to call on Taurus in the first place...let sleeping bulls lie!!

LOVE RELATIONSHIP

Sexy Sagittarius could sweet talk Taurus into bed, but those loving words would soon turn to sarcastic, blunt comments on your preformance the next morning!! If you don't want to get involved in a verbal war that you cannot win, Taurus, then just keep your distance, as this suspended note suggests, and you will be more than happy.

If, you as the Sagittarius, would like more from Taurus, then you will have to somehow find words of praise for all that Taurus has done for you. It's a difficult task methinks!

If Taurus can't win the battle of words then our horse, the Sag, had better get out of the stalls pretty quick, with a raging bull not far behind!

CHORD COMBINATION
Csus 4th
C/E AND F

SAGITTARIUS/ARIES AND TAURUS

Overall, this is a difficult combination. They both have a high regard for honesty, but in their different ways. Sagittarius will be brutally honest and Taurus trustworthy honest. Will this trait be a starting point for a longer term relationship?

FOR TAURUS AND SAGITTARIUS
SEE CHAPTER 5   THE G NOTE

CAPRICORN AND GEMINI
SUSPENSE?

GENERAL RELATIONSHIP

Cautious Capricorns eventually get to where they want to go. Whether its a rocky road or a mountain to climb, they generally get there in the end.

So, life at times has been a struggle, and basically it is hard work that gets them through. So, they are a little jealous of Gemini's ability to seemingly get what is wanted without too much hard work at all!

If Gemini pops around with a get rich quick scheme, a younger and ambitious Capricorn may fall for it, and then generally suffer the consequences when he or she finds out that Gemini had not followed the scheme anyway! Older and wiser Capricorns would not fall for it now, and perhaps an older wiser Gemini may even be able to give sound advice after all.

After all...miracles sometimes happen!!

LOVE RELATIONSHIP

Capricorns normally like to build a relationship slowly and look for a reliable and trustworthy partner for life! So does our Gemini fit the bill?

I don't think so! Geminis can be unreliable and extravagant and leave a lot of hearts broken, and they normally get in to a long term relationship only if it's for their own benefit.

Capricorns, in the short term, could benefit from the clever Gemini in business, who could show them how to succeed without really trying. But in LOVE?... I think there are too many differences for a serious relationship. It would be hot and cold all the time, leaving the Capricorn to look elsewhere for a permanent mate!

CHORD COMBINATION
Csus 4th   C/E AND F
CAPRICORN/TAURUS AND GEMINI

Capricorn is Gemini's "ROCK" in the G note situation. I'm not sure if Gemini can be the same to Capricorn. Both signs are clever and intriguing personalities, who could be very strong together—but who's the boss?

FOR GEMINI AND CAPRICORN SEE CHAPTER 5
THE G NOTE

AQUARIUS AND CANCER
SUSPENSE?

GENERAL RELATIONSHIP

Here we have the sometimes quiet and thoughtful Aquarian with Cancer jumping in and out of the Aquarian's life. This could confuse a potentially unstable Aquarian, such that the crazy side of Aquarius could then come out and surprise everyone.

Cancer would throw emotions into the Aquarian brain, and then when the Aquarius is trying to analyze it and wants to ask questions, Cancer can't handle it and is off and running! Then, when Aquarius is getting over this, back comes Cancer again, with more mind bending emotions to sort out—and off the two of them go again!

There are only so many times this can happen, before the pressure cooker boils over and then watch out!!

Don't think too much,
Aquarius—it can give you headaches!!

LOVE RELATIONSHIP

If you want this to work, Aquarius, you will have to be prepared to have your emotions thrown in the air and down to earth with a bang!

The Cancerian will be more than happy to pour out heart and soul to you, and even when you can't take any more, he or she will grab you by the sleeve and say, "Hold on—I haven't finished yet!!"

Cancer may already be in an affair with someone else who has destroyed his or her life for the 3rd time this week, and our poor Aquarian may just be a shoulder to cry on.

Aquarians will not, however, be too sympathetic to an emotional crab and may just tell the crab to get over it and get on with life. The good news in this relationship for Aquarians, is that will now be just an occasional visit by the Cancerian. You don't have to be with him or her all the time......phew!!

CHORD COMBINATION
Csus 4th   C/E AND F
AQUARIUS/GEMINI AND CANCER

There may be just too many negative emotions here to succeed, but if any sign could sort out a problem it's Aquarius. Normally this would be a logical question that is not based on emotions, Aquarius is the Water Carrier, so perhaps he or she could carry our Cancerian crab's emotional baggage OK?....perhaps it's likely to be a tough job!!

FOR CANCER AND AQUARIUS
SEE CHAPTER 5   THE G NOTE

♓ ♌ PISCES AND LEO
SUSPENSE?

GENERAL RELATIONSHIP

Pisces will definitely want more from King Leo than he is probably prepared to give!!

"Sorry old chap—I'VE just got a press conference and a TV interview to do. Check with my secretary and I'll try to fit you in sometime."

Pisces will not be amused—and as much as they are animal lovers, they may try to cage their Lion!

This is most likely not a wise thing to do, however, because Leo needs to be free!!

LADY LEO may be a bit more understanding and try to be around a bit more since Lady Leos have such busy lives.

Anyway, it is likely that the challenge of trying to fit in an emotional Pisces, who can be somewhat controlling, as well, might be more than she wants to, or is able to handle!!

Don't lose the plot, Pisces!

With this relationship, it may be your best option to just accept that it may be no more than an occasional quick cup of coffee together!

LOVE RELATIONSHIP

King Leo is of course a seducer and an amazing lover!
He says so himself to whomever wants to listen!

Pisceans may be taken off guard by Leo's brash approach, and wake up in the den of the Lion or Lioness!!

Then, the King or Queen will sleep all day and wake up ravenous. "Bring food, slave!" is then the order, and you may see the other side of the fish, who turns into a fierce shark!

Now, some Leos—male or female—can also be very laid back and quiet at times. So, Pisces, if you are lucky enough to find this type of Leo, then all that was said here could be a different story!

CHORD COMBINATION

Csus 4th
C/E AND F

PISCES/CANCER AND LEO

In general, there are too many emotional differences to make a lasting relationship likely, and even Lady Leo might find the fussy, niggly ways of a Pisces a bit too much. As this chord suggests, a Leo would be in and out of your life, Pisces—so it may be best not to plan on the love of your life being in this relationship!

FOR LEO AND PISCES SEE CHAPTER 5 THE G NOTE

CHAPTER 10
THE DIMINISHED CHORD
Cdim or Co ...The note of Gb

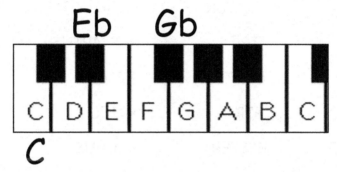

Now the DIMINISHED chord can only really work when all notes are linked to each other, and then is more of a team scenario!

This chord is made up of the base (root) note, (C being our example) +the minor 3rd(Eb) which we have covered (Cminor chord) plus the minor 5th(Gb).

All the notes are 3 semitones apart, and very often the sequence of music continues up every 3 semitones, i.e., add on the note of A and then up to C (octave) etc., to create quite an eerie effect!

The diminished chord can be very interesting and can enhance a piece of music or can even sound threatening! For example, horror/suspense movies often use this chord effect during a tense moment.

Really, this combination is better when all the notes are played together or in their correct order, starting at C and moving up. So, this could be a fascinating team together OR it could give you the creeps!!

We will look at the relationship with the base note C and the Gb third note in this chord.

So let's look at all the Cdim combinations.

SUN SIGN	ELEMENT	AUG Gb	ELEMENT
ARIES	FIRE	LIBRA	AIR
TAURUS	EARTH	SCORPIO	WATER
GEMINI	AIR	SAGITTARIUS	FIRE
CANCER	WATER	CAPRICORN	EARTH
LEO	FIRE	AQUARIUS	AIR
VIRGO	EARTH	PISCES	WATER
LIBRA	AIR	ARIES	FIRE
SCORPIO	WATER	TAURUS	EARTH
SAGITTARIUS	FIRE	GEMINI	AIR
CAPRICORN	EARTH	CANCER	WATER
AQUARIUS	AIR	LEO	FIRE
PISCES	WATER	VIRGO	EARTH

PLEASE NOTE THAT ONLY ON THIS OCCASION, YOU ARE THE SAME COMBINATION WHEN THE SIGNS ARE REVERSED!!

i.e.,ARIES and LIBRA is the same when LIBRA is the base note
e.g., LIBRA and ARIES.
So I will give you both sides in my interpretation!

What is also interesting here is that AIR and FIRE elements are drawn together and WATER and EARTH elements drawn together.

Now AIR can ignite the FIRE and cause an explosion or can blow the FIRE out!! Likewise WATER can feed the EARTH or can dampen and even drown the spirit!

212

ANTICIPATION?

GENERAL RELATIONSHIP

ARIES AND LIBRA

In this case I don't see too much blowing out of Aries fire especially with them in control so Librans could actually add to the Aries way of life and certainly not put too many obstacles in the way or huff and puff and moan about Aries flying off to do the next challenge! As long as Aries give Libra a little space and a bit of pocket money they will be ok and they would be quite happy to join social Aries entertaining friends etc., even if it wasn't their party!!

LIBRA AND ARIES

Librans actually rarely like to control in a strong way any situation so could end up just being Libran and let Aries have their own way anyhow! "Well" if that's what you think, my Arian friend or lover, it's ok by me¨. Now everyone has a breaking point to what they can take and Libra may eventually get tired trying to catch up with their 100mph Arian and suddenly blow Aries off the track! Arians will fly into a temper and then calm down as quick as they took off and apologize and then wonder what all the fuss was about. If Aries can involve their sometimes indecisive and uncertain Libra then this could work for both sides but you gotta put your foot down sometimes, Libra!!

LOVE RELATIONSHIP
ARIES and LIBRA

The fascinating diminished chord will attract both of these signs at first and Librans could be swept away by the sheer energy and sexual magnetism of Aries,but as in every vampire horror movie, you are waiting for the vital bite! Dracula is so charming and sensual, how could you resist, but to live in his world you have to be the same and Librans are just not like our fiery rams! Cover your neck Libra or an eternity of trying to be what you are not!

LIBRA and ARIES

Libra in charge in the bedroom?? Not much chance of that, methinks!! If you don't have a say in your everyday life with your Aries partner, Libra, then at least try to be forceful in the lovemaking department!! You have a lot of charm to sooth the rampant Aries, Libra and make him or her see the softer, gentler side of life......then go out together and have a party!!

CHORD COMBINATION 1
Cdim   C/Eb AND Gb
ARIES/CANCER AND LIBRA

In a team situation with Cancer as the Minor note you have Fire, Water and Air all mixed together bubbling up in anticipation. Could be a fun night out!!!! Next morning however is a different question!!

CHORD COMBINATION 2
Cdim   C/Eb AND Gb
LIBRA/CAPRICORN AND ARIES

In this situation Libra has their Capricorn Minor note to back them up if Aries goes too far. You will probably need the Goat Libra to bail you out on several occasions!!

TAURUS & SCORPIO   SCORPIO & TAURUS

ANTICIPATION?

GENERAL RELATIONSHIP
TAURUS AND SCORPIO

Taureans like directness and honesty, even if to their own detriment. They cannot lie and so are quite direct, but sometimes even a scathing Scorpio could be an agreeable partner. The secretive nature of Scorpio,

however, might not be a welcome trait that the Taurus partner would like, because Taurus loves being open about everything.

So on the one hand, there can be a strong connection, but a long term partner? I question if Scorpions are able to give enough of themselves to please a demanding Taurean!

SCORPIO and TAURUS

Now, many of the personality traits mentioned above could still be the downfall of this relationship. It's all about give and take. If Scorpions can open up a bit, and Taureans be a little less demanding of actual 100% honesty, then this could also work. Scorpions will be a friend and lover for life with total commitment, as long as they can have their own private and solo moments which sometimes Taurus does not agree on... total time and attention together...now! Everyone needs their own space at times, and even a few personal secrets, so don't be too contolling, Taurus, or you will lose a great friend!

LOVE RELATIONSHIP
TAURUS AND SCORPIO

Taurus can be very passionate lovers when they find someone they can trust but then can overdo the possessive side of the relationship.

Scorpions can also be obsessive in love, perhaps more emotionally than physically.

With the Bull in charge in this love situation they may be just too demanding in the bedroom, as well, and Scorpions do not take "orders" easily!! Tread carefully, Taurus— a Scorpion's sting can be pretty painful in the wrong place!!

SCORPIO and TAURUS

Now we have Scorpio calling the shots!! Is there any difference from what was said for Taurus and Scorpio?

Scorpios and Taureans can be extremely jealous in relationships. Scorpio will be verbally "stinging" if cheated on, OUCH!!

Taureans are unlikely to cheat on Scorpios, though, as they would hate it being done to them. In the end, both of these Sun signs probably would be too suspicious and too paranoid of any possibility of the other one leaving to actually see how very well this relationship could work!

Say you're sorry, when you ought to!!
BOTH of you !!

CHORD
COMBINATION 1
Cdim   C/Eb/Gb
TAURUS/LEO AND SCORPIO

In this team situation Leo may well get caught up in the middle of an emotional battle between Taurus and Scorpio. Who will Leo side with? Escape while you can. our Lion—back to the jungle, before they even ask! Impossible decision!!

CHORD COMBINATION 2

Cdim   C/Eb/Gb
SCORPIO/AQUARIUS/TAURUS

Aquarians would need the wisdom of Solomon to judge between these two, if either of them requested a court hearing!!

    Come on, Scorpio and Taurus—get your act TOGETHER, and learn to understand how the Aquarians' mental ability wants to soar onwards and upwards!

GEMINI/SAGITTARIUS   SAGITTARIUS/GEMINI

ANTICIPATION?

Sagittarius would be a strong and handy weapon on your team,
Gemini, if you can keep in charge?

GENERAL RELATIONSHIP

GEMINI AND SAGITTARIUS

Oh boy!...Fan the flame! It wouldn't take much to get these two alight! Gemini would have to control Sagittarius direct and often sarcastic opinions or could lead to trouble! However the best people to get themselves out of a hole are Geminis as they have a knack of coming up smelling of roses even in hard times. Even if on trial for murder, they'd convince the Jury that the poison, 23 stab wounds and gunshot to the head were self inflicted by the deceased!!

"Now I'm in charge!" says fiery half horse Sagittarian, as he or she rears up to whinny and neigh to heart's content and the gallops off into the night (the favorite time for Sag).

Gemini just soaks it up and waits for the right opportunity to take control again often without Sagittarius knowing it! Actually if these two form a strong bond they could have a whale of a time together and go on many adventures!!

The problem may be a financial deficit for "socializing." Both of them, however, are more than capable of earning and spending a great deal!! This is a dynamic duo when they are not each trying to out think the other. They could be like Batman and Bat Woman, but are likely more like Bonnie and Clyde!!

SAGITTARIUS AND GEMINI

If our half horse is clever, he or she they will stick by the Gemini lover, even if it's just to learn more "tricks of the trade of life"—of which the Gemini knows many!! His relationship can be hot and steamy to start with, but may fizzle out as soon as one or BOTH of them need to move on to other conquests!! They are similar in that they can get bored with the same routine—but they would probably remain in contact after an amicable split!. Quite likely they would end up as "friends with benefits!!"

His relationship can be hot and steamy to start with, but may fizzle out as soon as one or BOTH of them need to move on to other conquests!! They are similar in that they can get bored with the same routine—but they would probably remain in contact after an amicable split!. Quite likely they would end up as "friends with benefits!!"

CHORD COMBINATION 1
Cdim   C/C/Eb AND Gb
GEMINI/VIRGO AND SAGITTARIUS

The nervous anticipation would probably come from team member Virgo in the middle of these two!! Virgo may well end up doing all the physical work while the other two are out gallivanting! Someone's got to do it!

CHORD COMBINATION 2 Cdim C/Eb AND Gb
SAGITTARIUS/PISCES AND GEMINI

In this team our Pisces may well end up in an institution trying to play middle person to these swashbuckling guys and gals!! Hold on to your emotions Pisces and join in...you may be glad you did and have a great night out! Watch out though for our Sagittarians blunt tongue!! Don't take it too much to heart if it's aimed at you!

CANCER/CAPRICORN   CAPRICORN/CANCER
ANTICIPATION?

GENERAL RELATIONSHIP
CANCER AND CAPRICORN

Cancerians may find Capricorns too emotionally controlled in a relation-ship situation and may find them hard to talk to on any deep level. How-ever they will find the reliability and hard working nature of Capricorns

a useful tool and something the often lack! So in a work situa-tion a great member of staff to have on your team although watch out that Capricorn hasn't got their eye on your job!!

CAPRICORN AND CANCER

Thank god I am back in control says Capricorn! There's too much emotional stuff when Cancer has his or her way, and you are not really built for that, are you Capricorn?!

Learning from life's experiences is very important and these two

together would almost make the perfect person! Just think of the strong reliable hard working and strangely gentle nature of Capricorn together with the very caring and home loving and romantic personality of Cancer!!

Cancerians can become frustrated with life if they have no one to talk with on an emotional level, and might turn to alcohol or drugs to escape.

Can Capricorn open the door and let the Cancerian in? Capricorns can be good listeners if they don't have to reveal too much about themselves!

221

LOVE RELATIONSHIP
CANCER AND CAPRICORN

They say opposites attract. Initially, I think that may be true sexually. Capricorn will not feel threatened by our Crab and will relax more in the relationship. Cancer will need their people caring skills to somehow break down the many Capricorn barriers for any long term romance

however and may feel hurt occasionally by sometimes distant Capricorn ways if our Goat trots back up the mountain. It's nothing personal against you, Cancer. The Goat just wants to be alone sometimes!!

CAPRICORN AND CANCER

If these two fall in love and want a long term relationship they may need a prenuptial agreement!! Capricorn insists on running the budget and working 7 days a week if necessary and Cancer just....agrees!! Well

of course if Cancer want a stress free life just at home looking after the general domestic chores...fine! Hold on my Capricorn, friend, it is now the 21st Century, so beware a crabby Crab, if you get too tyrannical!!

Actually a lot of Capricorns are quite easy going and only like to do everything, so their partner has to do nothing, especially worry!! Have faith in your Cancer and let loose the chains!!

CHORD COMBINATION 1 Cdim   C/Eb AND Gb
CANCER/LIBRA AND CAPRICORN

If Cancer needs someone to run to for emotional support and talks with Libra they will get all the support they need and say "you are right, Cancer.That old goat needs a talking to." So off goes Libra to Capricorn and says "I think you are right, Capricorn that Crab is far too emotional." In trying to be fair to both sides, Libra is gonna make an enemy of both.

CHORD COMBINATION   2 Cdim   C/Eb AND Gb
CAPRICORN/ARIES AND CANCER

In this team scenario Cancer may actually get support from fiery Aries if Capricorn goes to far with their control!! Aries will not be afraid to speak their mind so Capricorn you had better show that gentler side that you possess inside but rarely show the world.!!

LEO/AQUARIUS

AQUARIUS/LEO

ANTICIPATION?

GENERAL RELATIONSHIP
LEO AND AQUARIUS

KING LEO will benefit from servant Aquarius in an advisory capacity although he will probably not take any notice and do it his way anyhow! Aquarians will tolerate this behavior to a point as they will believe he is like the "EMPERORS NEW CLOTHES" story and believe what only he believes in but comes an embarrassing figure in the end so justice is served!

LADY LEO would appreciate more the intelligent offering from clever Aquarius and use the info wisely. Aquarians would actually benefit a fiery Leo personality as they would not use up their own air supply in one go but just add little by little to keep the fire alight for a long time!

AQUARIUS AND LEO

KING LEO would probably not relinquish power and want to stay the boss and ruler even if they are in the other persons territory! Aquarians have patience, though and keep the Leo amused whilst cleverly controlling the situation anyway! A Leo ally or partner would definitely strengthen any business concerns so again this could be an effective combination, If Leo finds out that its not 50/50 however then be prepared for a severing of ties!

LADY LEO will be very happy to have a bit of "Intel" on the team even as a boss... "Just tell me what to do, boss—and away they go to fit it in to their already busy routine.

Leos definitely have the "like ability" factor, and Aquarians don't normally want to be center of attention, so this could be a happy compromise!

LOVE RELATIONSHIP
LEO AND AQUARIUS

Of all the Fire signs Leo is the most laid back, perhaps even lazy? Well if you are the King why do the work!! Aquarians will attract the Leo initially with their smart mind and probably talk the King into bed. Not that the King would need much tempting!! King Leo will find later that our Aquarius refuses to be another concubine and is out the Palace gates in a flash!

LADY LEO would appreciate a little more of the Aquarians intellect and not be shy to ask forhelp, academically if needed.
Our Aquarius would then feel needed and hang around a lot longer!!

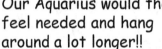

AQUARIUS AND LEO

"You are in MY domain now little Lion so behave¨ says our Water carrier. Aquarians in charge would be anticipating an explosive romance at first. Their Air and Leo's Fire has all the ingredients for lust and more lust!!

Will the fire keep burning? If Aquarius is still fascinated by their captive Lion do with as they please then....Olympic flame!! Will King Leo be subservient?....Fun to start with but wanna be King of the Castle again soon!!

LADY LEO will be happy to play second fiddle in this relationship and find the Aquarius mental strength very sexy!!

Will Aquarius be able to keep up this admiration society for long? Probably our Aquarius will seek new mental challenges eventually!!

QUANTUS QUERIES

HIGGS BOSON
$M(H^2) = \pi . \frac{1}{37}$
$3987^{12} + 4365$
$\Omega(+) \neq 1$

CHORD COMBINATION 1
Cdim   C/Eb AND G

LEO/SCORPIO AND AQUARIUS

In this combination our King better be careful that Scorpio does not protect Aquarius here. A long drawn out bloody battle could ensue! Play it cool Leo and negotiate with ALL parties for a peaceful reign! Our Lady Leo would make friends and allies of BOTH signs to protect her No1 priority her cubs!! In fact Scorpio and Aquarius would be well advised to do the same as our Lioness would be prepared to fight to the end for her family. You have been warned!!

CHORD COMBINATION 2
Cdi   C/Eb AND Gb

AQUARIUS/TAURUS AND LEO

If you needed any help to get away from the castle Aquarius the Bull in this situation could well defend you until you got away. That's if you were telling the truth your reason to leave otherwise the Bull and Lion may unite against you. Be careful!!

If you are dealing with Lady Leo you would have more chance of survival so just explain that you need to move on.......quickly!!

VIRGO/PISCES   PISCES/VIRGO
ANTICIPATION?

STAND BACK and PREPARE
for WAR of THE BOSSYBOOTS!!

GENERAL RELATIONSHIP
VIRGO AND PISCES

Ok I am exaggerating a little or am I?

I believe these two to have the bossiest personality traits in the Zodiac! Virgo (as always) in control in this situation, could find it unusually tough going to get his or her message over to the sometimes strangely stubborn and bossy Pisceans can be.

If the Piscean is are working together with the Virgo for the same end, then don't get in their way! You have been warned!! Together they make a very strong combination.

The clash comes when Pisces will simply not take any more orders—or probably will not like Virgo being too harsh on someone else. So Pisces will support the overworked friend or colleague and then let the battle commence!— as is usual in a bloodbath!!!

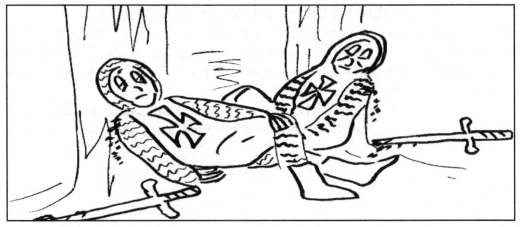

PISCES AND VIRGO

"Ok—now I am the boss," says Pisces... "That's what you think!" says Virgo under his or her breath!

Come on you guys and gals, sort out your power trips, you could be so good together an unbeatable partnership!

So if Pisces and Virgo can each just do their thing and come together on important issues, then the sky's the limit!

Pisces, you control the kids/school/pets etc.... and Virgo, you run the finances and the home. Unless you are 24/7 at work (possible!), in which case Pisces are great housekeepers!

Basically sort out your individual likes and dislikes and delegate individual jobs and this relationship can be heaven!!

LOVE RELATIONSHIP

VIRGO AND PISCES

Virgo is a down to Earth, practical sign and in love everything must also be practical. Falling in love has to be of some benefit to them and not just for the fun of it!! Like all Earth signs they need someone to set them free from their own personal struggle of not losing control and initially Pisces can do this and show them another side of life. Pisceans can be dreamers and into alternative religions, especially Spirituality and this will intrigue our Virgo from a mental point of view. Pisces can also experiment sexually and this may excite Virgo initially but frighten them to death eventually!!

PISCES AND VIRGO

Pisces lives with his or her heart on sleeve, while the Virgo lives entirely from his or her head!! This relationship could be the excitement that Virgo really longs for and Pisces will enjoy the mental challenge of trying to break down Virgo's tough exterior, especially in the bedroom!! Result? Lots of ups and downs in this relationship. If you BOTH played your cards right and enjoyed each others strengths and accept each others differences then together, and over time, a strong relationship could develop!

227

So, the development of this union could take time—but time is what we all have, so don't make it your enemy!!

CHORD COMBINATION 1
Cdim   C/Eb AND Gb
VIRGO/SAGITTARIUS AND PISCES

This combination for our Virgo could be quite daunting, because the Sagittarius normally would not be in agreement with the Virgo's plans. And, Pisces is possibly only after your body, and not your mind, so this could could be the Hammer House of Horrors!!

CHORD COMBINATION 2
Cdim   C/Eb AND Gb
PISCES/GEMINI AND VIRGO

This combination may not suit either sign, because the Gemini would possibly play Virgo and Pisces against each other for his or her own means!!

Anticipation, suspense and not knowing what is going to happen next would upset Virgo more than a Piscean, who could be excited by the uncertainty of it all!!

Gemini you hold the Ace here, so how are you gonna play the game?

CHAPTER 11

C PLUS (C+) or C AUGMENTED (Caug)

The note G#

Here we have the opposite combination of your perfect harmony E.

So whilst you may be someone's perfect harmony, when that other person is in in control it doesn't mean that her or she will be the same for you if or when you are in control!

They work out to be the note G# (G SHARP) in the chord C+ (C PLUS) OR Caug (C AUGMENTED).

This is also known as Ab (A FLAT) as explained in the music theory, but in this context I will call it a "SHARP," becuase the note is almost always used going up (higher) on the keyboard.

Therefore when going up to the next note or chord this person will assist you in achieving your ambitions and will be a plus in your life to augment everything you do.

The definition of augment is to make bigger, or add to, or move up! So, certainly you are better off with him or her than without!

You already have a perfect harmony connection and whilst this may be slightly different with the boot on the other foot it makes sense that this will be a very positive partnership and will mean progress in your life with this person.

So let's look at these combinations, as shown below, and again...

The only way is UP↑

notice the compatible elements!

SUN SIGN	ELEMENT	+NOTE	ELEMENT
ARIES	FIRE	SAGITTARIUS	FIRE
TAURUS	EARTH	CAPRICORN	EARTH
GEMINI	AIR	AQUARIUS	AIR
CANCER	WATER	PISCES	WATER
LEO	FIRE	ARIES	FIRE
VIRGO	EARTH	TAURUS	EARTH
LIBRA	AIR	GEMINI	AIR
SCORPIO	WATER	CANCER	WATER
SAGITTARIUS	FIRE	LEO	FIRE
CAPRICORN	EARTH	VIRGO	EARTH
AQUARIUS	AIR	LIBRA	AIR
PISCES	WATER	SCORPIO	WATER

Birds of a feather stick together. Same signs think alike. So this is your perfect partner in many ways. You are THEIR perfect harmony and in this combination you help THEM to achieve happiness or their goals in life or just be there as a helping hand. Onwards and upwards!!

The CHORD COMBINATION in this case also brings ALL three signs of each element together.

FIRE, EARTH, AIR and WATER
Strength in depth!

ARIES and SAGITTARIUS
HELP AT HAND

GENERAL RELATIONSHIP

When these two get together there is normally fireworks or a great party going on and certainly nothing boring in this combination.

With Sagittarius to help you up to the next level, Aries, who can stop you? If anyone tries, he or she will get short, sharp shrift from your galloping partner!

People with Sun in Aries have enough energy to cope with the possible stresses and strains of life. They can take a lot in their stride and brush off adversity as if it had never happened. With a strong, good looking sporty Sagittarius to help them, "There ain't no stopping us now!!

LOVE RELATIONSHIP

As in their perfect harmony pairing, these two sexy beasts will have no trouble getting everything on and everything off!! Keep the local fire brigade handy to douse the flames of passion! Sometimes passions could overflow and the occasional high octane disagreement could occur but normally only for a short space of time and all is forgotten and the making up is soooooooo good!!

CHORD COMBINATION   C+   C/E AND G#
ARIES/LEO AND SAGITTARIUS

Imagine the scene of three gunfighters walking through the town heading for the Sheriff's office. The Sheriff is long gone if he has any sense.

So what do these "outlaws" do?...
Buy everyone a drink in the saloon of course!! If you are in the company of these three, you're in for a great night!

Just don't try to come between them, or it will be the gunfight at the OK Corral all over again!!

FOR SAGITTARIUS AND ARIES
SEE CHAPTER 4 THE NOTE E

TAURUS AND CAPRICORN
HELP AT HAND

GENERAL RELATIONSHIP

Capricorns needed Taurean honesty and strength in their own perfect harmony and whilst they may not give as much when Taureans rule the roost they can and will help them on their way albeit in the slow plodding methodical way of the goat which does at times irritate the Bull.

Taureans should take note sometimes that careful planning can reap dividends and not be too impatient in this partnership. One thing for sure these 2 will work till the cows (bulls and goats) come home sometimes forgetting about other "lighter" things in life! Fun could be a little down on the list of essentials here!

LOVE RELATIONSHIP

Let Taurus control the bedroom Capricorn and you won't regret it! For once submit to a more powerful partner—well, as far as love goes!

Just be honest and tell the Bull how you feel. It's difficult thing to do, I know, for you secretive goats.

But, Taurus will not reveal any of your inhibitions, Just open up a bit more and bliss!!

It could take a while for BOTH these signs to fall totally in love, because they can both be insecure and not trust anyone until they really get to know them well. But when it all clicks into place, a long, long relationship normally develops. 30/40/50 years together? It's possible!

CHORD COMBINATION
C +   C/E AND G#

TAURUS/VIRGO AND CAPRICORN

In this combination we have ALL 3 Earth signs together. Strength, reliability, organized, obsessed with security!! Most Earth signs need to feel secure, at home, in work and even when they are socializing they rarely really let their hair down in case they lose self control. They need to lighten up a little!! At the same time they can be the most generous, normally in a quiet way to the underprivileged and people going through hardship as that situation frightens them to death!!

FOR CAPRICORN AND TAURUS
SEE CHAPTER 4 THE NOTE E

GEMINI AND AQUARIUS
HELP AT HAND

GENERAL RELATIONSHIP

This is a meeting of minds that will probably benefit Gemini more than Aquarius although Geminis do not normally need any help up the ladder of life a little touch of Aquarian crazy genius logic may well come in handy to them just when they needed it!

Geminis will store all useful information to use when it suits them best. The only drawback to this combination may well be an excess of alcohol or other addictive substances a trait often found in both of these intelligent but sometimes inexplicable signs!

LOVE RELATIONSHIP

A fascinating combination for both signs who will find each other attractive physically but more so mentally! Aquarius will give the freedom to our gregarious Gemini because that is also what they need. This openness will attract each other more and probably keep them together longer! If you feel trapped you want to break free so neither sign will have this problem together. There could be many a night in the bedroom after lovemaking where the conversation could go off the wall. You both can talk about anything especially about the meaning of life and perhaps the occult! WARNING..... If you drag your perfect harmony Libra into the night(a very willing cohort!) to make up a threesome then all sorts of shenanigans could happen! You have been warned!

CHORD COMBINATION
C +   C/E AND G#
GEMINI/LIBRA AND AQUARIUS

Here we have all the Air signs together and as you know Air can blow hot or cold!!

When hot, these three will party all week until the funds run out!! When cold they could be depressed from not having the funds to get out again!!

It is appropriate that Libra is in the middle of the two more daring Air signs to perhaps balance things out, but Libra could be so undecided which to follow, if Gemini or Aquarius each went in different directions.

These three signs could start a debating society or an underground protesting movement, but they would get other signs to do the physical work!!

FOR AQUARIUS AND GEMINI
SEE CHAPTER 4 THE NOTE E

CANCER AND PISCES   HELP AT HAND

GENERAL RELATIONSHIP
."Woe,woe and thrice woe!!"

Could there ever be a better combination than these two signs to cry on each others shoulders?

These emotional, but very caring creatures, will appreciate each other's depth of feeling, and Pisces will definitely add something to the Cancerian way of life—and give his or her Cancerean friends or family a lift when needed, especially when Cancer may be feeling a little down-trodden.

In will come the inner strength of Pisces, fighting for justice and problem solved,,, albeit perhaps emotionally bashed around a bit!

If you also involve your perfect harmony Scorpio to fight for you, then heaven help those who oppose you! I hope the local hospital is on alert!

LOVE RELATIONSHIP

They both will understand each other and the emotions could run riot in the sex department! Cancer can totally give all of their incredible sensitivity to this partnership and Pisces will respond not only sexually but will listen to all your grievances Cancer.

If Pisces is THE one then you could not find a better defender or protector in times of trouble Cancer. Just don''t lay it on too thick or Pisces may just get a bit bored of the complaining! Love each other as you love your animals and all will be rosy on the farm!

CHORD COMBINATION
C +   C/E AND G#
CANCER/SCORPIO AND PISCES

The three Water signs could wash away any troubles in their path when they're together.

Scorpio and Pisces have the inner strength, and even our caring Cancer could turn really "crabby" in the event of adversity.
Cancer in particular would benefit from a team scenario, as Scorpio and Pisces could probably fend for themselves!!

They should start an animal rescue center—or perhaps a consumer protection service, or maybe even a political party for the downtrodden!!

FOR PISCES AND CANCER
SEE CHAPTER 4 THE NOTE E

LEO AND ARIES   HELP AT HAND

GENERAL RELATIONSHIP
Again, I will split male from female....

A LEO MALE will undoubtedly get a boost from an Arian's constant flow of energy, and will be happy to reap any benefits or treasure won by loyal Aries minions!!

Don't bite the hand that feeds you, though, King Leo —even if you are partial to a bit of Ram or sheep, and will miss it when it's gone!

LEO FEMALES will benefit greatly from this Arian all action guy or girl and be pleased to have the help to get up and get on with life, even if it's just taking some of the strain off Lady Leos domestic duties... Help gratefully received and rewarded later!!

LOVE RELATIONSHIP

I have actually been quite hard on LEO MALES and admit that there are many who can be quite reserved and laid back. To some that could appear lazy?

Actually if they find the right Lioness they can be a pussycat and will work hard to provide for them and be very caring. It's just that there is so much on the menu!!

Could Aries be your sexy and tasty love partner? Absolutely! Along with your Sagittarian "ROCK" harmony, Aries will have all the ingredients for an amazing sex life. Aries can definitely help you to get where you want to go Leo if you can keep up!

LADY LEO would also be attracted to her Aries partner, who will add a sometimes needed boost of energy either in bed or just around the house! Now Aries could have made that mess themselves first but who cares? You are in love!!

CHORD COMBINATION   C +   C/E AND G#
LEO/SAGITTARIUS AND ARIES

The three gunslingers are back together...
Doc Holiday/Billy the kid and Calamity Jane!!

With our Lion leading the troops this time. Pure energy! Who needs electricity? If you connect with these three balls of fire, you could live forever!! Don;t get burnt though!!

FOR ARIES AND LEO SEE CHAPTER 4 THE NOTE E

VIRGO AND TAURUS   HELP AT HAND

GENERAL RELATIONSHIP

Taureans just can't help being the slave labor to whichever boss is in control, although if treated badly, will react like the worst case of Trade Union dispute you have ever seen.

However there will be a lot of mutual respect for the also hard working Virgo, who will be happy to follow the Taurus through thick and thin!

A few kind words of appreciation, though, will not go unnoticed by the workaholic Taurean.

The Virgo will have to display a less bossy than normal attitude to get the best out of Taurus, otherwise he or she may have a raging mad Taurus to deal with !!

LOVE RELATIONSHIP

Taureans can be very sensual, and could bring out a hidden sexy side to a Virgo who knows that his or her Taurean would be faithful and not "kiss and tell !!"

Romantically this could be a slow moving process, as bit by bit the two of them come to trust each other more, and this would relax them both in the bedroom.

Virgo, you will be rewarded with your trust by your Taurean's devotion and honesty. And if you want to reward your amorous Taurus?

Buy your love a fast car—a sports car, preferably!!

CHORD COMBINATION   C+   C/E AND G#
VIRGO/CAPRICORN AND TAURUS

All the EARTH signs are now back together!

If I were a King, defending my castle, I would put these three at the front of defenses. A solid wall of determination. Strength in depth!!

A bit boring perhaps? Boring can be very useful in your life at times of extreme stress believe me!! OK you probably wouldn't go to a salsa party with these chicos and chicas but you never know when you would need them!! Keep their cell phone details....just in case!!

FOR TAURUS AND VIRGO
SEE CHAPTER 4 THE NOTE E

LIBRA AND GEMINI   HELP AT HAND

GENERAL RELATIONSHIP

This + note is to assist getting a little higher in life, work etc., and Libra will be very glad of Gemini's help in this, as their sometimes insecure trait can leave them swimming against the tide and getting nowhere.

Who better than to amazingly, and with a miracle, split the waters so that Libra can just walk through to the promised land than General Gemini!

Make sure, though, that whatever you agreed to "pay" for services rendered is paid in full—or halfway across the sea, the waters could suddenly return!!

Now who would do that dirty trick?

LOVE RELATIONSHIP

These two could actually hit it off very well, just as long as the Libra knows where they stand, and can be decisive for once. As drinking partners on quiz night down at the local "hang out" is probably where they met!

"Fun" is the operative word in this relationship, which may over time build into a deeper romance, as long as they are having...FUN!!

Both of these two signs are charmers and can flirt with the best of them, but neither are particularly jealous as long as they are having...FUN!!

Gemini may well lead the way in the bedroom to start with, and easy going Libra will be eager to please!!

This is a happy go lucky relationship, but keep one eye open, Libra, for your sometimes deceitful partner!!

CHORD COMBINATION   C+   C/E AND G#
LIBRA/AQUARIUS AND GEMINI

Now we have all the AIR signs floating through life without a care in the world!! How do they do it? Perhaps we should take a leaf from their book and chill out as well?......Probably get nothing done but what the heck we had FUN!!

Actually these Air amigos are very clever and may not appear at times to be enthusiastic about work etc.,but know how to get on without too much physical effort!!

Leave that to the Earth signs!! Together they may have invented the next best thing after sliced bread to make everyone's life easier so don't pass judgment yet!!

FOR GEMINI AND LIBRA, SEE CHAPTER 4 THE NOTE E

GENERAL RELATIONSHIP

Scorpions do not often need any help getting on as they do it in their own way and just get on with life through thick and thin.
"Don't look back, what's gone is gone," etc.

However, occasionally everyone needs someone to talk to, and Cancerians will be only too happy to oblige! So, in this case, it is not really a matter of materially getting on, but more for emotional comfort and support! This should be a great friendship at first that Scorpios will take to their grave, if not cheated on!

If Cancer can keep the secrets of Scorpio's inner temple, then, perfection! If not, the Scorpion guillotine will descend and all ties—and probably heads—will be severed!!

LOVE RELATIONSHIP

Scorpio may, at last, have found someone they can trust—and then let the lovemaking begin!! Our Crab will be delighted to offer emotional and sensual company and to have found someone they can rely on and explain all the problems they have in life. But don't go on too much, Cancer, even if you have caught our Scorpion in a mellow mood. Scorpions are not enamored with "drama queens!"

CHORD COMBINATION   C+   C/E AND G#
SCORPIO/PISCES AND CANCER

Scorpios normally would not need anyone in their lives to get what is most wanted because they rarely trust anybody!!

Occasionally, however, after a long apprenticeship of proving loyalty to a Scorpion, both Cancer and Pisces could provide that missing piece of humanity that the Scorpio is prone to lack!!

Don't think everyone is trying to find out all your secrets, Scorpio. Most people have enough going on in their own lives to be bothered about yours. At least you have your loyal fellow Water signs to moan to with your "conspiracy theories!!"

FOR CANCER AND SCORPIO
SEE CHAPTER 4 THE NOTE E

GENERAL RELATIONSHIP

""Sporty, socially outgoing, fun personality, good looking.....well—hey—that's enough about me." says the "modest" Sagittarius!!

"Well, I can beat that!" says King Leo. "I'm handsome, debonair, regal, great with the opposite sex, have a commanding presence and am center of everyone's attention"...(or else!!)....Only one person in the bathroom can get ready at one time so there could be a rush to the door!

KING LEO could help Sagittarius to progress in social status, if he wants to. He may find Sagittarius irresistible and a possible new addition to his harem?
Sagittarius will not like being 2nd, 3rd or 4th on the list so only a monogamous arrangement is possible here!

LADY LEO will as usual assist where possible although in a more

practical way and our Sagittarius will be happy to accept this physical help if it gets them where they want to be i.e., a winner in the race of life! Add a little praise and "sincere" thanks, not the usual sarcasm and on you go!

LOVE RELATIONSHIP

These two sexy fire people will have no trouble in the "love game." Both will be attracted to each other physically and mentally, as they love the challenge of life and personal freedom to express their views!! Just try stopping them!!

There may be a few skirmishes along the way, as Fire signs do that, but as always, the making up is worth it. Sagittarians can actually "goad" people into an argument just for the sake of it, and to show off their oratory skills.

KING LEO is likely to take the bait and then laugh about it in bed later.

LADY LEO would not be fooled so easily and just tell Sagittarius to make them a nice cup of coffee and shut up!!

When these 2 met initially it may have been LUST at first sight and a lift home could have ended in "steamy windows!!"

CHORD COMBINATION

C+   C/E AND G#
SAGITTARIUS/ARIES
AND LEO

Just get these three together and watch the fireworks. On a night out, it's a blast all night until the "downside" of alcohol kicks in. Then, in particular with Sagittarius, a tirade of sarcastic remarks to all within earshot is likely. Not pleasant!

So, Sagittarius, you may be better off as the designated driver for the night and avoid the demon drink. Yes? No! That may make you even worse but you may avoid conflict! Leo and Aries will come to your aid regardless and bail you out if necessary!!

FOR
LEO AND SAGITTARIUS

SEE CHAPTER 4
THE NOTE E

CAPRICORN AND VIRGO   HELP AT HAND

GENERAL RELATIONSHIP

Capricorns can be very solitary and introvert creatures and rarely accept help until they desperately need it, so if a crisis occurs who better than a Virgo to get them out of any mess!!

Capricorns are seldom wrong (so they tell me!!), but IF they have a weakness occasionally, then Virgo will cover all indiscretions and lift them them up to the next ridge on their mountain!

Self control is so important to sometimes very moody and deep Capricorns that they often need to lighten up in order to enjoy life. they can be very serious and "old" children. As they as they get older, they realize this, and then often act younger!!

Virgo, in this partnership, will just strengthen the work ethic and organization of careful Capricorn, and by doing so, will and take a little of the stress off their backs.

As long as Virgos don't go for complete control themselves this could be a very strong, if somewhat dull combination!!

LOVE RELATIONSHIP

It could take a while for these two to really get it together in romance, as neither are particularly romantic!! Doing nice things for each other would probably involve paying the bills on time, doing the household chores, etc. Wow!!

Actually, neither will feel comfortable going out and spending money, unless it is included in the household budget. In the bedroom they could surprise one another and actually be spontaneous for a change. As long as you don't tell anyone!!

They will feel relaxed together, as both have similar ideas on the home and security and money and blah,blah,blah...If it makes you happy, then that is all that matters!!

CHORD COMBINATION   C+   C/E AND G#
CAPRICORN/TAURUS AND VIRGO

Would you have a night out with these guys or the FIRE signs?.....
Answer....FIRE

Would you be safe getting home with these guys or FIRE signs?...
Answer...These guys!

You need all sorts of people in YOUR life to make you happy and content. These EARTH signs will feel very "safe" together, as most adventurous action requires RISK!!

This would frighten our Earth team to death...unless....it's a calculated risk with a chance of making money??

FOR VIRGO AND CAPRICORN
SEE CHAPTER 4 THE NOTE E

250

AQUARIUS AND LIBRA   HELP AT HAND

GENERAL RELATIONSHIP

These two like-minded gentle souls may just be a little too light to get any really big physical job done! Libra will happily agree all the time with Aquarians and ok will lead them upwards, probably up the stairs to the wine bar where they can discuss and dream and plan to their hearts content and tomorrow...they can discuss and dream and plan to their hearts content and so on! Practically they could both probably need a Taurean housekeeper and Virgo financial adviser and then joy to the world!!

They're interesting and nice "dreamers" though—most of the time!

LOVE RELATIONSHIP

A fairy tale romance of these dreamers is possible. Aquarians will love Libra's open approach to love and life in general, and together they could experiment in every aspect of their love affair. They could write new chapters in the Kama Sutra, perhaps!!.

Librans will enhance our Water Carrier's life, and listen intently to all the crazy ideas coming from the Aquarian's naturally intellectual brain. Neither will be jealous of the other, perhaps even having an "open" relationship.

Aquarians are the original "hippys." Free thinking, free love, etc., etc.

Peace and love to all....

CHORD COMBINATION   C+   C/E and G#
AQUARIUS/GEMINI AND LIBRA

Blow, wind, blow! A rush of AIR—
all together—could change the face of this planet!

These mentally charged creatures could instigate mind revolutions and be protagonists against injustice! Well, they may have some "interesting" ideas, but the world needs "thinkers" to instigate change when there is a stagnation of thought. So, go for it, gang....bring it on.... Genius ideas though come with a "crazy"streak at times, so be a little careful you don't blow yourself up in the lab, while finding a cure for everything!!

FOR LIBRA AND AQUARIUS, SEE CHAPTER 4, THE NOTE E

GENERAL RELATIONSHIP

This is actually a strong combination, even though both are water and potentially too emotional they both have an inner strength that is hard to beat!!

Pisces have probably been through many hardships (or so they will tell you!) and they will always come out ok but emotionally scarred!

Scorpios will however, even if they have been through REAL hardship, will not disclose this to just anyone and get on with the here and now so they will jolt Pisces off their sometimes self pitying routine and help them get on with life as it should be. They will admire the Piscean sense of fighting to help the underdog and those that can't help themselves but add practical rather than emotional solutions and just do it!

LOVE RELATIONSHIP

Pisces will love our Scorpion coming in to their life to bring some emotional stability, and even though Scorpio can be insanely jealous at times, Pisces will view this as being wanted and needed!!

Both of them are possibly interested in "out of the box" ideas and even spiritual or occult themes.

In the Pisces boudoir it will be very sensual—almost bordello type of furnishings with perhaps a few implements at hand!! Don't ask!! In general, this is a strong love relationship if, as always, you don't reveal the sexy Scorpion's secrets!! Blackmail is not an option, if you wish to survive, Pisces—or you may end up "grilled or fried!!"

CHORD COMBINATION   C+   C/E AND G#
PISCES/CANCER AND SCORPIO

All good for our Pisces here. Scorpio to provide all the tools necessary to get on in life and Cancer the understanding shoulder to cry on in difficult times.

We are all 7/10ths water anyway and can't live without it so ALL the other signs actually need some of the above at some time. All together though may be a little too much to bear or you could be crying for months!!

FOR SCORPIO AND PISCES SEE CHAPTER 4 THE NOTE E

CHAPTER 12

THE 6TH CHORD C6

THE NOTE OF A

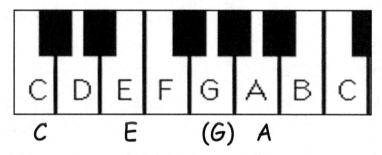

The 6th note is often played without the 5th as they clash when played together! So the 6th person can take you a little higher and help you progress a little in life, but the 5th will bring you back down to earth. Don't use them or put them in a situation together!

These combinations are opposites, but if they are used wisely, they can be very beneficial.

So if a happy partnership can be reached by respecting each others differences, then this could be the help that you needed—iust at the right time!

So here are the 6th note combinations!

BASE NOTE	ELEMENT	6TH NOTE	ELEMENT
ARIES	FIRE	CAPRICORN	EARTH
TAURUS	EARTH	AQUARIUS	AIR
GEMINI	AIR	PISCES	WATER
CANCER	WATER	ARIES	FIRE
LEO	FIRE	TAURUS	EARTH
VIRGO	EARTH	GEMINI	AIR
LIBRA	AIR	CANCER	WATER
SCORPIO	WATER	LEO	FIRE
SAGITTARIUS	FIRE	VIRGO	EARTH
CAPRICORN	EARTH	LIBRA	AIR
AQUARIUS	AIR	SCORPIO	WATER
PISCES	WATER	SAGITTARIUS	FIRE

As stated above, these two have to respect each other because in normal relationship circumstances, they just do not get on.

In the team scenario, however, they could be a useful stepping stone to success!

So in this case.

FIRE must slowly heat the EARTH
EARTH must be scattered gently by the AIR
AIR must invigorate the WATER with oxygen
WATER must not put out the flames of FIRE

ARIES AND CAPRICORN   A LITTLE HELP?

GENERAL RELATIONSHIP

Ok, fire and earth are never good together!

But when the Earth sign is helping the Fire to get ahead, then there is no better sign to do it than a Capricorn!

As long as these two are playing their respective roles in achieving the end result, then fine. Just let Capricorn take you onwards and upwards, and as long as there is a bit of distance between the two of you, then there is no problem.

However, Aries, if you try and interfere too much in HOW the Capricorn is doing this or that, then be prepared for icy replies, or just no reply at all, or even just a sulk from the secretive Capricorn, who does not like too much questioning about anything he or she is doing!! Leave it to the Lone Ranger!!

LOVE RELATIONSHIP

Aries' passion and Capricorn's "take it easy" approach do not bode well for a sexy affair. This relationship would have to build slowly to have a chance, and Aries just does not do SLOW!

Capricorns can be attractive because of their "shyness," which is really more about being secretive and not revealing their true thoughts. This could intrigue our Ram into either battering Capricorn for answers—or for once, realize that this might a time when it could be best to just wait and see!

If you do decide wait and see, Aries, then you may be surprised that in time Capricorn would be a most useful friend to help you on your way, even if not also providing the sexual fireworks that you crave!

CHORD COMBINATION   C6   C/E/(G) AND A
ARIES/LEO/(SCORPIO)
AND CAPRICORN

This partnership works best in a team situation. You have your loyal, sexy perfect harmony Leo at your side, Aries, and then the Goat to give you that little push in the right direction......upwards!!!

Scorpio in the background as your ROCK will be there to catch you if you fall! It's nice to have a safety net!

FOR CAPRICORN AND ARIES
SEE CHAPTER 8
THE MINOR CHORD

TAURUS AND AQUARIUS A LITTLE HELP?

GENERAL RELATIONSHIP

Aquarians can be an intelligent choice for Taurus to help them succeed. Taurus, an earth sign, can be the best "doer" in the Zodiac, and Aquarius, an air sign, can be a best "thinker." So Aquarius may plan the way ahead first, rather than being like a Bull, just charging in!!

      Taureans are no slouches in the brain department, either—but they need gratification right away. An Aquarian may urge Taurus to slow down a fraction and think about everything very thoroughly first, and this may irritate the Taurus somewhat, but it could be to advantage of both of them, if they are to work well together.

LOVE RELATIONSHIP

Brawn versus Brain? Don't ever tell a Taurus that he or she is just all muscle because Taureans are sensuous, caring souls who long for a nice home and security in a relationship with openness plus honesty. Can our free spirited Aquarian provide any of this?

Doubtful, I think—although if used within THIS scenario, the Aquarian could come up with some brilliant ideas to help you progress steadily through life, Taurus, and you could find that to your liking.

In the boudoir you could be talking as much as lovemaking, and be "satisfied" in other ways! However, you must let Aquarius have a free reign on his or her life, if you want a long term partner.

Taureans would have to give more in this "love relationship" for it to work well, so eventually that may just be too much of a strain for our faithful Bull and end in tears!!

CHORD COMBINATION   C6 C/E/(G) AND A

TAURUS/VIRGO/(SAGITTARIUS) AND AQUARIUS

Ok, this may not be the most romantic of connections , but if you need a little extra love in your life Taurus, without commitment, then Aquarius could be the perfect partner.

Virgo will always be there to keep your feet on the ground, so you can't get into too much trouble and you'll keep feeling secure.

Sagittarius? He or she should be your ROCK here, but may be tempted into seeing what our intriguing Aquarian is up to!!

Play it cool Taurus, without your normal "bull in a china shop"reaction, and you may be surprised at what you can achieve here!

FOR AQUARIUS AND TAURUS
SEE CHAPTER 8 THE MINOR CHORD

GEMINI AND PISCES

A LITTLE HELP?

GENERAL RELATIONSHIP

Geminis in general do not need too much help in achieving their aims but sometimes other people become "useful" in their quest!

Pisces Sun signs have a very emotional trait, but have an inner strength and sheer "bloody mindedness" when they are fighting for what or who they believe in.

Gemini may sit back and use this Piscean "talent" to their own ends when getting into tricky situations, and certainly would know how to press the right Piscean buttons! If Pisceans don't get used too often in this way, then OK—but beware if one button too many is pushed, or the Gemini might get into hot water with a steaming piranha!!

LOVE RELATIONSHIP

There is Plenty of attraction here at first. Gemini could seduce our Pisces into bed with promises of everlasting love, but then up and leave for the next adventure, saying, "I didn't say it was forever... really."

So here is our fish, then— out of water and flapping around to get some answers, and plan revenge!!

You will have to be so careful, Gemini, if you want anything from this relationship. Pisces types can seem to be sensitive, harmless creatures— but hell hath a furious fish with a devil inside, if he or she feels personally wronged OR also if an injustice has been done to one of their close friends or or a family member.

Or, if if you play your cards very carefully, you could have a partner that will back you to the hilt.

The trouble is, though, that you don't like just one partner, do you, Gemini?

CHORD COMBINATION   C6   C/E/(G) AND A
GEMINI/LIBRA/(CAPRICORN)AND PISCES

Well, Team Gemini.—there can be only one captain here! Libra will be happy to go along with "the boss," as long as there is no stress attached. Capricorn, your ROCK, will be in the office doing the books, keeping the accounts in order, and your Pisces will be swimming you upstream to where the gold is!!

Bliss for you Gemini, as long as your alter ego doesn't upset the Goat and the Fish...or be prepared to go missing for a while!!

FOR PISCES AND GEMINI
SEE CHAPTER 8 THE MINOR CHORD

CANCER AND ARIES   A LITTLE HELP?

GENERAL RELATIONSHIP

Cancer could benefit greatly from Arian energy in this combination and be dragged up to the next level quite quickly but check the foundations are solid or could come crashing back down just as fast by Arian impetuosity!! The ride could be amazing and a lot of fun but save something in the tank or the bank for later!

　　　The only problem could be that Cancer gets worn out with the next event that Aries has planned and may have to use some of their "water" element to dampen the fiery Aries down a bit!

　　　However they would also enjoy the social side of this encounter as long as they are not dragged into many alcoholic celebrations!

LOVE RELATIONSHIP

Aries would certainly have the Crab's passions boiling over here! The trouble is that with too much "boiling over," you could end up like the unfortunate lobster!

The emotional Cancer could get very hurt if our Aries is their normal foot loose and fancy free character that Aries can be. Still, Aries also has a caring side, especially with animals— and so does the Cancerian. So, this could be a common thread to a longer romance than at first may seem viable!

Our Cancer will have to "toughen up" a bit in the emotional stakes, though, and not take too much to heart, as Aries can be as equally as hurtful as he or she can be caring, almost in the same breath!

Be kind, Aries if YOU want to help this caring soul—or just help out a bit and then move on before you break our Cancerian's heart!

CHORD COMBINATION   C6   C/E/(G) AND A
CANCER/SCORPIO/(AQUARIUS) AND ARIES

This combination is quite strong for Cancerians, because they have their loyal Scorpion on hand to fight in their corner, if the headstrong Aries gets out of hand. Scorpio will provide a good back up!!

Aquarians won't be too involved in this type of situation unless asked, and the Aries, with his or her childlike enthusiasm and energy, could propel our Crab into the stratosphere and beyond!! If so, Cancer, make sure you have a parachute!!

FOR ARIES AND CANCER
SEE CHAPTER 8 THE MINOR CHORD

LEO AND TAURUS   A LITTLE HELP?

GENERAL RELATIONSHIP

Male Leos will enjoy a workaholic Taurean getting them what they want when they want it. Both signs can be impatient for results and since both are proud animals of stature, they will have a mutual respect!

Taureans may tire of King Leo's commands, however, and a bitter battle could ensue!.

A Leo female would, I think, have a better chance in in relating to a Taurus—either male or female—as both of them would be pre-pared to give and to work hard for something they both care about. So, this could be a happy association—although they may prefer to be just friends or colleagues at work, rather than roommates.

LOVE RELATIONSHIP

If our KING LEO is a flirtatious show off, then he is headed for a fall if he thinks his Taurean lady will give him adulation. Taureans will not be attracted to this kind of self importance, even if the Lion is a handsome fellow! If, however, our Leo is the more laid back type, then perhaps they could start off on the right foot, but probably not for long. The Leo trait of leaving things that need to be done until later will annoy the Taurus, who wants to have things clean and tidy. Love and respect for Taureans has to be earned, so while for a short time there could be a physical attraction between Leo and Taurus, it doesn't bode well for a long term relationship.

Our LADY LEO will have a better chance of keeping the Taurus Bull happy, as their work ethic is very similar and the Taurean will go the extra mile for someone who gives more than she takes. At first the Bull may like the excitement of a partner who has totally different views, but if a relationship is to develop, the Lioness definitely has the better chance to make it succeed!

CHORD COMBINATION   C6   C/E/(G) AND A LEO/SAGITTARIUS/(PISCES) AND TAURUS

The opposites of some signs are exposed more than others, and I think FIRE and EARTH are really "chalk and cheese." Life, however, is a balance, and even these signs need a bit of strengths of other signs at times. So, our King Leo might do well to think like King Solomon, and then wisely use Taurus to the mutual benefit of all concerned.

Sagittarius will always be there to keep the frivolity going when you need it, so none of you have to be boring. Be wise!!

FOR TAURUS AND LEO
SEE CHAPTER 8 THE MINOR CHORD

VIRGO AND GEMINI   A LITTLE HELP?

GENERAL RELATIONSHIP

For Gemini to help Virgo achieve a little more in life is more than possible—but read the small print, Virgo, or you may have to pay your "pound of flesh" for such help!!

Geminis will normally and willingly help others, as long as there is also something in it for them! If you are happy to go more than 50/50, Virgo, then no problem—the price could well be worth it, as you are almost guaranteed to succeed..

Just make sure that contracts are not signed in the bar!!

LOVE RELATIONSHIP

This is in your hands, Virgo! Your Gemini is a very attractive, sexy and smooth operator. Now, if you know this you will also know that Gemini is unlikely to stay faithful, or at least will want some freedom.

Sexually, if you are a bit too careful in the bedroom, as well as in life in general, your Gemini will probably get a bit bored with the same routine.

In my opinion, a clever Virgo will use his or her Gemini partner only as a step ladder to greater things. Combine your talents and you could go far, but you will also have to let your Gemini have his or her space, and keep your Virgo controlling nature to a minimum! You will achieve much more this way, and possibly your Gemini will want to get closer, as now that the gate is open, he or she doesn't want to leave!!

CHORD COMBINATION   C6   C/E/(G) AND A VIRGO/CAPRICORN/(ARIES) AND GEMINI

It's a strong combination here! With Gemini getting you to the next level, Virgo, and your supportive solid Capricorn pushing you up the ladder, how could you not succeed!!

Still, You could be your own worst enemy here, with your some-times controlling attitude. Gemini and Capricorn are equally strong signs, so are much better as friends than foes!!

Be careful that your ROCK, Aries, doesn't run off with Gemini just for the fun of it all, or because he or she got fed up with watching over you in front of the TV every night!!

FOR GEMINI AND VIRGO
SEE CHAPTER 8 THE MINOR CHORD

LIBRA AND CANCER

GENERAL RELATIONSHIP

On the face of it this could be a happy and gentle partnership. Librans will not be tested too much or asked to give too much in this pairing, and Cancer could use an emotional card to get on to the next level in life. If it all comes crashing down, the two of them will have a good cry together—and there's always tomorrow!

A Libran will be a good listener to the Cancer's concerns, and this could be all that the Cancerian will need to carry on. If things do go badly, however, they could both drown their sorrows a little too much!!!

LOVE RELATIONSHIP

Sexually these two could be good lovers, as Librans will always try to please and Cancer is happy to be pleasured!! Possibly, though, Cancer will want to take it to the next level a bit too fast for our uncertain Libran, and Libra could then be lured into a relationship he or she is not yet ready to feel sure about!

Although Cancerians are, in general, home lovers, they can party with the rest of them, often to express their emotions, and then Libra will be happy to be brought out whenever and wherever he or she is needed! Your Cancerian will be very caring towards you, Libra, it's in the nature of this Sun sign. You will respond, of course to this kindness, but in the long term, it could frighten you, causing your indecisiveness to rear it's ugly head. Then your Cancerian will get "crabby" when you can't make up your mind.

Don't push too quick, though, Cancer or you could lose a possible good friend, if not a long term partner!

CHORD COMBINATION   C6   C/E/(G) AND A LIBRA/AQUARIUS/(TAURUS) AND CANCER

This is a very light, easy going combination of signs. No one is in too much hurry to go scrambling up the ladder of success. If it happens, it happens!!

This is all very well, but someone still has to pay the bills to live! Which one? It may be necessary to have to call on your ROCK harmony Taurus, who is not really involved in this chord, but may be able to come to the rescue financially. Come on, Cancer! Give your loving Libra a kick in the pants to get things moving!!

SCORPIO AND LEO   A LITTLE HELP?

GENERAL RELATIONSHIP

LEO MALES will have to get out of bed early, if this is to work! (Work being the hardest word in Leo's dictionary!) Scorpio will have to praise the sensitive Leo ego to get the best out of this relationship, and to achieve things together. It may work well, or they may decide they can do as well and maybe better if each continues on alone.

If, however, Scorpio needs a salesman to sell the next best thing in designer clothing, etc., then just leave it to Mr. Leo and Company!

Scorpios can be a little dry and too "straight" for selling—there's no kidding around with this Sun sign. So, in that case, an association with Leo could be an answer to the Scorpio's prayers.

LEO FEMALES should not have problems in working with the straight-forwardness of Scorpio, as long as they also can get out of bed. This is not a work shy thing—it's just that Lions hate mornings! They are great on a night shift, though or when entertaining 'till the early hours!

271

The Lioness does have to get up to do the chores, though, and look after the cubs, but after all, most lions are night animals, and Lady Leo will have been out all night getting the breakfast. So, she deserves a rest in the morning!

LOVE RELATIONSHIP

Sensual but secretive Scorpio will be attracted to a strong Lion, and KING LEO may well want to discover all the Scorpio's secrets with a little "pillow talk," perhaps? Try to get blood from a stone, Leo—you will have more chance!!

Initially Leo and Scorpio could be a strong connection, as each may try to outdo the other. The competition fascinates, but Scorpio won't bear allegiance to "his majesty," who appears to expect to be the one in control. So, the Leo may move on toward easier foes to defeat!

If these two signs do get their heads together, they could be formidable as a partnership, but the Scorpio may not let the Leo close enough for a lasting romance! So, OK, Scorpio—just have your Leo as an ally to help you progress in life.

LADY LEO may fear she won't be able to break down the defenses of Scorpio for fear of being stung! If she cares for her Scorpio, though, she will realize that the so-called Scorpio "sting" is only an old-fashioned Sun sign idea that doesn't apply to her own abilities to charm her mate. She will go happily on with their relationship, confident in her queenly ability to handle things well.

Scorpios rarely need or accept help, and some may feel offended if help is offered that they did not request. This tends to be an independent and self-sufficient Sun sign—but again, we must all realize that the Sun sign is only ONE factor in one's total personality and in one's total astrological chart.

Again, as was said in Chapter 3 of this book, your Sun sign, while important, is only ONE part of your total horoscope. When you have had your whole chart calculated and read by a competent astrologer, or you have learned more about astrology yourself, you will realize that a true full understanding and a fair judgment of anyone else should NEVER be made on the basis of ONLY his or her Sun sign.

In any case, with this chord combination, you will have a devoted Pisces as a back up, and a Gemini friend may also be waiting in the wings to also assist you

CHORD COMBINATION   C6   C/E/(G) AND A SCORPIO/PISCES/(GEMINI) AND LEO

So, Scorpio, do you really need Leo to help you succeed? Maybe you do, or maybe you do not. Again, as was said in Chapter 3 of this book, your Sun sign, while important, is only ONE part of your total horoscope. When you have had your whole chart calculated and read by a competent astrologer, or have learned more about astrology yourself, you will realize that a true full understanding and a fair judgment of anyone else should NEVER be based of ONLY on the Sun sign.

In any case, with this chord combination, you will have a devoted Pisces as a back up, who shares your water sign nature, and a Gemini friend may also be ready to assist you.

As for the Leo, is a Lion better at helping you or hindering you? Leo shares your fixed determination, so more likely will help you, especially if you offer friendship.

Remember that there are so many options when you have learned how to read and understand an entire astrological chart. Astrological lore, has three symbols for Scorpio—a serpent, representing the lowest expression of the sign, the most widely known symbol of a scorpion with evil looking claws, an eagle, which has been said to represent the Scorpio who has risen above the serpent and scorpion expressions of this complex Sun sign, and soars to the heights of its most positive expression. Which symbol you represent is your choice, Scorpio! of your own choice. Another old saying applies here: "The stars impel; they do not compel."

FOR LEO AND SCORPIO SEE CHAPTER 8, THE MINOR CHORD

SAGITTARIUS and VIRGO   A LITTLE HELP?

GENERAL RELATIONSHIP

This is not the best of combinations, so these two may be best apart most of the time! Still, as long as both respect the other's position, in this case with the Sagittarians in chart, then it should be ok!

Sagittarius will have to keep their brutal honesty under control to get the best out of a Virgo partner, who will not let them down, if spoken to nicely!! The Virgo will need to think his or her ideas are accepted by the Sagittarian, even if Sag is the one who previously planted the seed. This relationship could be very successful, or it could end in tears or even in a few blows, if the extremes of both signs come to the fore! Can Sagittarians hone their "person management" skills to get the best results?

LOVE RELATIONSHIP

Earth and Fire rarely combine well in a long term love relationship so all does not bode well here either! There is a chance with their mutual love of intellectual conversation, but Sagittarians will then want some excitement and to be adventurous in the bedroom, which may meet with reluctance from a prudish Virgo.

A Virgo could help enable our Sagittarian to progress in life, and would be a great friend if a disaster should ever occur. So, Sagittarius, can you control your sarcastic, hurting, personal remarks and be patient

274

towards your Virgo? If this relationship is ever to blossom into a fine romance, then BOTH of you will have to go against some of your normal Sun sign instincts and personality traits. It's a tough job, but if you care for each other, you can do it!!

CHORD COMBINATION
C 6   C/E/(G)
SAGITTARIUS/ARIES/(CANCER)
AND VIRGO

This will primarily be up to Sagittarius to make this relationship work. Sagittarians don't normally need any help up the ladder, but if a crisis arises, then Virgo can be your best back up to have.

So, don't upset the team! Aries is always there to give you a good time and extra energy, and although Virgos may bring you back down to earth, what they have to say or do may take you higher than you've ever been before!!

FOR VIRGO AND SAGITTARIUS
SEE CHAPTER 8
THE MINOR CHORD

CAPRICORN and LIBRA   A LITTLE HELP?

GENERAL RELATIONSHIP

Well, the only way that I can see Libra helping Capricorn to get along is by being Libra! Does that sounds daft? Let me explain.

Librans are, in general, kind and caring people who are very good with other people, can communicate well, and have good taste.

These skills sometimes are lacking in Capricorns. It's not that they don't have a soft caring side. They do care, and very much, but they tend to have difficulty in showing it to the world because they do not want to expose any "weakness or loss of self control. So, if someone else can play this role for them, all the better, and in steps a Libra to fill this gap!

This could be a friendly partnership, as in general Libra will not threaten Capricorn's need to control things. Also, Libra will be happy that Capricorn will "be there" to assist, if Libra's own efforts fail to achieve what he or she intended.

Although this relationship is not likely set the world on fire, you will not come away offended if you meet these two, and you will be pleased to have them as your Facebook friends!

LOVE RELATIONSHIP

How can we be lovers if we can't be friends? Well, in this case a love relationship may well develop from being friends at first.

Librans will not sweep you off your feet but you will be attracted by their laid back and caring attitude to life, and not feel threatened that they will try to change you.

Capricorns will then be happy to

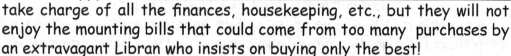

take charge of all the finances, housekeeping, etc., but they will not enjoy the mounting bills that could come from too many purchases by an extravagant Libran who insists on buying only the best!

So in conclusion...yes, a Libran and a Capricorn could fall in love and also be good friends. But, over time it may become apparent that these two also have quite totally different points of view on how to live life!

So, in the end there could be a very amicable parting of the ways— but they will still keep in touch with each other!

CHORD COMBINATION   C 6   C/E/(G) AND A

CAPRICORN/TAURUS/(LEO)
AND LIBRA

If you need a PR manager, Capricorn, then your Libra in this combination will wax lyrical about all your achievements and plus points. If you are a politician, for example, a Libra spin doctor would do just fine. Libra might also be a good person to ask to choose your clothes and home, if such things are important for your career. Taurus would probably disagree with this appointment, though, since Librans tend to be very good at spending money—especially someone else's!

FOR LIBRA AND CAPRICORN
SEE CHAPTER 8 THE MINOR CHORD

AQUARIUS and SCORPIO   A LITTLE HELP?

GENERAL RELATIONSHIP

If a Scorpio is 100% sure of his or her Aquarian partner, nothing will stop them from getting closer and closer— and woe betide anyone who tries to come between them! The Aquarian's only folly here would be for his or her crazy side to emerge, such that straightforward Scorpio will wonder what is going on! But in general, with the clever Aquarian brain in full flow and the Scorpio to get them where they want to be, I would not bet against this duo!

It could be fun to be at dinner parties with these two, if you are looking to stretch your imagination and perhaps learn a few things.

LOVE RELATIONSHIP

Both of these signs can be very secretive and give nothing away. Aquarians can be happy by simply being in their own space—it's not a deliberate thing, it's "just being me!" Scorpios, however, can intentionally preserve their innermost secrets at all costs!!

So in love? Who will give in first? Well, neither, so stalemate! At first there will be physical attraction and probably a few mind games, as they are fascinated by each others privacy. Aquarians will soon get fed up, though, with their inability to penetrate Scorpio's defenses — and why waste the effort anyway!! Scorpios can be overly jealous if the free thinking, free love, do your own thing Aquarian angers the Scorpio such that the green eyed monster appears!!

CHORD COMBINATION
C 6   C/E/(G) AND A
AQUARIUS/GEMINI/
(VIRGO) AND SCORPIO

Aquarians have a good chance to progress in life with a Scorpio partner, but may be nervous about the "way" that the Scorpion would work to help get them there!

Aquarians can be very easy going types who think, "Live and let live, etc.,, but Scorpios sometimes can bend the rules to get results, and Aquarian may not agree with that type of behavior!!

Gemini is your perfect partner to protect your interests, Aquarius, but be careful that you don't get tempted by a scheming Scorpio's plan to make everyone rich!!

So....state the rules firmly, our Water Carrier, before you engage the services or get involved too deeply with the Scorpion, and you may avoid facing the possible "law suit" later!!

FOR SCORPIO AND AQUARIUS
SEE CHAPTER 8 THE MINOR CHORD

PISCES and SAGITTARIUS   A LITTLE HELP?

GENERAL RELATIONSHIP

Sagittarians will definitely help Pisceans rise on the social calender, and be happy to arrange lots of ways to achieve this! They also would benefit from it, of course, but they'll do it mainly to help their emotional and shy partner!

Pisceans are well capable of looking after themselves when push comes to shove, though, and somehow I can't see Sagittarians responding to bossy leaders!

Be prepared for many "wars of words," in this relationship. The Pisces will find it hard to hold his or her tongue with a typical sarcastic Sagittarian on the prowl!!

If, however, they can find a way to work or live together, then please don't criticize anything they do, or you may be in for a rough ride!!

LOVE RELATIONSHIP

If these two are able to get their act together, they would be a quite formidable pair.

Sexually they would be very active, because the Sagittarian's natural ego and strength would be like a rock for Pisces to fall back on, and that will attract our emotional fish. Sagittarians are very good at "fishing," so don't get caught hook, line and sinker, Pisces!!

Emotion does not play a large part in a Sagittarian's life, as he

280

or she will say, "Just get over it and move on," which they do on MANY occasions!

Our Pisces, however, could be in a deep depression for weeks if his or her lover was unfaithful or just walked out. Afterwards, the Pisces would then plan revenge!! So, Sagittarius, if you are going to do this to our gentle fish, you had better have your horse saddled and ready, or your fastest shoes on, or be a very good swimmer, if you expect to escape the "shark" that is not far behind you!!

CHORD COMBINATION   C 6   C/E/(G) AND A
PISCES/CANCER/(LIBRA) and SAGITTARIUS

In this team scenario, Pisces, your Sagittarian may drag you kicking and screaming into the 21st Century—but it would be worth it, in the long run! Sagittarians are intelligent and "on the ball. " They can be right about a lot of things....BUT, it's just the WAY that they do it that upsets some people. Diplomatic they are not!

Still, sometimes the hoped for results will come, but at what cost? Lose a few friends? Make a few enemies? You could get alternative advice from your loyal Cancer friend and then make a wise decision.

If you do decide to go against the Archer be prepared for sarcastic, stinging arrows aimed at your heart!!

FOR SAGITTARIUS and PISCES
SEE CHAPTER 8
THE MINOR CHORD

CHAPTER 13

THE 7TH

This, in posh music terms,
is called a
DOMINANT SEVENTH

This is made up of the normal basic chord of 1ST/3RD/5TH(C/E/G) plus the flattened or minor 7th which in the case of the key of C is the note Bb (B flat).

It is more commonly called just the 7th to distinguish between the note of B which forms the MAJOR 7th which I will be covering in the next chapter!!

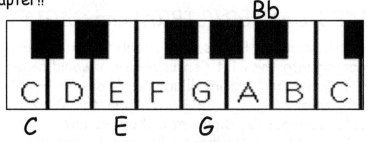

Now a 7th is very often used in ROCK N ROLL so this person could really lighten up your life and get things moving for you!!

Alternatively this person could be dancing all over you and just want to party!! The 7th can also be used in THE BLUES, so this person could be emotional and bring you down OR add a bit of "soul" in your life!

A very common chord is also a MINOR SEVENTH e.g., Cm7. This is made up of C/Eb/G AND Bb, and is common in a lot of genres of music including Disco and Jazz, so this person could have you boogying the night away or lost in some crazy music.

What type of 7th is yours? Rock 'n Roll or the Blues?

We have compared the C/E AND G already so here are your 7th pairings.

BASE NOTE C	ELEMENT	7TH NOTE	ELEMENT
ARIES	FIRE	AQUARIUS	AIR
TAURUS	EARTH	PISCES	WATER
GEMINI	AIR	ARIES	FIRE
CANCER	WATER	TAURUS	EARTH
LEO	FIRE	GEMINI	AIR
VIRGO	EARTH	CANCER	WATER
LIBRA	AIR	LEO	FIRE
SCORPIO	WATER	VIRGO	EARTH
SAGITTARIUS	FIRE	LIBRA	AIR
CAPRICORN	EARTH	SCORPIO	WATER
AQUARIUS	AIR	SAGITTARIUS	FIR
PISCES	WATER	CAPRICORN	EARTH

There are only two combinations of ELEMENTS in the 7th pairings. So we have the explosive FIRE and AIR combination (rock 'n roll) or AIR blowing out the FIRE (the blues). The EARTH could be a fun mud bath with too much WATER (rock 'n roll), or a barren desert with not enough (the blues).

ARIES and AQUARIUS ROCK N ROLL or the BLUES

GENERAL RELATIONSHIP

Ok—the Fire and Air combination could really ignite here, especially if the Aries drags out the crazy side of the Aquarians nature. Then, this relationship could really rock n roll!!

Eventually, however, it could turn into the blues for Aquarians who would prefer a more subtle and laid back approach to life. If the constant Aries energy is controlling things, then the Aquarian could feel a little overwhelmed!

LOVE RELATIONSHIP

Aries will be excited and intrigued by the Aquarian, who can be a little myste- rious. Neither Aries nor Aquarius give much away, as both are free spirits who would be very adventurous.

Neither of these two Sun signs likes to feel trapped, so they would re- spect each others privacy

—although Aries may, in the long run, wear out our cool Aquarian! If you want a longer relationship, Aries, you may have to slow down a little to give your Aquarian a chance to digest all that is happening. Other- wise, this could be an explosive love affair that is finished almost as quickly as it started!

CHORD COMBINATION 1   C 7
C/E/G AND Bb
ARIES/LEO/SCORPIO AND AQUARIUS

Probably there is too much FIRE power in this combination for our Aquarian, with Leo adding to the Aries ball of energy! It's the blues for Aquarius, unless the Scorpio's water can dampen the fiery Aries and Leo friends!!

CHORD COMBINATION 2   Cm7
C/Eb/G AND Bb
ARIES/CANCER/SCORPIO AND AQUARIUS

In this combination, Cancer replaces Leo to add more water to the Aries flame and so could our Ram calm down a little? Well at least 10 seconds!! It depends what YOU want in these combinations Aries..... don't burn yourself out!!

FOR AQUARIUS AND ARIES
SEE CHAPTER 7 THE NOTE D

TAURUS and PISCES ROCK N ROLL or the BLUES

GENERAL RELATIONSHIP

Here I imagine a slow heavy blues partnership with Taurus at the helm. Pisces is not great at being given orders, so emotions may come to the forefront, and a few confrontations are likely.

But Taureans do have a hidden soft side, so could feel sympathy for the Piscean's need to tell anyone all about his or her personal troubles and then expect or even demand help!

Trust and honesty would have to play a major part in the relationship for Taurus, but Pisces could drift off into his or her own world of mystery, while giving Taurus the "cold shoulder treatment." This could hurt the feelings of a "giving" Taurus, who would store the experience in away in memory banks for future reference. Do not expect any second chances here!

LOVE RELATIONSHIP

With a passionate Bull and a sensual Fish, there shouldn't be a problem in the physical part of this union! Taurus will be fascinated and attracted by a mysterious and clever Pisces, and once the relationship starts, will help in any way that helps them to build a home together and will work 'till the cows (and bulls) come home!" Pisces may not put in the same amount of effort, unless he or she is getting enough attention !!

Both of these signs are animal lovers. This could connect them even more, but eventually our Taurus may not know where he or she stands, or will feel overwhelmed by the flood of emotions created by the Pisces.

So, is this a short term affair?
...Rock 'n Roll baby!!
Or is it a long term affair?

My bet......
they'll both
be singing
the blues!

CHORD COMBINATION 1   C7   C/E/G AND Bb
TAURUS/VIRGO/SAGITTARIUS AND PISCES

Team Taurus 1.......Solid loyal Virgo should help keep things on track here if Piscean emotion gets too much for the sometimes quite sensitive Taurus. who can take anything said very personally!! Sagittarius should also be your ROCK defense, so our Fish would be wise to go along with whatever plan the rest of them have!

CHORD COMBINATION 2   Cm7   C/Eb/G AND Bb
TAURUS/LEO/SAGITTARIUS AND PISCES

Team Taurus 2.......Leo comes in to replace Virgo and could put a very big spanner in the works as both of these signs have loyalties to the friendly Sagittarian and could drag both the Horse and the Fish out for the night (or a week) and leave you stranded, Taurus! Always remember to have your bus fare home!!

FOR PISCES AND TAURUS SEE CHAPTER 7 THE NOTE D

GEMINI and ARIES   ROCK N ROLL or the BLUES

GENERAL RELATIONSHIP
Stand back and watch the Air ignite the Fire!

This is rock 'n roll at double tempo!! Aries will happily go along with the cunning Gemini's constant ideas for enhancing their lives and bank balance, even if they spend most of it going out on the town! "Let's party" could be the motto for this couple. That's OK, since both of these signs have great energy levels.

But be wary, Aries, that you don't fall for scheming by our clever Gemini that involves YOUR money!! Get it checked out first and don't rush in as you would normally do!!

LOVE RELATIONSHIP

Love at first sight!! These two probably met at a disco or a nightclub of some sort. I doubt if they met in the morning, unless maybe it was on the way home from the previous night!

These two will most likely be will be attracted to each other from their first meeting, and will enjoy the fun as they have great times together. Sex will be adventurous and exciting—and each of them will give the other space, when that is what is needed.

This "rock 'n roll" type of lifestyle always comes with a price, though, both financially and physically.

How long can Gemini's air keep the Aries flames alight?

CHORD COMBINATION 1   C7   C/E/G AND Bb
GEMINI/LIBRA/CAPRICORN AND ARIES

In this team situation you may just decide to leave Capricorn behind in anything you are up to Gemini, because you are afraid the goat would put a stop to your fun!! That could be by someone in the group you are with asking, "Who is gonna pay for this?"

Sometimes it's wise to take sound advice, and sometimes you just want to take a chance!! Are you a gambler Gemini? Of course you are....stupid question!!

CHORD COMBINATION 2   Cm7   C/Eb/G AND Bb
GEMINI/VIRGO/CAPRICORN AND ARIES

Capricorn has some back up in Virgo to stop Gemini from making huge mistakes, but will you listen to your Virgo friend, Gemini?

Probably not, and off you'll go with Aries, into the night, leaving those miserable people behind.

But, don't go running to them the next day, Gemini, when you have no money and a huge headache from the night before!! Now you've got the blues!!

FOR ARIES AND GEMINI
SEE CHAPTER 7
THE NOTE D

CANCER and TAURUS   ROCK N ROLL or the BLUES

GENERAL RELATIONSHIP

This is similar in many ways to the Taurus and Pisces combination with some heavy blues going on, except that Cancer's control, in this case, will lessen the "dour" work ethic of the Taurean!

Don't get me wrong, though. Taurus will carry out all that needs to be done, and since they both like a nice home, then "Do It Yourself" could be at the top of the entertainment schedule here!

Again, this can be a caring and animal loving combination, but don't work the bull too hard, Cancer, especially if you drown your sorrows too much while you're out partying with your friends! Taurus will come looking and break up the party!!

LOVE RELATIONSHIP

This could be a very romantic affair, as each provides something the other needs. Taureans can be passionate lovers when they have found the partner they can trust, and Cancerians are sensual. They don't hide their feelings and will feel safe with their Taurus love!

There may not be a major Rock 'n Roll event here, but it wil be swinging along all the same. If there's a main problem in this gentle relationship, it could be the "blues!!"Taureans are worriers, as in general most Earth signs can be, and Cancer can feel that his or her world is coming apart every other day! If you can't keep the positive sides of this relationship going by caring for each other and building a lovely home together, etc., then depression could creep in, and at times could be severe!!

CHORD COMBINATION 1   C7   C/E/G AND Bb
CANCER/SCORPIO/AQUARIUS AND TAURUS

This 7th combination is quite strong for our Crab but will not set the world on fire!! The Cancerean will feel fairly secure with strong Scorpio and Taurus friends in their ranks. Aquarius will add some intellect and contentment! If you do get restless Cancer or feel you are not being listened to then be careful that you don't go over the top, such that these three other signs think you are being a "drama queen... or king!!"

CHORD COMBINATION 2   Cm7   C/Eb/G AND A
CANCER/LIBRA/AQUARIUSAND TAURUS

You may get more joy and comfort from this combination, Cancer, as Libra replaces Scorpio with a far gentler approach to life and is more sympathetic to emotional problems. The Cm7 can be a lovely sounding chord depending on how you "feel" it!!

You are the base (root) note, Cancer, and you are calling the tune. The song could sound different every time, though, depending on your moods. How are YOU feeling today??

FOR TAURUS AND CANCER
SEE CHAPTER 7 THE NOTE D

LEO and GEMINI   ROCK N ROLL or the BLUES

GENERAL RELATIONSHIP

These two should really set the stage alight with their Fire and Air combination, but as said before I'm going to separate the men from the ladies on the Leo side!

LEO MALES initially will get along with their Gemini partner as the Gemini will cleverly give compliments to boost his ego and perhaps even get the lazy Leo to do all the work?? Such as...."You do that far better than me, your highness!!"

This will rock along for a while until the Leo figures out that he's been had! If you tread on his tail —watch out!

LEO FEMALES, however, will not tolerate a sly Gemini attitude. She will see through the plan quite quickly, demand an equal role and use the Gemini's intellect to their mutual advantage. When this is established, then she'll be happy to work her heart out for the cause!

It's give and take, Gemini, or the Lioness will just take...probably you for dinner!!

LOVE RELATIONSHIP

Dance and make love until dawn. These two could just enjoy life and all it's pleasures, and not really worry about tomorrow. Then when the bills come in they'll make a plan to rob a bank or some such scheme!! This Rock 'n Roll combination could party all day and all night—and most certainly they will enjoy each other!

KING LEO will only stop to eat, and Gemini stop to drink! When the King falls asleep, however, Gemini could be on the prowl for another partner...and if a jealous Lion awakes from his sleep what then?

LADY LEO would sleep with one or even both eyes open if she could, because she would not be so trusting of a sweet talking rogue.

In general, this could be a really fun partnership, if Gemini doesn't stray!!

CHORD COMBINATION 1   C7   C/E/G AND Bb
LEO/SAGITTARIUS/PISCES AND GEMINI
This combination could really rock any party!! You may have to leave Pisces at home unless they are in one of their mysterious "let's try anything" mood, and then anything can and probably will happen. Enjoy tonight......pay tomorrow!!

CHORD COMBINATION 2   Cm7   C/Eb/G AND Bb
LEO/SCORPIO/PISCES AND GEMINI
Scorpio replaces Sagittarius in this combination so puts a damper on any possible plans that Leo and Gemini have hatched!! This may still work for you, Leo, but don't let the charming Gemini lead you astray, or you may find that the credit card bill at the end of the month is in YOUR name only!!

FOR GEMINI AND LEO
SEE CHAPTER 7 THE NOTE D

VIRGO and CANCER   ROCK N ROLL or the BLUES

GENERAL RELATIONSHIP
This is definitely blues time!!

Virgo will control things right from the start, and despite Cancer's plea for compassion, plus a few tantrums, he or she will have to just put up with it for this relationship to survive!

Although the Cancerian may be a little hard "done to" in this partnership, he or she will probably be thankful on several occasions for Virgo's ability to "be there" in an emotional or physical crisis—and Cancerians are often prone to feeling that they are in crisis.

But, on the other hand, Virgos can learn a lot from Cancer's caring side. They need "water" from a Cancer partner to feed their earth, which leads to personal growth.

LOVE RELATIONSHIP

Deep down every Earth sign wants to break free from his or her workaholic and general dour demeanor, and just let loose. If our Cancer can crack the steel barricade around Virgo with his or her gentle, caring ways, then it may be surprising how the Virgo can go out and party with the best of them! They may even become Disco divas!!

Probably, though, Virgo will regret everything the next day and bring on the blues again with a hangover, a pile of accounts to do, or some other very practical ideas. This could make our Crab very crabby, such that the atmosphere could feel threatening!

Come on Virgo, lighten up your load and enjoy life! Your Cancer will then help you most willingly! Our Crab may have to do all the seducing here, but after all, wouldn't any of us more likely give our hearts to someone who shows us love.

CHORD COMBINATION 1   C7   C/E/G AND Bb
VIRGO/CAPRICORN/ARIESAND CANCER
This combination gives you a 50/50 choice! Capricorn will keep you down to earth and tell you how much a night out or buying a new car, etc., would cost you. Aries and Cancer would look on in disbelief and tell you how life is too short to worry so much. Which way do you go Virgo? The devil or the angel?

CHORD COMBINATION 2 Cm7   C/Eb/G AND Bb
VIRGO/SAGITTARIUS/ARIES AND CANCER
In your Cm7 combination, you have Sagittarius and Aries with Cancer and you would surely stand no chance of not enjoying yourself, Virgo. Likely you'll be carried home by them all at the end of the night! You will hate yourself in the morning, but may try it again in six months? Check my diary!!......Spontaneity is not your strong point!!

FOR CANCER AND VIRGO SEE CHAPTER 7 THE NOTE D

LIBRA and LEO   ROCK N ROLL or the BLUES

GENERAL RELATIONSHIP
Ok, this could actually be swing time!!

Libra will be out dancing, having a great time, while her Leo partner (male) will be happy to have an audience to perform for! The problem is, who's looking after everything else? You can't party all week without having to clear up the mess. If Libra tries to tell Leo that it's his turn, perhaps he'll employ a housekeeper? And also a good accountant?

The Leo female, however, will enjoy the laid back style and fairness of a Libra love, who should really control this situation, but will probably just give in to whatever the Lioness wants! The female Leo will not stand for a messy home, however, so if the Libra is just passing through life, he will get a wake up call!

LOVE RELATIONSHIP

All Air and Fire combinations are explosive in the bedroom and this is no different. We'll rock out on the town, and roll in the bed!

Also these two have got an eye for quality, so if the passion continues after the "one night stand" and develops into something long term, they would have a beautiful home, a lovely car and fancy clothes, etc. So, who is going to pay and who is going to clean?

In steps, it's Lady Leo for the cleaning, for generally keeping the house in order and for getting our Libran out of bed and off to work ASAP!! If finances are kept in check, then there is no reason why these two could not have a really good life together, and dance the night away every weekend. If money becomes a problem, though, then the Blues could set in. They might then just shrug their shoulders, and move on to new pastures new....apart!! They would keep each others cell phone numbers, though...just in case!!

CHORD COMBINATION   1C7   C/E/G AND Bb
LIBRA/AQUARIUS/TAURUS AND LEO

Libra will love this combination with only Taurus there to stop total chaos!! They will dance the "week" away, let alone the night, and have intellectual conversations with their "perfect" Aquarian and flirt with a sexy Lion! What more could a Libran want? Well...a few thousand in the bank, a good housekeeper and a mansion in Beverly Hills...that's not much to ask for, is it?

CHORD COMBINATION 2   Cm7   C/Eb/G AND Bb
LIBRA/CAPRICORN/TAURUS AND LEO

The Cm7 combination here would involve Capricorn and Taurus which would help you keep your feet AND finances on the ground. Don't be afraid to call them, Libra—even if your Hollywood bubble has been burst!! They could get you there in the end!!

FOR LEO AND LIBRA SEE CHAPTER 7 THE NOTE D

SCORPIO and VIRGO ROCK 'n ROLL or the BLUES

GENERAL RELATIONSHIP
What a combination we have here!! Heavy rock!!
This is really strong, or a clash of the giants!! Both will respect each other's general view that you just get on with things, even if you have just lost your home to an earthquake or a nuclear war has broken out!!! Virgos will have to temper their control freak nature with Scorpio being the captain of the team, or otherwise there could be some titanic arguments. Still, I figure they will just get on with it as usual, and heaven help anyone or anything in their way!! "Steamroller blues" could be their theme song!!

LOVE RELATIONSHIP
I find that Scorpions have a lot in common with all the Earth signs and this can make their relationships that much stronger. So Scorpio and Virgo can be a very strong combination. They may not set the world on

fire or the bed alight, but both have intelligent, inquiring minds, and between them they would be able to sort out any problem.

Ok, it's hardly sex in the city, although you may be surprised that behind closed doors, and with no security cameras, these two could really get it on!! You may never hear about it, or even think to look at them, as they won't display public shows of emotion, but if you were a fly on the wall in the bedroom, you could be amazed.

CHORD COMBINATION 1   C7   C/E/G AND Bb
SCORPIO/PISCES/GEMINI AND VIRGO

Heavy man, heavy!! Get the guitars and long hair and leather trousers and groupies!!

But don't film it!! This group could organize a "secret" concert for their own enjoyment, but then the video is leaked to the press!! Where were you Gemini? Filming?

CHORD COMBINATION 2   Cm7   C/Eb/G AND A
SCORPIO/AQUARIUS/GEMINI AND VIRGO

The Cm7 combination in this case would involve Aquarius into the mix but I don''t think they would get involved in the lifestyle of Scorpio and just let them get on with it. Can Virgo keep their love secrets from the world? If they do turn traitor, they better find a good "safe house" from a betrayed Scorpion!!

FOR VIRGO AND SCORPIO SEE CHAPTER 7
THE NOTE D

SAGITTARIUS and LIBRA
ROCK N ROLL or the BLUES

GENERAL RELATIONSHIP

This should rock along quite nicely...well quite nicely for Sagittarius more than for Libra, who may well feel a little intimidated by the forceful and straightforward Sagittarian nature!!

This should be OK, though, because socially, Libra will not question the Sagittarian's actions, even if he or she stays out all night...but with someone else?? That could cause some questions...

I think that Sagittarius may not find this combination quite challenging enough, though, so may swiftly move on to try another form of music!

LOVE RELATIONSHIP

As always, the Fire and Air combination could be explosive in the bedroom, with the Sagittarian taking the lead and the Libran happy to follow. Both of them are "social animals" and probably more night than day people. As there is normally more action at night, then happy, happy nights!!

So intimately, this sign pair is a good match. They could have a great time going out together. But, back in the home, in everyday, boring life, can the happy-go-lucky Libran put up with the sarcastic comments of a Sagittarian master of putting people down?

Sag, if you like or even possibly love your Libra, then you will have to be kind to make this relationship last. A few compliments and gifts now and then could do the trick!!

CHORD COMBINATION   1 C7C/E/G AND Bb
SAGITTARIUS/ARIES/CANCER AND LIBRA

Has your Libra enough air to keep Sagittarius AND Aries alight? Probably not, and also our Libran may feel under pressure from these two strong Fire signs and start singing the blues to the caring Cancer.

CHORD COMBINATION 2 Cm7 C/Eb/G AND Bb
SAGITTARIUS/PISCES/CANCER AND LIBRA

The Cm7 combination would involve Pisces instead of Aries and is more likely to favor a downtrodden Libra and stand up to the sarcastic Sagittarius and then a battle of words and a heavy metal challenge would be heard for miles around!

FOR LIBRA AND SAGITTARIUS SEE CHAPTER 7 THE NOTE D

CAPRICORN and SCORPIO
ROCK N ROLL or the BLUES

GENERAL RELATIONSHIP

This is meant to be one of the strongest combinations in the Zodiac and may well be, as long as the Scorpio is a friend and not a foe!

Scorpios will back up their partners to the death and also not reveal "boardroom"secrets. They'll work hard to achieve a mutual aim.

Surprisingly both of these signs have a real soft and emotional side that is rarely seen, certainly not in public, where image is so all essential!

Charitable causes could benefit from these two, once they have accumulated enough to give! Control is very important to Capricorns and rarely will you see them in a vulnerable position. If they do slip, Scorpio will guard their back and prevent embarrassment!!!

Don't do "the dirty" on your Scorpion pal, Capricorn or you WILL feel that sting in the tail !!

LOVE RELATIONSHIP

You will most likely not know how these two are getting on!! They won't tell you intimate details about their sexual relationship, or more likely will not say anything at all! It's none of your business!

So is it Heavy rock/Country/Pop or the bedroom blues? It could be all of them, as these two will make a great team—and if they really get along well, will climb the goat's mountain to success, even if it takes a while. A Scorpio could actually speed up this process for Capricorn who is a bit less of a risk taker than the Scorpio!

So...in love? They won't shout it from the mountain tops but a have a steady, respectful love relationship that could last for years.

How can you be lovers, if you can't be friends/business partners??

CHORD COMBINATION 1   C7   C/E/G AND Bb
CAPRICORN/TAURUS/LEO AND SCORPIO

There are no lightweights here!! A Goat/Bull/Lion and deadly Scorpion —all on the same side—are destined for the Rock n Roll Hall of Fame!! Does anyone want to stop them? Not many would bet against this team. It might take a few years, but success is guaranteed!!

CHORD COMBINATION 2   Cm7   C/Eb/G AND Bb
CAPRICORN/ARIES/LEO AND SCORPIO

The Cm7 combination would involve Aries who would try and get our Goat away from the herd and just live a little! Beware of the Scorpion following your trail to bring Capricorn back down to earth and then deal with the Ram afterwards. Leo could desert the ranks and support their Fiery Aries friend. Heavy Blues man!!

FOR SCORPIO AND CAPRICORN
SEE CHAPTER 7 THE NOTE D

AQUARIUS and SAGITTARIUS
ROCK N ROLL or the BLUES

GENERAL RELATIONSHIP
Slow rock with clever chord changes here!

Is it a battle of wits, perhaps? Aquarians in control of this situation will take in a lot of Sagittarian straightforward energy, but not be battered by Sagittarian sarcasm!

In fact the controlled intelligent air of Aquarius could enhance the fiery Sagittarian spirit to both their advantages. Aquarians would have to watch that Sagittarians don't get them in a situation where their CRAZY side comes out, as that could mean fireworks or a big explosion!!

LOVE RELATIONSHIP

Neither of these two signs are particularly jealous types and both have a live and let live attitude. So Aquarius is probably one of the few signs that doesn't really care if the Sagittarius gets very personal in their criticism! Aquarians will just shrug their shoulders and get on with life anyway.

This is another Air and Fire combination for bedroom frolics, so it's Rock 'n Roll all the way and in any way!! Long term, these two will be fascinated by each other's intellect, although Sagittarius will be right every time, of course!! So with "freedom" being their password, together, it could be a total orgy with many partners each, or they may decide that just this one satisfies all of their needs.

CHORD COMBINATION 1   C7   C/E/G AND Bb
   AQUARIUS/GEMINI/VIRGO AND SAGITTARIUS

Virgo might not receive an invitation to the Aquarian party if he or she wants to change the music from Dance to a Strauss Waltz!! Aquarius, Gemini and Sagittarius would sneak out the back and off to one of their houses without leaving a forwarding address for Virgo.

CHORD COMBINATION 2   Cm7   C/Eb/G AND Bb
   AQUARIUS/TAURUS/VIRGO AND SAGITTARIUS

In this combination, who knocks at the door? Taurus!! Virgo will be delighted to see the loyal Earth sign and they can play the classics together. Aquarians may feel the next day that they made the wrong choice and should have stayed, or so their blinding headache is telling them. It's from Disco/Classical/Rock to the Blues—all in one night!!

Kick everyone out and go to bed Aquarius. It's been too much even for YOUR over developed brain cells!!

For SAGITTARIUS and AQUARIUS
SEE CHAPTER 7 THE NOTE D

PISCES and CAPRICORN
ROCK N ROLL or the BLUES

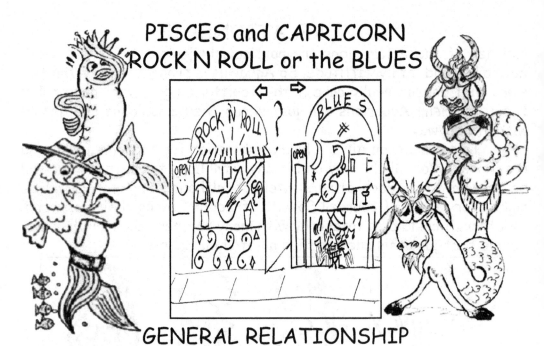

GENERAL RELATIONSHIP

Pisceans will find a willing rock 'n roll partner here, as long as they don't try to control the dance too much!

Capricorns will take just so much "instruction" and then want to do their own thing anyway! They can be a good team player for a while, but eventually will always have their eye on the Manager's position!!

Pisceans are usually good bosses, if they can keep their emotions in check. That may be easier said than done, especially if they get their teeth into a lost cause by try-ing to help someone, or to as-sist an animal that can't help itself!!

LOVE RELATIONSHIP

Pisces, in love with Capricorn, could find that he or she gives stability to the Picean's some-times fragile and volatile life. Capricorn may not be the great-

est romancer of all times, but he or she could learn a thing or two from Pisces, who could have had more heartbreaks than hot dinners!!

These two Sun signs could compliment each other, and whilst the relationship may not be explosive, it will swing along nicely—that is, as long as the one negative trait that they both share does not raise it's ugly head... and that is CONTROL!

Pisceans give the impression of being caring, loving souls, but if you hurt them or their friends or family, then beware, as the cute goldfish can turn into a killer whale!!

Capricorns also can go over the top in their stubborn "I am always right" moods! They are also great defenders of their "kin," so watch out for a charging Billy goat with horns sharpened! If the battle is between Capricorn and Pisces, I would not want to be the referee!!

CHORD COMBINATION 1   C7   C/E/G AND Bb
PISCES/CANCER/LIBRA AND CAPRICORN

Pisces will definitely need decisive Capricorn in this team scenario. Who will make a decision without emotion? Pisces? Cancer? Libra?....So most of the pressure to get things done will fall on the Goat's shoulders but Capricorns are used to this and just get on with it. Pisces will gather up the rest of the troops whilst Capricorn is working away and have their own "social occasion!!"

Capricorn may turn up later and find them all in tears reminiscing on past loves blah, blah, blah, etc. It's YOUR party Pisces, and you'll cry if you want to!!

CHORD COMBINATION 2   Cm7   C/Eb/G AND Bb
PISCES/GEMINI/LIBRA AND CAPRICORN

The Cm7 combination may throw up the "stubborn" side of Pisces and Capricorn and will involve Gemini who may well offer to referee any confrontation between the Fish and the Goat and then just sit back and collect his winnings from side bets he made on BOTH sides!! Clever Gemini!! Probably there are no winners, and everyone but Gemini is singing the blues!!

FOR CAPRICORN AND PISCES SEE CHAPTER 7 THE NOTE D

CHAPTER 14
The MAJOR 7TH

The note of B in the chord of Cmaj7

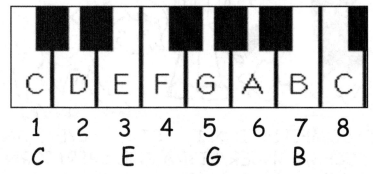

This one of my favorite chords. It's made up of the first/third and fifth (C/E and G) as normal plus the (major) 7th note in the scale which is B. (see chapter on the 7th Chord which uses the Flattened 7th note) Played all together they make the major 7th.

Now the person who makes up the major 7th really enhances your life and could add the "cherry on the cake," so to speak!!

This is also similar to the Maj9 combination, as both notes, when played next to each other. clash badly!! (See chapter 6 C#)

But apart, they can sound heavenly!!

This, in a home situation, could be a friend or a family member who, whenever he or she appears, adds a little sparkle.

Or in a work situation, this could be the member of your team who just adds the finishing touch to whatever your team is doing.

WARNING!!
If you get too close, though, or interfere in each other's job, you WILL clash!!

So keep your distance and you can make sweet music together!!

Here are
the maj 7th
combinations

BASE	ELEMENT	MAJ 7TH	ELEMENT
ARIES	FIRE	PISCES	WATER
TAURUS	EARTH	ARIES	FIRE
GEMINI	AIR	TAURUS	EARTH
CANCER	WATER	GEMINI	AIR
LEO	FIRE	CANCER	WATER
VIRGO	EARTH	LEO	FIRE
LIBRA	AIR	VIRGO	EARTH
SCORPIO	WATER	LIBRA	AIR
SAGITTARIUS	FIRE	SCORPIO	WATER
CAPRICORN	EARTH	SAGITTARIUS	FIRE
AQUARIUS	AIR	CAPRICORN	EARTH
PISCES	WATER	AQUARIUS	AIR

In this situation......
FIRE should gently heat the WATER
EARTH should not put out the FIRE
AIR should not blow the EARTH
to the 4 corners of the world
WATER should fall like gentle rain from the AIR

ARIES AND PISCES
HARMONY in SEPARATE JOBS

GENERAL RELATIONSHIP

Pisces can add a little emotion and perhaps a slight dampening down when used in a team situation, if Aries gets too carried away with things! Aries acting impatiently? Surely not?

In a family situation, Pisces could be the one Aries will turn to for guidance, or for how to react to certain situations.

If Pisces thinks that the Arian needs backing up, Pisces will be there with all guns blazing!

As an individual partnership, there may be too many differences to make this combination work on a long term basis. Aries will not like the slightly bossy control of the Piscean, even when he or she knows that Pisces could be only doing it to be helpful!

Just go to the Piscean advice bureau, Aries, but it may be best to not share the same home!

LOVE RELATIONSHIP

Aries may well be attracted to our mysterious Fish, who could drag Aries to depths where he or she has never been before!! It's exciting for Aries, who would love the sexual adventure. Pisces also may find the self-assured Aries to be someone to rely on, and a bit of strength. So, on the face of it they could compliment each other...BUT....(there's always a but). Initially this could be a fascinating partnership for both, but in life's ups and downs, it's how you react together as a team that counts. Aries could be a little too free spirited with life in general and be, for example, overly generous with the cash. Then Pisces will worry about how to pay the bills, etc.

Aries will just shrug it off and say, "There is always tomorrow. " Then Pisces says, "The bills are here today..." and so on until a heated argument ensues and all hell breaks loose with neither giving in. Aries will go off to cool down, which takes about five minutes! Pisces will smolder for a lot longer, retaining word for word what was said and by whom!! So, for these two to have a chance at a lasting relationship, focus on the positives that you both have, and don't work together!!

CHORD COMBINATION C MAJ 7 C/E/G AND B
ARIES/LEO/SCORPIO AND PISCES

In this situation you have Aries perfect harmony Leo and Scorpio's perfect harmony Pisces. If you don't split down the middle and work as a team, then it is harmony indeed!

The danger is in wanting it all YOUR way or nothing, Aries and then getting into a tantrum when no one does as you demand!! So, listen to the team for best results, as they are doing this for you—and you can have your cake AND eat it!! The choice is yours!

FOR PISCES AND ARIES SEE CHAPTER 6 THE NOTE C#

TAURUS AND ARIES
HARMONY in SEPARATE JOBS

GENERAL RELATIONSHIP

Taureans envy the Aries energy, but could well use it if they are working together or if they need just a little more to get a certain thing done. Aries will be happy to oblige and work all hours if necessary, especially at night to complete the task. As long as they can have a little play afterwards or even during, then no problem! Aries could also lighten up the sometimes stressful and anxious Taurean who worries about everything! The childlike qualities in the Arian could lift the dour spirit of the bull and even make him laugh! However sharing a life or a home together may be chaos as the Bull charging around and the Ram running at 100mph could end up like a bad traffic accident!!

Have plenty of plasters and bandages in the 1st aid kit!!!

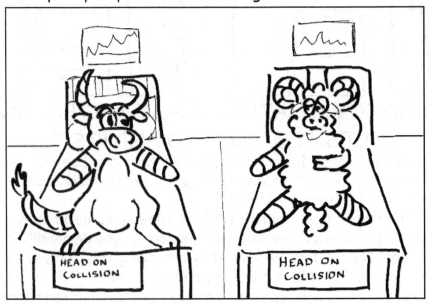

LOVE RELATIONSHIP

Both animals are, of course, amorous lovers, so this could be a fantastic 1 or 2 or 3 or more nights of passion. Will they fall in love? Well, they fell in lust so that's a start. Sexual compatibility is not the only requirement in a long term relationship, of course, so here are a few compatibility questions for our "horny" lovers to consider!

1. Are you careful with money?
    TAURUS— "of course" ARIES— "not important"
2. Are you a day or night person?
    TAURUS— "day"   ARIES— "night is always more fun"
3. Do you worry about the future?
    TAURUS— "naturally" ARIES— "never"
4. Do you believe in one partner?
    TAURUS— "absolutely" ARIES— "per night?"

        MADE FOR EACH OTHER....What do you think?

CHORD COMBINATION
C MAJ 7   C/E/G AND B

TAURUS/VIRGO/
SAGITTARIUS
AND ARIES

This combination throws the Earth and Fire signs together, and a Taurus/Virgo duo could certainly keep the flames down. Normally this could be a total mismatch....but, as in life, with everyone giving a little and not taking too much, then everyone is happy.

If only it were that easy!! Team Taurus together may not be a "dream" team, but its certainly hard to beat. Aries could add just that final spark to complete the task at hand and then there could be Gold medals for all !!

FOR ARIES AND TAURUS
SEE CHAPTER 6
THE NOTE C#

GEMINI and TAURUS
HARMONY in SEPARATE JOBS

GENERAL RELATIONSHIP

Gemini will use the Taurean strength as a reserve in his army! And a powerful reserve would be used to good effect. If the Taurean was happy with the plan and what was required, he or she will follow the Gemini leader into battle willingly, sacrificing self for the cause, if necessary.

If, however, General Gemini has led them into a massacre just to pursue his own needs, then the Taurus will round up the remnants and charge back to base with a vengeance!

Taureans are the best workers for a good boss, but don't treat them like fools!

In a relationship Gemini would have to prove that he or she is not the dictator that Gemini can sometimes be, or it will not work for long...and then beware the Taurean temper!!

LOVE RELATIONSHIP

Geminis are attractive people in general or at the very least...."charmers!!" Getting someone into the bedroom may not be a problem...but keeping them there is!!

In this case our Taurus would admire and be jealous of the ease at which Gemini floats through life, and so Taurus believes that his or her alliance with Gemini might have the same effect.

Wrong!! You will be attracted to Gemini at first, Taurus, but your honesty and reliability does not match our sometimes devious Gemini's traits! It's just that a Gemini needs to "feel" free, even in a relationship. If you can let your Gemini go off and do what he or she wants, as long as it means coming home to you, Taurus, then you've got a chance!

I think, however, that your jealous streak could kick in and demand to know every detail of what your Gemini has been up to. Of course, you'll be told that it is "the whole truth and nothing but the truth!!"

CHORD COMBINATION
C MAJ 7   C/E/G AND B

GEMINI/LIBRA/
CAPRICORN AND TAURUS

Here we have two Earth and two Air signs trying their best to come together as a team. For me, there is too much wind confusing our Earth signs to easily make this combination a success, as both Taurus and Capricorn like their feet on the ground, and **not** their head in the air!!

Geminis will have to be the sly foxes that they can be at times, to entice their Earth buddies to stay in the team. You'll need all the charm that you possess, I think!!

FOR TAURUS AND GEMINI
SEE CHAPTER 6 THE NOTE C#

315

CANCER and GEMINI
HARMONY in SEPARATE JOBS

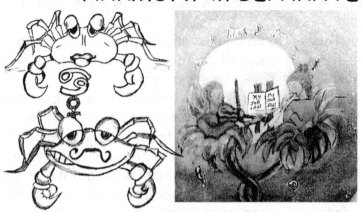

GENERAL RELATIONSHIP

The caring Cancer could well need the clever Gemini to help out in certain situations where Cancer may not have the emotional strength required. If, for example, the animal loving Cancer was faced with the final decision on an animal's life, for health reasons, etc., he or she may well not be able to decide. Although Geminis are sometimes tainted with a callous reputation, they will weigh everything up so as to make the decision easier and clearer, and then probably do the right thing!

LOVE RELATIONSHIP

Geminis air could "bubble" up a Cancerian's emotional water element and make him or her cry with laughter rather than with sadness—and this can be very appealing, and even sexy, to our Crab!!

But...together in a relationship?

If the laughter continues, then perhaps all will be OK, but Cancerians wear their hearts on their sleeves, and could eventually be deceived by the Gemini's ultimately selfish aims!

You may be seduced into bed, my dear Cancer, but you may have to kick Gemini out of your bed—and your home, once you find out what he or she has been up to!!

CHORD COMBINATION
C MAJ 7   C/E/G AND B
CANCER/SCORPIO/AQUARIUS
AND GEMINI

A Gemini certainly has the skill to add the final touch to your plans, Cancer. As long as you don't mix work with pleasure, and keep your distance from the charmer, then you will be fine.

If you need an emotional fix, then your Scorpio is on hand and by your side—and with the intellectual Aquarius coming up with the master plan of your life, you have harmony indeed!!

If Gemini suggests a private meeting with you then make sure you have hidden cameras and taped conversation!!,

FOR GEMINI AND CANCER
SEE CHAPTER 6 THE NOTE C#

LEO and CANCER
HARMONY in SEPARATE JOBS

GENERAL RELATIONSHIP

MALE LEOS could well need the Cancerian emotional side within their Royal court! If they like the lovable Leo, then they could add to the praise already given to him by his faithful followers!!

Cancer could also prevent Leo's ego from getting a bit out of hand, and advise him to do or say something a bit more appropriate, "Your Highness."

Together, Cancerians would definitely pour water on all of the Leo's posturing, which may then leave him wanting new advisers!!

LEO FEMALES may well endure this combination better, by accepting the Cancerian's kind nature and being happy they can work together.

From a distance, as this chord suggests, though, our Lady Leo may well accept the Crab into her Den primarily to have a babysitter for the kids!

LOVE RELATIONSHIP

KING LEO may well fancy a bit of Crab now and then, and Cancer may be tempted by offers of a secure and luxurious home. Seduced by the whole glamour and glitz of his highness may sweep you off your feet, our Cancer!!

   But the trouble is.....the next morning!! Leo may already be looking for more conquests once he is out of bed!! This could leave our Cancer saying, "Oops, I've done it again!!"

LADY LEO can be a bit of a devil in the "love" stakes!! She also could tempt many a Crab into the Den with her sexual energy. Once you get in Cancer it may be harder to get out!!.............
   Perhaps you don't want to!!

CHORD COMBINATION   C MAJ 7   C/E/G AND B
LEO/SAGITTARIUS/PISCES and CANCER

A question is, Leo, "Do you need anyone else in your life? You have your perfect harmony Sagittarius by your side and your "emotional" ROCK Pisces there to catch you, if you fall. What possibly could a sometimes nervous wreck Crab do for you?

   Everyone has his or her own individual talents and Cancerians make friends in all walks of life. There may be a "country club" you want to join, so send in your Crab to make friends with the secretary and "Bingo"....your membership is in the post!

   Once you have secured this favor, don't let Leo get too close, Cancer, or you may end up "dish of the day!!" Some reward huh??

FOR CANCER AND LEO
SEE CHAPTER 6 THE NOTE C#

VIRGO and LEO
HARMONY in SEPARATE JOBS

GENERAL RELATIONSHIP

LEO MALES could add that touch of grandeur to assist a sometimes dour Virgo personality, and in the right situation both signs will benefit from each other.

Virgo's undoubted organizing abilities and Leo's strength and likability could be irresistible! However, in the end there can be only one king, and Virgos could bury him with their earthy element and claim the crown! So this sign combination could be a bloody battle at first!

The FEMALE LEO will be a more willing accomplice in any Virgo business strategy and also add a touch of glamour when needed e.g., in any promotional work etc.!!

This combination together would have a chance but only if Lady Leo is happy to be bossed around a bit!

Virgo may get away with this for a while but eventually will tread on the tail of the Lioness!! Watch out!

LOVE RELATIONSHIP

They say that opposites attract and you couldn't get too more opposites here!! Perhaps the Lion's magnetism could spark some sensual feeling into our Virgo or perhaps the King is fascinated by the solid, secure personality of Virgo.

For one night only, are you tempted Virgo?

With KING LEO it is more likely to be a passing affair and fizzle out rapidly, but with LADY LEO there is a slim chance of adding a few more nights in the hope that Virgo may unleash an inner passion not seen for many a year!! Chalk and cheese, I'm afraid!!

CHORD COMBINATION   C MAJ 7   C/E/G AND B
VIRGO/CAPRICORN/ARIES AND LEO

Working with a Leo in this combination will only work if you leave them to do what they do best Virgo......show off!! They may be the final piece of your plan to build a new commercial center or football stadium... whatever and you need to sell it to your investors!! Come on Leo, the stage is yours!! Contracts signed!! No problem!!

Now if you get too involved with Leo's presentation then Leo may just tell you to do it yourself and run back to the Jungle!! What's Plan B Virgo?

FOR LEO AND VIRGO SEE CHAPTER 6 THE NOTE C#

LIBRA and VIRGO
HARMONY in SEPARATE JOBS

GENERAL RELATIONSHIP

Librans like to please everyone, and of course sometimes you end up pleasing no one! Virgos are only pleased when they are in control. If Virgo can just please help the Libran on a practical level and not get involved in their whole life, then fine—this will please everybody!

Will Virgos not get involved? If Virgo is your trusted adviser and you only see him or her on appointment, then this will work OK.

If, however, you are thinking of living together, then be prepared, Libra, to give more than you take!! Come on Libra, you can do it, be assertive and say what you want and perhaps you will surprise Virgo into submission??   ha!ha!ha!ha!.......

LOVE RELATIONSHIP

Librans are normally well liked socially as they try and keep the peace-and in general don't like to have problems in their life.

Virgos are attracted to "crisis" situations like a magnet. So? are there romantic goings on between these two opposites!! Probably not, but Virgo may feel that Libra needs a secure friend and possible lover/ Libra would respond well to feeling safe in the arms of a strong partner.

Will this relationship last the test of time? It's difficult, I feel, if Virgo does not control his or her natural instinct to want to run everything in everyone's life! Libra could start to feel totally trapped and at first opportunity run for the hills (or move back in with the parents) to escape!!

CHORD COMBINATION   C MAJ 7   C/E/G and B
LIBRA/AQUARIUS/TAURUS AND VIRGO

Now you know you can't work closely with your Virgo, can you Libra? So just give them the accounts, etc., and an office as far as way from yours as possible, so you just get together for monthly meetings!!

You have your "perfect" Aquarian by your side, and a strong Bull to get all the physical stuff done whilst you go out and enjoy life!!

Too good to be true? It may depend on whether you can control your own spending, as you have expensive tastes that Virgo would NOT approve of!!

FOR VIRGO AND LIBRA
SEE CHAPTER 6, THE NOTE C#

SCORPIO and LIBRA
HARMONY in SEPARATE JOBS

GENERAL RELATIONSHIP

Scorpios can be the strong silent types and not give any of their inner-most secrets away—and they also won't give any of YOUR innermost secrets away either! As long as you don't betray them, they will not betray you.

Librans will add a lighter touch to the sometimes stern outward Scorpion appearance, and this could be a friendly association. Librans in this situation will try to please and enhance the life of the Scorpio, but can they keep secrets?

Fail once, Libra and bye bye! Only ONE strike and you're out!!

LOVE RELATIONSHIP

This could start out as a friendly acquaintance and build over time until Scorpio would be able to trust Libra long enough for a full blown affair!! Our Libra will feel intrigued by the secret Scorpio as they en-joy meeting ¨unusual¨ people. Libra will give their all in the bedroom but perhaps not as much as a committed partner. If Scorpio responds to a sensitive but sensual Libra, and is happy to let Libra out to play when they want, OK! Is this likely to happen, though? Scorpio's jealous streak and insecurity in relationships would more likely put shackles on this liaison!!

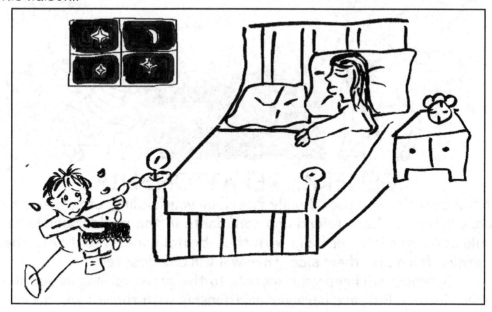

CHORD COMBINATION C MAJ 7
C/E/G AND B
SCORPIO/PISCES/GEMINI AND LIBRA

Scorpios rarely need any help and may dismiss any offers from Libra in this team situation. This would be a shame as part of Libra''s personality could be very useful to a Scorpio that not everyone likes!! You're a friend or a foe."For or against?" says the stinging Scorpion!

So if you need that someone with better "people skills" than yourself, Scorpio, then don't rule out our likable Libra. It may be the difference between getting ALL that you want from just SOME of what you want!! So shake hands, partners!!

FOR LIBRA AND SCORPIO
SEE CHAPTER 6   THE NOTE C#

SAGITTARIUS and SCORPIO HARMONY in SEPARATE JOBS

GENERAL RELATIONSHIP

If the Scorpion is a good family friend or your sibling, etc., then he or she will be your best friend and confidante in the world. Sagittarians could often get into conflicts with their brutal honesty, but with their Scorpion friend by their side, they will win any debate!

Scorpios will keep your secrets to the grave, as long as you show similar loyalty. But, in a personal relationship with these two, it's more than possible that the Sagittarian could let slip a personal piece of Scorpio's information. The Sag probably didn't mean to do it, but he or she just had to tell... was just being honest!!

Sagittarians are well known for sporting achievements, and could well need a good pair of running shoes when Scorpio finds out what Sagittarius told !!

LOVE RELATIONSHIP

Scorpio may well be tempted sexually by our good looking Archer, and with the Scorpio's own sensual passion, this could be a LONG "one night stand!!"

Can it be more than one night? Will Sagittarius keep the bedroom secrets?

There are lots of permutations here, as I think there could be a mutual respect between these two, at least with their direct, hard hitting comments, which to most other signs would appear hurtful and insensitive.

It's up to Sagittarius to keep this romance going by keeping the steamy details private—and NOT on Facebook!!

Ultimately, I think that Scorpio's possessive, jealous streak and the Sagittarian's love of freedom would lead to too many conflicts.

Make sure the war of words does not become physical!!......Just agree to disagree, and then go your separate ways.

CHORD COMBINATION   C MAJ 7   C/E/G AND B

SAGITTARIUS/ARIES/CANCER AND SCORPIO

If the love relationship doesn't work out, Sagittarius, you may be advised to be as amicable as possible and keep Scorpio in the team, but from a distance, as suggested in this combination! Just leave them to do what is required without your "opinion," and you will benefit from their skills! You always have your perfect partner Aries to go out and enjoy life with you, so why create conflict? Pass any "constructive criticism" of Scorpio via Cancer who will "gently" suggest your ideas to their friend, the Scorpio, without any blood being spilled!!

FOR SCORPIO AND SAGITTARIUS
SEE CHAPTER 6 THE NOTE C#

CAPRICORN and SAGITTARIUS
HARMONY SEPARATE JOBS

GENERAL RELATIONSHIP

Opposites attract, so they say, and this is definitely true in this case! When these two signs are on the same team, but doing their own thing, there is no problem. They could even admire each other from a distance. Capricorns could be taken in by the flamboyant energetic and even glamorous Sagittarian, and this could work for both signs at first. Capricorn's control, however, would eventually make the restless Sagittarius look for a new team, and a transfer request would likely be handed in after they have signed the new contract

LOVE RELATIONSHIP

Capricorn will be attracted by an enigmatic Sagittarian who is every-thing they are not!! Well, in the "love game," anyway! Inside, our cautious Goat will want to break all the rules made for himself or herself in the past, and just go wild!!

Our sexy Archer would fulfill all of Capricorn's private fantasies and some of his or her own, as Capricorn may be seen as a challenge that Sag would just love to win!

This relationship will fly along at a gallop initially, but calm down to a canter eventually. OK, Sagittarius, you won the challenge, so off to the next one!! Capricorn may feel a little deflated, even stupid for going along with the ride, but will soon pick himself or herself up, dust off, and then get on with climbing the next mountain....and this time, most likely alone!!

Initially and socially, this is a fun combination, but one that will likely expose too many differences within a close relationship.

CHORD COMBINATION
C MAJ 7   C/E/G AND B
CAPRICORN/TAURUS/LEO AND SAGITTARIUS

In a team situation use your Sagittarian wisely to achieve best results, Capricorn. Let the Sag work away on his or her own or perhaps with a buddy Leo, as well, in organizing social events for you. These fire signs love being the life and soul of the party, and you like avoiding them on most occasions so.....perfect!

Make sure you give them a budget, though, or your "expense account" may have some unusual items added after all their "socializing!"

FOR SAGITTARIUS AND CAPRICORN
SEE CHAPTER 6
THE NOTE C#

AQUARIUS and CAPRICORN
HARMONY in SEPARATE JOBS

GENERAL RELATIONSHIP

Aquarians could well turn to the careful, organized Capricorn to run their organization and this could work very well as long as Capricorn is given the control! Perhaps as an adviser would be a better proposition in this case, and Capricorns could offer many words of wisdom or solutions to problems.

As usual the Capricorn control may cause a rift in a personal relationship, although the sometimes quirky crazy Aquarian could release a different side to the workaholic earth sign and scatter him to the winds with an Airy blow!

Eventually, though, the Capricorn would return to his or her senses, and all would be as before.

However, a good friendship is more than possible with these two, even if it is from a distance!

LOVE RELATIONSHIP

Certainly a meeting of the minds will be possible here, as Capricorn will crave the information that our clever Aquarian has in his or her data base!!

Aquarians will also be attracted to Capricorn's intelligence and straight-forward arguments in a debate which the Aquarian could even find to be sexy!!

So, both will want to gain information on each other's life experiences, which could lead to a personal relationship.

However, Capricorns will be more reluctant to share their "true" innermost secrets, which would frustrate our Aquarian, who then would tire of the effort.

It's just not worth the hard mental work, is it Aquarius!! It wears you out!!

CHORD COMBINATION   C MAJ 7   C/E/G and B
AQUARIUS/GEMINI/VIRGO
and CAPRICORN

Played all together, this is a lovely sound. But can this team play "together?"

It might be a case of one half against the other. Aquarius and Gemini have their own "perfect harmony," as does Virgo with Capricorn. Can the intricate classical music of the Air signs blend with a bit of heavy blues? Well, anything is possible with compromise!!

Capricorn will have to take direction from the Aquarian leader of the orchestra, and just play what is written......no jazz!!

The result is a sweet symphony!!

FOR CAPRICORN AND AQUARIUS
SEE CHAPTER 6 THE NOTE C#

PISCES and AQUARIUS
HARMONY in SEPARATE JOBS

GENERAL RELATIONSHIP

For an Aquarius to be the final part of the jigsaw for Piscean puzzle lovers, would be ideal, as their deep and clever thought process could solve any murder mystery, or perhaps the "Times" crossword!

This could be just what Pisces needs to complete his or her inner journey, and also form a spiritual relationship, if not a particularly personal one!

Pisces sometimes struggles to control emotions, and in this situation where Pisces is the "boss" (and Pisces likes to be in charge), the Aquarian would just think it all through and then give an alternative view for the Pisces to think about!

LOVE RELATIONSHIP

Pisceans often are involved in the "alternative" side to life, whether spiritual, alternative medicines, natural remedies or even the occult!

Aquarians may also investigate with their inquiring minds into similar territory, and this may be a base to form a relationship with Pisces! The romantic and emotional Pisces may then want to dictate the terms of their affair.

Wrong move, Pisces! You should take this slowly, and also allow some freedom to the Water Carrier, or else you may drain him or her emotionally, so much that your potential friend or lover will disappear somewhere into the quiet to get recharged—and may decide not to return!!

CHORD
COMBINATION
C MAJ 7
C/E/G AND B

PISCES/CANCER/
LIBRA and AQUARIUS

In my opinion, this combination of Sun signs could work together for the better good of the human race, and they could possibly even find some amazing cure for all diseases or end world hunger!

They have all the "lighter" elements to think differently than the tried and tested methods probably preferred by the old fuddy duddies Earth signs.

The Fire signs would be totally opposite in their approach and just try out vaccines, for example, without testing first!!

So if you can keep your emotions in check, Pisces,Cancer and get your "out of the box" ideas together with Libra and Aquarius, then who knows what the world's next greatest invention you could come up with!!

FOR AQUARIUS AND PISCES
SEE CHAPTER 6 THE NOTE C#

CHAPTER 15
and finally!

THE OCTAVE and
SAME SIGN COMPARISONS

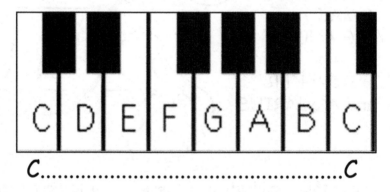

C...C

Together at last.....comparisons of the same sign.

On a keyboard, this would be the octave above or the octave below. It is the same note but played higher or lower. This strengthens the

sound and emphasizes the note, sometimes in a dramatic way.

Obviously two people with the same personalities and the same views will have a lot in common, but nearly always there has to be a boss!

Some signs will be very comfortable with this and agree on everything.

334

Some signs will think there is only ONE boss.....ME!!

All these signs have the same element, of course, so just to refresh your memory, here are their elements again:

SUN SIGN	ELEMENT
ARIES	FIRE
TAURUS	EARTH
GEMINI	AIR
CANCER	WATER
LEO	FIRE
VIRGO	EARTH
LIBRA	AIR
SCORPIO	WATER
SAGITTARIUS	FIRE
CAPRICORN	EARTH
AQUARIUS	AIR
PISCES	WATER

If you are in to Trivia quizzes etc., remember this combination...

FIRE/EARTH/AIR/WATER

2 FIRES can bring a brilliant firework display or high octave explosion!!

2 EARTHS can bring strength in depth or buried secrets!!

2 AIRS can bring a welcome strong breeze in a heat wave
    or blow up a storm!!

2 WATERS can bring welcome relief to a drought or cause terrible
    flooding!!

Let's find out which is YOUR scenario!

ARIES with ARIES

GENERAL RELATIONSHIP

When these two get together...mayhem!!!

If these two "kids"start playing, don't get in their way, or you will be run over or trodden on or bumped into or just literally run off your feet!!

It's show time, folks, so stand back and enjoy the show, but don't turn away for a second, or you may miss something! These two will have a great time together, but the Aries leadership qualities could be tested by the other Aries, who also wants to be leader!

Also, who will pay the bills for all the partying??............MOM ?

LOVE RELATIONSHIP

There is serious attraction here, and passionate nights, especially during the "honeymoon" period of every relationship. This one could last a long time, with both energy levels at full throttle!!

If the relationship gets serious, then the competition to be on top starts!! Only one would survive an all out leadership contest, so if you really want "peace and harmony," do separate occupations to start with and have separate roles in the house, etc. This plan will keep you the boss of your own area, and when you get romantically together it will be just a load of fun in the bedroom! Who, then, will be on top???

CHORD COMBINATION
C MAJOR WITH OCTAVE C/E/G AND C
ARIES/LEO/SCORPIO AND ARIES

So in a team situation you can only have one captain! Competition for this role will be fierce and you may have to end up "job sharing!!" It's not entirely satisfactory, but leaves you both time to do the million other things in life you need to do!!

Leo may be stuck in the middle of two Arians vying for attention. Whom do you go to?

Well.....both. Can you imagine these three walking into a night club or bar? The atmosphere would be electric! You may have to bring your ROCK harmony, Scorpio, as personal protection, as it normally ends in some confrontation or another!!

337

TAURUS with TAURUS

GENERAL RELATIONSHIP

Two "bulls" would be a match for any matador. so don't try to harm these beefy guys and gals! Together they will work hard and long hours to build a secure and beautiful home or solid business. The only problem may be when they get in each other's way! Crash, bang, wallop!

But they would clean up well and then get on with their routine. Taureans need a schedule or routine or they could slip into unusually lazy ways for their earth pedigree! If they clash and lock horns it could be messy, but most of the time they will be too busy working to argue!!

LOVE RELATIONSHIP

Probably this is not the most exciting of love affairs, but both find a secure, trustworthy partner who is just as sexy as they are. Once they feel this sense of security, they can open up, enjoy life together and even spend some money!!

If they don't feel secure for any reason, it may affect their relationship with possible bouts of depression! As is normal for Earth signs, their worries are seldom founded, so they should lighten up for their health!!

Once they totally trust their partner, it will probably be for life, and it would be unlikely for either male or female Taurus to stray!

While this relationship may not set the world on fire, both male and female Taureans have plenty of stamina and muscles for bedroom frolics!!

CHORD COMBINATION
C MAJOR WITH OCTAVE C/E/G AND C

TAURUS/VIRGO/SAGITTARIUS AND TAURUS

GEMINI with GEMINI

GENERAL RELATIONSHIP

This could be heaven on earth or eternal damnation! In nearly every partnership there is one who is dominant, even to a small degree over the other, and Geminis hate being controlled or manipulated—after all, that's their job! So, two of them together could be a huge clash of personalities and intrigues, with both trying to outwit each other, and of course their own twin!! Very complicated!!

On the other hand, if you have a Gemini with a "softer" rising sign, and with a little emotion and caring, and one who is happy to be second in command, then this relationship could work really well.

But, if these are two strong Geminis who each want to rule the world, don't bet against them!!

LOVE RELATIONSHIP

Geminis are great social animals who can talk anyone into their boudoir if you let them! Charming, attractive and clever. Smooth talkers!

So will one Gemini "out charm" the other? These Twins know each other inside out and backwards! So they can relax with each other and not try to "trick" the other into bed! They will enjoy each others company and not mind if the other one wants a night on his or her own. If, however, these two went out together for a night, they may even have a competition to see who gets the most phone numbers, then go home together, laughing all the way!!

CHORD COMBINATION
C MAJOR WITH OCTAVE   C/E/G AND C

GEMINI/AQUARIUS/TAURUS and GEMINI

This team will use all the intelligent and tactical experience at their disposal! Two Geminis plus clever Aquarius should outwit any opposition! Taurus will be there to defend the rear or go charging to the front line, if ordered!!

Perhaps your only downfall, Gemini, could be a clash with yourself! One General Gemini is enough in any army. Too many Generals and not enough troops to actually do the fighting could leave your defenses weak.

Taurus can only do so much as a lone Bull! Aquarians are on the computer or at a spiritualist meeting.

Reinforcements are needed, Gemini—but from where ? May I suggest a truce!!

CANCER with CANCER

GENERAL RELATIONSHIP

Roy Orbison's song, "Crying," comes to mind in this partnership! Cancers are known to be very caring, and if two of them together can control their emotions to achieve a better world for all, then "paradise."

If, however, they just get carried away on an emotional tide, then nothing is likely to be achieved except frustration and anger!

If you use your head with your heart, you can achieve a great deal, Cancerians. You can talk to each other on a mutually emotional level—but don't cry over too many glasses of wine!!

You might consider opening a shelter for animals—but it's best that you not let too many "human" strays into your life. That could drain both your energy and your resources!!

LOVE RELATIONSHIP

This sign combination is sensual and erotic in the bedroom. Passionate feelings are flying all over the place. Both of you love to love, so you're off to a great start— but is it enough in this partnership?

Cancers need to be wanted, so Crab 1 says "I need you to need me." Crab 2 says exactly the same thing. You both have to need the other, as well !!

If you can get this simple solution together, then you may have each found your soul mate. You both enjoy a comfortable home and probably want loads of little crab kids. But if both of you are just **taking** from each other, then it can be stalemate, frustration and as usual...tears!!

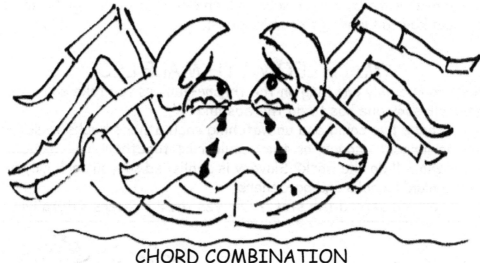

CHORD COMBINATION
C MAJOR WITH OCTAVE C/E/G AND C
CANCER/SCORPIO/AQUARIUS AND CANCER

Team Cancer!....mmmmm......Life, as we all know, is up, down, OK, rough, paradise and everything in between. It's how you cope with everything thrown at you that could be the difference between just surviving, or perhaps even enjoying your short stay in this world!!

Cancerians may struggle, in times of stress, with an overload of emotions, and could even appear weak. Your "perfect partner" Scorpio will help you and defend you in difficult times, and Aquarius will find the solution to your "practical" problems. So, you have protection in this scenario Cancer. Don't worry, be happy!!

LEO with LEO

GENERAL RELATIONSHIP

Ok, it's the Kings and Queens of the jungle that they call civilization! As you are aware by now, I separate the boys from the girls, so here we could have all kinds of combinations!

MALE LEO WITH MALE LEO

There can be only one King on the throne—unless you take equal turns. After all, someone has to do the washing up!

     These two could end up watching each other's backs to see who has the longest dagger, or they could rule together! The trouble is, then—who will do the work? Slavery is abolished so you each may need several maids, cooks and gardeners!

     Can you afford the staff? Oh, yes...hairdressers naturally!

MALE LEO WITH FEMALE LEO

Well this should be perfect, OK for a male Leo more than a female, as she will probably still do all the chores and go to work and look after the kids!! You know the problem is that everyone loves a Leo! You just can't help it! There are actually some quite shy Leos whom you want to give a cuddle and then take them home to Mother.

FEMALE LEO WITH FEMALE LEO

Girls rule!!! yeah!! These two grafters will kick ass, if needed and get the job done in no time at all! They are great in the workforce, as a team together, or if they are single...party on! Fire signs know how to do this well!

They attract males like bees around the proverbial honey pot and can normally pick and choose!!

LOVE RELATIONSHIP

As with all Fire signs. they are attractive, energetic and have magnetic personalities, so finding a "mate" is not very difficult for these sexy creatures! Finding a partner for life is so very different from a one night stand, so will the Leo and Leo corporation work? There will be a power struggle, but probably not in the bedroom—more likely it's in the boardroom!

Behind closed doors at home, anything goes, and it's fun—but someone has to be the CEO of the home or the business, etc., etc. If you want a longer relationship that could be very successful and happy, then the old adage of "give and take" is definitely the way to go here!

CHORD COMBINATION
C MAJOR WITH OCTAVE C/E/G AND C
LEO/SAGITTARIUS/PISCES AND LEO

In this combination, there can be only one President, Captain, Boss or Leader! Which one will emerge the victor? Think about the consequences, Leo. If you are waging a battle for control, you may get injured or weakened and other rivals could take over. Power share with your other Leo and become twice as strong. Sagittarius is there to back you both up with fiery arrows, and even the emotional Fish would become a school of Piranha to defend you.

VIRGO with VIRGO

GENERAL RELATIONSHIP

"Virgos are the kindest, gentlest, most caring and lovable people you could ever wish to meet!!" (I have been told to write this by a Virgo on pain of execution, if I don't!)

The truth?....Virgos are among the most controlling and bossy people you could ever wish to meet...but...boy are they great to have around in dark times, and especially in an emergency!! They could organize a plan to save the world, even with atomic missiles and earthquakes going off around them. So, two of them together?

Well, they may have actually sent the atomic missiles at each other! But Virgos together normally end up doing their own jobs to perfection, and as long as there is this separation, they are a great team. Don't intrude on the other's work, and life -long respect will be achieved.

The trouble is that one of them nearly always starts getting nosy!!

LOVE RELATIONSHIP

There is a strong earthy attraction here and a lot of respect for each other. They may not set their Earth on fire, as such, in the bedroom, but they will be attracted to each other's mental abilities. Nights in the boudoir may even consist of talking most of the time. Well, it is a form of oral sex, I suppose!!

This could be a long term partnership built more on similar qualities and admiration for each other, and as long as they have separate roles to play in the household or at work, then they can feel totally secure in their lives. Security is No 1 on their check list!! The drawback may be if one Virgo tries to dominate the other in ALL walks of their life. This could lead to several nasty arguments and a bitter separation!!

CHORD
COMBINATION
C MAJOR
with
OCTAVE
C/E/G AND C

VIRGO/CAPRICORN/ARIES AND VIRGO

This combination has strength from top to bottom—two Virgos controlling the events, with careful Capricorn keeping the accounts straight and a Ram as the Rock! All is OK at the moment, Virgo, but as usual, you may upset the apple cart by being too bossy a boss!! It takes a lot to upset Capricorns, as they can be quite calm, but then you don't know what has hit you, when an angry Goat is charging your way!

First to attack will be the Aries Ram, who will just not put up with any criticism at all!

Then, even your other Virgo turns on you in order to secure the leadership for him or herself!! Now, you have your own personal crisis. Somehow, though, you always have the answer in critical times.

LIBRA with LIBRA

GENERAL RELATIONSHIP

Two Librans together would be a lovely carefree partnership of loving carefree people! Neither of them will put any stress on the other and they'll be content and happy together...until the bills come in!

"I thought you had paid that?"........"Me?—.I thought it was your turn?"

Here we go again, with Libra being a little indecisive...."After you," "No..after you—I insist! "Well, unless you really want me to go first?" ...and so on. and on....

As explained in the beginning, I do over emphasize the stronger traits shown in each sign, so perhaps your Libra has a positive rising sign to counteract this kind of uncertainty!

Actually, Librans are normally nice people, so don't give them a hard time. They only want to please and to be fair to everyone.

LOVE RELATIONSHIP

If two Librans meet for a romantic liaison, it will probably be just that....romantic.They would buy each other "expensive" gifts, even if they couldn't really afford them— and then worry about the credit card bill later!!

Quality is very important to Librans, but they don't like feeling trapped in a relationship, so two Librans would give each other the space they need.

For a long term partnership they each may be better off with a more down to Earth partner who could draw up a budget for them to

348

stick to......mmmmm..... it is not so sure that they will keep to it....but you can only try!

Librans like to entertain and to be entertained. Often they can be professional entertainers, or artistically talented in one or more art forms. They love to express themselves, and like to have quality possessions. All of them, but especially the Lady Librans, often love to "dance the night away!"

That is, as long as they don't dance into the arms of someone else who may have been able to charm them? Remember, Librans like to please!! So...how far do you go?

CHORD COMBINATION
C MAJOR WITH OCTAVE C/E/G AND C
LIBRA/AQUARIUS/TAURUS AND LIBRA

Normally two signs clash over who will be the "boss!" In this case, probably neither of them want to take on that responsibility.

So, the Libra would let Aquarius assume the CEO position, with Taurus keeping everything else in order, and then take a background role!

BUT...sometimes you have to step up to the plate in life, Libra —with no support around you! So, take some responsibility and you will feel better for it. If not, you probably will continue to just float through life.......good luck!!

SCORPIO with SCORPIO

GENERAL RELATIONSHIP

Scorpions are your best friend or your worst enemy so this could be either "friends forever.com" or "sting in the tail.com."

Scorpions, in general, just get on with things even in the depths of despair. They may be hurting inside, but will not show it!

Together? If they are friends forever, then this will be a very strong partnership, so don't try to come between these two!

If they lose trust in each other, then let battle commence and it will be stingers at 20 paces!!

LOVE RELATIONSHIP

Sometimes Scorpions love to hate!! They can be possessive, jealous, somewhat controlling, and because of all that, may find it difficult to find a partner whom they think comes up to their standards!!

So, another Scorpio should be their equal...? Yes or no?

Scorpios will be attracted to other Scorpios, and this is not because of the size of their...sting!! They understand each other far too well, and know what each is capable of doing, if sufficiently provoked.

In love?...trust, and above all secrecy. is of the utmost importance to both these "double agents," who could turn on each other in an instant.

Once all the skirmishes are out of the way, though, and they find that they CAN actually trust each other, then it is possible for a pair of Scorpios to be lovers for life.

CHORD COMBINATION
C MAJOR WITH OCTAVE C/E/G AND C
SCORPIO/PISCES/GEMINI AND SCORPIO

Why do Scorpions distrust everybody? It is a form of insecurity, as Water signs, in general, are caring and emotional. Inside, Scorpios are like this, but think it's a weakness, and therefore they give off a more aggressive demeanor! I, personally, wouldn't approach two Scorpions together without defenses!!

In this combination, as well, Scorpio has the back up of a loyal, brave Pisces and the cunning Gemini! Phew!! In business, you would be wise to make partners, not enemies, of this team and make sure all the details are 200% correct on any contract. Better have some small print with an "out clause." Also, you had better not default on the contract, or Gemini could sue the pants off you and the others would have you running for the next state—or maybe even the next country!!

SAGITTARIUS with SAGITTARIUS

GENERAL RELATIONSHIP
Watch out there's a Sagittarian about!

You can't fail to notice these enticing creatures, because they will make sure they get noticed!

So, two together? Well, it could be a swell party for however long it lasts, and there's a lot of mutual admiration going on here....as long as they give each other the freedom and space that they both crave so badly. You have to remember that Sagittarians love attention, socializing, and being a little spoilt— but above all they love their freedom to do whatever they please and whenever they please to do it!

Sagittarians can be great sports people and entertainers.

You will likely be fascinated and even adore these people—but to live with a Sagittarian is to play second fiddle!

LOVE RELATIONSHIP

Sagittarians definitely understand each other, and as both are "social animals" with that sexy magnetism that flows from them, they will naturally be attracted to each other. No sarcasm is needed here, since both males and females of this sign have high energy levels that need an outlet. So with two Sags together in a relationship, the sparks will fly for a long time. Each of them appreciates that all Sagittarians need freedom to do and be what they want, so they will not be jealous or possessive in this scenario. What more do you need Sagittarius?

"Nothing, really"... except each must realize that Sagittarians are on the constant look out for different experiences, so this could lead to long spells of each doing separate things, and that may mean the relationship ultimately fizzles out! If this does happen, both will be very understanding, will probably say "until we meet again" and then...

Hasta la vista!!

CHORD COMBINATION
C MAJOR WITH OCTAVE   C/E/G AND C
SAGITTARIUS/ARIES/CANCER and SAGITTARIUS

This team could win an Olympics on their own!! Sagittarians can be the best sportsmen and women of the world, and with the 100 mph Aries in the athletics team.—you try and catch them!! Cancer will refresh them well with their Water element and with their Fire sign energy levels full......unbeatable!

Our Archers may well fight over who stands on the podium and gets the glory, as there is probably not enough room for two fiery horse people!!

The party after the medal ceremony may be just as big and spectacular as the actual event, so be sure not to miss it. Some may find Sagittarian's sometimes selfish lifestyle to be a bit too much for them to be friends...but does our Sagittarian care?

What do you think?

CAPRICORN with CAPRICORN

GENERAL RELATIONSHIP

Capricorns can be their own worst enemy. They can sit and brood and worry themselves into an early grave, if they are not careful! So two Capricorns together, in an emotional sense, might be like trying to get blood from a stone! They tend to keep their emotions under control—control is their God! Their belief is that one must not lose control especially of oneself. So, one must just keep it all inside until the ulcer starts kicking in. For this reason, Capricorns can make great actors and actresses because they rarely play themselves!

Two Capricorns can make a nice, comfortable partnership, and certainly neither of them will be afraid to work and earn sometimes a very good living, because as they can be depended upon. They also tend to climb in their chosen profession.

But there is more to life than work, Capricorn, so go out and take a look sometime. You may be...surprised!

LOVE RELATIONSHIP

Mutual respect rather than sizzling romance is most likely the case in this relationship, I think! These two have the same feelings about life, security, reliability and so on, but they rarely let their hair down and open up completely! As two stubborn goats slowly moving up the mountain of life, they may not be Romeo and Juliet, but they will not feel threatened or pressured into trying to be what they are not! So, this can be a comfortable relationship. When the two of them have achieved a reasonable level of financial security, they can be very philanthropic!

Quietly caring is a secret Capricorn trait, but don't tell anyone that they actually have emotions!! A summary of this relationship would be.....steady, secure and stable! If there is trouble, it may be because after several years of togetherness, the predictability of it all could drive one or both of them to bouts of depression.

CHORD
COMBINATION
C MAJOR WITH
OCTAVE
C/E/G AND C
CAPRICORN/TAURUS/
LEO and CAPRICORN

Capricorns can work equally well alone or in a team but usually they have to be left to do it their way. They can be stubborn to the death, if they think they are right.

In this team setting they will be helped a lot by their "perfect" Taurus, who shares some of the same ideals of our Goat, i.e., hard work, reliability, dependability, blah, blah and blah!! Leo, thank goodness, could lighten the whole scenario here and actually get the Goat and the Bull out of the house or office and...god forbid....they'll enjoy themselves!! While they are out, along comes the other Capricorn to remind them of the work schedule for the next day!!.......Oh dear!!

In all fairness, Capricorns can be some of the most charming people you have ever met, but finding out their TRUE feelings is a hard task for any sign to crack!!

You might reach your mountain top, Capricorn but don't be surprised if you are on your own when you get there!

AQUARIUS with AQUARIUS

GENERAL RELATIONSHIP

Two Aquarians will be a stimulating challenge for each other, and I can imagine a meeting of the minds here! As long as the "crazy" side doesn't kick in by one of them before the other, no problem—or perhaps they will go crazy together and then anything could happen!!

At home, the place could be a mess and a cleaner could need employment, but they will be kind and generous bosses! Most Air signs can be very spiritual and interested in after life experiences, psychic connections, etc., and most people who know these two will probably say they are already on another planet!

LOVE RELATIONSHIP

Aquarians have to be stimulated and they hate boredom! Always on the look out for new, interesting friends, who can be better than someone they already know so well....another Aquarian.

Now most "same sign" relationships normally have some battle for supremacy going on, but I feel that Aquarians will be different and not create challenges with someone else who is as crazy as they are!!

So, there will be a positive attraction both physically and mentally between two Aquarians, and they would enjoy each other's company and stimulating conversation. They also wouldn't mind the other one disappearing to do some research or a trek through a South American jungle to find their spiritual guru. "It's YOUR life....enjoy it!" is what the Aquarians would say.

CHORD COMBINATION
C MAJOR WITH OCTAVE C/E/G AND C

AQUARIUS/GEMINI/VIRGO
AND AQUARIUS

Aquarians are the most intelligent and interesting people, but just when you think you have met the reincarnation of Einstein, off they go on a tangent and you haven't a clue what they are on or about!!

So if, for example, a University employed the team above, they may discover a new planet (likely the one they were born on!) and Gemini would probably be the one to take the credit for this!

Virgo will have the contracts ready for media companies to sign quickly, and the world of Science will bow at their feet!!

On the other hand, they may blow up the Campus in a strange experiment!!

The world needs you Aquarians!!
Keep us all guessing about what's going to happen next!

PISCES with PISCES

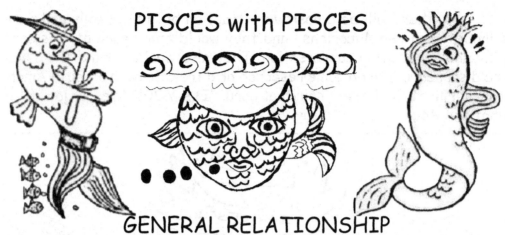

GENERAL RELATIONSHIP

If two Pisceans are swimming around, one could be a little goldfish and the other a shark! They can be a bit like "Jekyll and Hyde" creatures, who are, on one hand, the most caring and protective of people, and on the other hand "bossy boots" types, whose only way is theirs!! So, the two together could be founders of the biggest animal sanctuary in the world, as long as its done THEIR WAY!

The great thing about Piscean strength, is their ability to take on Goliath and support David to the death—or the supreme court or however far they need to go! So, Pisces types would make great "human rights" lawyers, etc.

LOVE RELATIONSHIP

Pisceans often release their worries through a sexual relationship, so another Pisces would want the same thing and emotions would run high in the bedroom!!

If life could be solved by lust, then these two have it made! Now, back down to Earth because you can't stay in the bedroom forever! John and Yoko tried it, and were fairly successful, but still had to go and do other things!

So, after making little fishes, you have to be able to feed them! The "ups" of life we can all cope with, but it's normally how you handle the "downs" that matters!! This could be tricky for these two sometimes emotionally unstable Pisceans.

CHORD
COMBINATION
C MAJOR WITH OCTAVE
C/E/G AND C

PISCES/CANCER/LIBRA
AND PISCES

This team, on paper, looks a little lightweight to tackle major problems. Two Pisceans and a Cancer alone might think Bambi is a horror movie!

Libra will just go along for the ride, so there's not a lot of strength in depth!

So, if you feel confident now in taking on this gang, let me warn you! All of this emotion can bring out amazing feats of endurance and toughness in adversity, and if Pisces types, in particular, are offended or feel that they or their personal friends are under attack, then be afraid.....be very afraid! The little "neon" in your Tropical tank has just become a yet undiscovered species from the depths of the Pacific ocean. Don't swim in these waters. Avoid at all costs!!

CAPRICORN

AQUARIUS

SAGITTARIUS

AND NOW
INTRODUCING

PISCES

"THE ZODIACS"

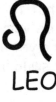
SCORPIO

WHICH MEMBER
OF THIS
SENSATIONAL
BAND ARE YOU?

ARIES

This chapter
is about the general
character and
personality traits
of each sign,
plus which instruments
I believe will be best
associated with each sign
within a band, group
or orchestra!

LIBRA

TAURUS

VIRGO

GEMINI

CANCER

LEO

♈ ARIES

My Aries musician would want the loudest instrument he or she could find—so bring on the drums and lets make some noise! Their enthusiasm and childlike quality will keep the energy going in any musical scenario, but more so in a rock band or heavy metal!!

General characteristics of these fiery but kind people are that they can flare up like their fire sign demands, but just as easily cool down and then wonder what all the fuss is about.

Aries are born leaders, but can rush into situations without first thinking it through carefully. They run at 100mph in most things, and probably had many little accidents when they were children! With loads of energy, Aries needs to keep occupied, otherwise he or she can feel down and depressed quite easily!

People with Aries as their Sun sign are self-motivated and get bored quickly, so they need to have no chains to hold them back—or stand back and relight the fire!

Aries types make great team motivators!

♉ TAURUS

A Taurean musician would probably play something that needs strength and endurance and a lot of wind! So bring on the TUBA! I can imagine the bull red cheeks bellowing and blowing thumping out those deep dark notes. Alternatively a trombone would require the same stamina perhaps in a soul band! Taureans actually prefer to be told what to do as long as you ask them nicely! A bit of praise but not condescension will go a long way with these down to earth workers.

   This is probably the most honest and open of signs, which does not always have the desired effect, as people often don't like to hear the truth! Even though they may complain of too much work being piled on them (mainly because bosses know they will do more than most!), they actually need this motivation, or they can slide into lazy habits, and many chocolate bars!! Fast cars delight these bulls!

Ⅱ
GEMINI

Behold the leader of the orchestra and controller of most things, so they have to be the conductor! Geminis will not take a back seat in a music group of any kind, and will soon take over, even if it is behind the scenes and perhaps a bit sneaky!

So the Conductor will control everything and get the praise at the end!

In a group, a Gemini will be the lead singer or at least run the band, perhaps as manager? With a Gemini you will be sure of success unless he or she believes his/her own publicity, and can slide into the next bar and tell many a story, his/her own story, of course!

As the "twin" sign suggests, a Gemini could be like Jekyll and Hyde! If you come across Jekyll, you will be charmed to death and may have to pay for the meal and the bar bill for the price of his/her company!

If Geminis are able to stay on the straight and narrow, they can be unbeatable in business, and they can be good team members, but normally most things they do will be because they think it will further their own ambitions!!

♋ CANCER

My Cancerian musican would have to be 1st Violin and gently, sweetly play those tender emotional sounds that would bring a tear to a glass eye! If not in an orchestra, then a folk singer/guitarist and songwriter is a possibility, as long as the music comes from the heart and means something! Cancerians are, of course, one of the most emotional signs and the heart rules the head, which can lead to a lot of kind and caring actions, especially with animals. It can also lead to heartbreak and despair in romance, since they can believe too much of those sweet nothings in the ear! This could lead to depression and some alcohol or drug abuse, if not careful, and require a good true friend in times of need! Cancerians also can be a support to others, since they will listen as they would want to be listened to! Cancers are nice people, so please don't break their heart or they can turn really "crabby"!!

♌ LEO

The long haired lead guitar of a rock band has to be our KING LEO!
With locks a flowing, guitar licks screaming out at the fanatical crowd
of adoring fans...and doesn't he just love it!.

KING LEO has to be Lord of the manor and loves attention. A
giant ego, you think? Well, OK—that's true, but everyone loves a Leo!
There's just something about them that you cant help but like. They
can be lazy, of course, and you may feel they are not pulling their
weight! But don't underestimate these laid back lions, and don't tread
on their tail or you will be on the menu for their next meal!

Our Lioness will be the rock chick dressed in leather and leading
the fan base where she'll have her fair share of male admirers! If they
are in the band and not the "groupies," then they will be the back up
singers and dancers, perhaps even playing a bit of percussion, such as
tom-toms,bongos or African instruments from their part of the jungle.!

LADY LEOS certainly pull their weight and are generally hard
workers, who will make sure there is always a meal on the table!

♍ VIRGO

Virgos would keep pounding out that bass rhythm and you had better keep in time with them or you will be given music homework of three hours on a metronome! They are reliable, hard working and often a pain in the proverbial...BUT you wouldn't be without a Virgo in times of crisis or emotional upheaval or even an atomic bomb falling on your town. They will be there first, organizing through the chaos. If some members or ALL of the band fail to turn up, Virgo will probably do a solo one man or one woman band act, as the show must go on. Secretly, I am sure Virgos would love to show a softer less organized side and let their hair down a little, so when they do relax eventually and get a chance to go wild, they paint the town red, then totally regret it the next day!!

Probably they will add up the money spent and more importantly, "Did I show myself up?" Loss of personal control would horrify these earthy creatures!!

LIBRA

Our MALE LIBRA could well be the laid back lounge singer with the smooth Sinatra or swing tones. Trying to keep the audience happy will always be on the mind of the Libra and so may need a few "confidence boosting" shots before the show!

Be careful you don't stay in the bar and miss your cue!!

Once our male Libras have overcome a bit of stage fright, they could make the ladies swoon!

FEMALE LIBRANS will possibly be the back up dancers, or indeed have their own dance troupe, as they love to boogie!! Quality is important to these guys and gals so expect the most expensive stage suit or dance outfits with plenty of "bling!"

They love to be out late, so don't wait up. They could bring back a few showbiz pals to see the dawn in. Some Librans can be quite shy, however. and if they don't drink or need any other substance,they may be very quiet individuals and very gentle souls!

SCORPIO

My Scorpion would be the Rhythm guitar player. You don't really know they are there, but without them there would be a gaping hole in the music! Scorpio is in the background, just getting on with keeping everything going along at the right tempo, with lots of self control and discipline! Don't ever tell these stingers that they played a wrong note, though, or you may find said guitar wrapped around your neck!

The Scorpio will be the most reliable member of the band, and will carry on playing to the end. Titanic springs to mind! He or she will expect this endurance from every other member, as well, and will defend the members of the band if a few bottles of beer come flying in from dissatisfied clients! This is not likely to happen, though, if the band leader is a Scorpio. He or she will demand a lot of rehearsal and perfection in performance. This could seem a bit too rigid for the Jazz muso who likes to jam around a bit!

SAGITTARIUS

For me, there's only one instrument...the sexy sax player! These normally good-looking and very flirtatious creatures can seduce you with their smooth sexy sax playing and have the audience eating out of their hands! Born entertainers! If they don't play an instrument, they will be dancing or singing or be the cynical sarcastic comedian who will make you the target of his jokes.

If it's all in fun, no problem. Or the problem can be that the Sagittarian really means it! Don't try and take them on in a verbal and/or a probable physical challenge, as you will most likely come off second best! If the Sag is a TV or film critic, then woe betide the actors they critique. Don't read the revue, if you want to stay in the business!

Altogether, though, if you meet these half horses out in a bar or disco, etc., you WILL be entertained and definitely charmed..perhaps into bed.... but living with a Sagittarius is a journey in self discipline! IF you can keep your Sag amused, and not feeling bored or tied down, then he or she may decideto stay!

369

♑
CAPRICORN

Capricorns would want to be in control. Firstly, of their own perfor-mance, and then of the band. They would not like to be involved if they didn't feel the standard was to their liking! In many cases they would go it alone and become a "one man band!" So keyboards/piano, etc., would give them a sense of total control without the need for any other musicians! They are quite happy in their own company, so being a re-cluse would not bother them, and they could spend the time composing music compositions or writing or even get involved in spirituality and the "alternative view" of life!

Be careful you don't get too involved on the darker side of life, Capricorn, as you can easily get depressed and moody if your life is not going in the direction you hoped! Capricorns are normally very careful over money and possessions, and will build their empire slowly without risk. They can be surprisingly generous and very kind, or have times of "not caring" about themselves, when they even become untidy and lazy!

Ultimately, though, Capricorns will pull themselves together and are known survivors of life!

♒ AQUARIUS

OK, you Aquarians, blow your own trumpet! Well, you would be entitled to, as you are the brains of the Zodiac!! So let us hear those complicated Jazz trumpet sounds or the muted trumpet of the orchestra!

The trouble is that the other side of genius is crazy, and our Aquarians could literally blow the house down with trumpet horns a blazing! Look what happened at Jericho!

I could imagine Aquarians writing Broadway shows, a new Opera or something challenging that would stimulate their craving for knowledge. Normally they would do this in their own quiet way until....yes, you've guessed it, the crazy pill kicks in and they go off the wall and everyone wonders what has happened to them!! Then, lo and behold, seconds later they are back to normal! Use these Aquarians wisely, and you will be well advised. They love questions and are surprised you didn't know the answer, as it comes easy to them! Apart from the trumpet they could also play clarinet and flute, or a range of other instruments, if they studied them, no doubt!

As with all AIR signs they are free spirits—only spirits in a bar don't come cheap! Careful on the alcohol, Aquarius, and your bank balance will also benefit!

♓ PISCES

These emotional creatures will be playing on YOUR harp strings and have you in tears with their music and wild emotions. They will play the harp like a heavenly angel, but probably bring you down to earth with a bump, if you are not visibly moved by the experience!

Along with Virgo, I class Pisces in the BOSSY league! Ok, they are great defenders of the underdog and undercat and undermouse, and sometimes underhuman! But, they can be so demanding for justice that they can really upset people—especially people in so-called "power positions" such as politicians, police, etc.

So, they will woo you with their harp music, telling their so sad tale of injustice suffered, but if you do nothing about it...it gets messy!!

But, OK, you definitely need Pisceans at certain times because they will create action when action is desperately wanted. It's just the way they go about it that can really rub you the wrong way!

Still, they are good as organizers and good in "sales," too. You really don't want to say NO to these Pisceans, and expect to remain healthy!

SO THERE
YOU HAVE IT...

MY ENTIRE ZODIAC PEOPLE!!

I hope you have some fun in my interpretations of who you may possibly be in or out of tune with. These are of course "generalizations."

It's like saying all Englishmen wear bowler hats and carry umbrellas or all Frenchmen ride a bike with onions round their neck and wearing a striped shirt!

When you have a cartoon caricature made, the artist will over-emphasize the obvious, e.g., if their ears are big or nose very long, etc., etc., and to an extent, this is what I have done in this book. It is, after all, hopefully to entertain you! You really need to get a full birth chart done if you really want to investigate further and see what YOUR real personality is!

If this book has whetted your appetite, and you want to know more about Astrology in general, have a full chart done, full compatibility comparisons etc., then please contact **www.astrocom.com** for a COMPLETE guide to all you need to know!!

It's always a good idea to ask friends and family what they think your personality traits are, as we always look at our own positives and negatives from OUR perspective and rarely know what others think of us. Most of us would not care, anyway, what people think, so just treat this in a lighthearted fun way and don't get upset...PLEASE!!

Some of us, however, might be taking personal notes of our enemies and making plans for revenge!!   (ONLY JOKING)

AUTHOR'S NOTE

There are positive and negative personality traits in each sign, and for me it is about recognizing in YOURSELF when you are being a bit negative., e.g....I am a Capricorn and we can be very moody and insular at times, which I admit and I so say to myself "stop being a grumpy Capricorn!" Perhaps you are a fiery Aries whose "childlike" qualities can brighten the whole day for someone!

We are ALL different, thank goodness, and we can at least try to be nice to each other, even if we don't really get on! No?

Bye bye!

See you later!

That's all, folks!!

Thanks for reading
and I hope you were entertained...
and perhaps even a smile or two
appeared on your face??

The world is full of negativity in so many walks of life,
but if you can bring a little bit of happiness to someone...
just do it!!

Keep YOUR faith and turn the music UP!!

Love and light....
Alan Hamilton

Index, by Chapter and Page of the Sign Combinations

This page is to assist you in locating specific two sign combinations in Chapters 4-15

About the Author
Alan Hamilton

Although born in Ireland, Alan considers himself a "plastic paddy, "as at the age of 3 his Irish father, who was in the British Army, took the whole family to Kenya, Africa, where they lived for the next four years.

So Alan's first education was in Kenya, until they returned to the south coast of England, where his Mother is from, and where she lives to this day.

Alan taught himself to play the piano from this early age, eventually working solo and in bands from the age of 14!! After completing grammar school education, he decided on a career in music—not realizing that some 48 years later he would still be "gigging!!"

Having worked all over the UK and Europe, Alan has been based in Spain since 1987. During this time, he obtained an interest in Astrology, mainly with regard to the personalities and compatibilities of people, which he observed whilst entertaining! Very soon his "party trick" was to guess the Sun signs of people, with with about an 80% success rate! From here he delved a little deeper into this fascinating world of Astrology, eventually connecting the twelve major notes in music with the twelve Sun signs, to produce the theory that is the basis for this book.

Alan has two children from his first marriage. His son, Adam, is a Forest Ranger in England and his daughter, Alexandra, is an Actress in Australia. Alan lived in Ibiza (Balearic Islands) for many years, but now live 20 miles north of Marbella on the Costa Del Sol in the "real" Spain with his wife Claire and their dogs and cats.

About the Illustrator
Marcella Kelly

THE
ORIGINAL
""SELFIE""

The task of drawing over 300 illustrations for this book fell to Marcella Kelly. Marcella was born and bred in Dublin's fair city, Ireland, home of "sweet Molly Malone." After completing her Irish education with many honors, including Art, she became a supervisor in Dublin's famous fishing industry in Howth.

She also spent some time working with her other passion of caring for animals and became a dog groomer and veterinary nurse, whilst also rescuing abandoned animals. She started painting and sketching people's pets and is now working as a full time freelance Illustrator.

Apart from her Honors in Art at college, Marcella also holds a merit diploma from the London Art College. She is currently working on other projects, including illustrating books for children.

Further information at
Marcella Kelly Illustrations

www.marcellakellyillustrations.com

Prices subject to change without notice

CPSIA information can be obtained
at www.ICGtesting.com
Printed in the USA
LVOW03s1004220616

493642LV00001B/1/P

9 781934 976662